The Purging

Richard Fisher

Richard Fisher was born in St.Pancras, grew up in Watford and settled with his family in North West Essex. Having studied at Cambridge he pursued a career in the voluntary sector in which he still works. "The Purging" is his first novel, and the first in a series featuring Inspector Wendy Pepper.

First published in 2014

The Purging

ISBN 978-1502965776

Acknowledgement

The book referred to in the text of this novel is "God's Own Country. Tales from the Bible Belt" by Stephen Bates, published in 2007 by Hodder & Stoughton.

"I know you well – you are neither hot nor cold; I wish you were one or the other. But since you are merely lukewarm, I will spit you out of my mouth!"

Revelation 3, verses 15 and 16

Dedicated to my wife and my boys

Sunday Morning

The atmosphere was solemn at the Quaker Meeting. The clerk was reporting back on the current state of relations with other local churches. Things were not good.

'The covenant is still a major issue. We have said we cannot sign up to the wording as it is, and even the rector is now questioning whether, if we don't say we believe in the doctrine of the Trinity, we can be part of a group of Christian organisations.'

Wendy and Catherine listened patiently, along with the rest of the meeting, as the depressing report continued.

'The Pentecostal Church is resigning from Churches Together because of our support for same sex marriages. Apparently we are an abomination and mired in the sin of Sodom.'

A gentle ripple of laughter lightened the mood in the Meeting Room.

'I fear we are about to be turned into salt. Sadly our good friends don't realise we are the salt of the earth.'

The laughter grew.

'And finally, I have been asked to remind you that somebody may be moved to speak during our meetings as we help each other to a clearer understanding and a deeper experience beyond our self. It's a convention that we speak only once in a meeting. We should all pay due regard to the principles that underlie our time together. Speak if you are moved to do so, but please pay due regard to others who are present. Silence says far more than ill considered words.'

Trevor Sandling sat down. And Luke Watson stood up. He was an active member of another local church, but he had convinced himself that he had a mission to convert the town's Quakers to the true faith. The collective groan in the Meeting Room was more felt than heard, but it was definitely there.

'I am moved to call you all to repent for your sins. You must come to know Jesus. You are all sinners and fornicators; you consort with sodomites and accept the devil as a friend.'

For the first time in his life, the gentle, mild mannered person that was Trevor Sandling lost his temper in public. He marched across to the other side of the Meeting Room, grabbed Luke Watson by the arm, and dragged him towards the door.

'Can't you take a hint?'

Well that's livened up the morning thought Wendy.

Sunday Evening

'Oh, you're lovely, you're such a lovely audience, I do so like coming to these concerts at Castle Lofts.'

The opera star, one of the main attractions at this year's season of open air concerts, was drawing towards the finale of her Sunday night performance and the crowd were loving it. Having joined in a hearty rendering of "I vow to thee my country," they were gearing up to give Jerusalem the full works.

Some of them near the front were getting a bit ahead of themselves, waving their union jacks aloft and singing a rather course sounding *"And did those feet."*

'Oh, be patient. I know you love this one, but let's do it properly.'

The crowd roared its approval and quietened down as Hubert Parry's music began to travel through the warm summer air.

At the side of the gently sloping field, some of the audience were dismantling their pergolas early. Collecting chairs, rugs and the remains of picnics, they were getting ready to make a quick dash to the car park so that they could escape before the queue grew too long.

Inspector Wendy Pepper was enjoying the evening. For once she was a guest, not on duty. These Castle Lofts concerts might be a celebration of everything the white middle classes held dear, but each year they brought their accompaniment of crime. The odd bag snatch, pickpockets and then the road rage as drivers fought over places in the queue out to Castle Lofts Road. Silly boys with silly toys thought Wendy. Last year one young constable had been hospitalised as two large cars had fought to get through the gate first. Both of the drivers had spent the night in the cells at the police station in Mound Street, and must have regretted their subsequent front page appearance in the local papers. When it became public that one of them was Lloyd Evans, a stalwart of the Rotary Club and Parish Church who lived on Commonside, and that he had consumed several too many glasses of champagne before attempting to drive home, Wendy had hoped an example would be made of him. But somehow he had got off. Typical she thought, that somebody like that would spend a fortune on a clever lawyer and get away with it.

But none of that tonight. This year she was here to just relax and enjoy. It had been suggested by Catherine, or Miss York as she was known to the students at Bonhunt Academy, the local secondary school where she worked. Wendy and Catherine had shared a small house in Granary Lane for five years now. It suited them both. Catherine could walk to the school and, although on some days it could be a bit of a slog driving to Braintree where she was usually based, Wendy loved the town as a place in which to live.

So this year they were here, relaxing in the warm summer air, enjoying some cheap White Zinfandel rosé and soaking up the atmosphere of the last night at the Castle Lofts Proms.

White Zinfandel. As the music marched towards Jerusalem, Wendy remembered the Rotary Club wine tasting she had attended with Catherine. It was a fund raiser for the school's Africa trip, and fair's fair, it had been a generous gesture getting so many of their members to fork out fifty quid each for an entertaining evening learning a bit about fine wines. The trouble was, Wendy and Catherine hadn't realised it was going to be competitive. Wendy enjoyed a good wine, and knew a bit about the subject. Back at Granary Lane they even had a small cellar with a few really good clarets, a taste she had inherited from her uncle.

But Lloyd Evans had been the host for the evening and he'd been such a wine snob.

As Wendy finished her glass of White Zinfandel, she turned to Catherine.

'Do you remember that tasting at the Bonhunt Hotel? I'm sure I drink more of this stuff just to spite Lloyd Evans. What did he say?'

Catherine laughed. She laughed so loudly that a few heads turned and some frowning faces stared at the two of them.

'Oh dear,' she giggled, 'I think the "tut tut" brigade are looking at us!' She lowered her voice, 'he said he'd rather drink cow's piss.'

'And I thought I was showing off my incredible wine expertise. That white wine we tasted couldn't have been White Zinfandel, because that as we both know so well is a rosé! Four ninety-nine on special offer at the supermarket. Great chilled on a summer evening. Mind you, this lot's pretty warm now, but who cares.'

'God he was a snob. No sense of humour and no idea that some of us can enjoy a cheap bottle and still know a bit about wine!'

Bring me my bow, of burning gold,
Bring me my arrows of desire.

Wendy and Catherine joined in the singing. They were just about to stand up when a young man with cropped hair and wearing a brown leather jacket and jeans ran straight through their picnic, kicking over the bottle of wine. He caught his breath, cursed and then disappeared off through the crowd.

Wendy hardly had time to size him up, but was sure that his left hand and tee shirt were covered in bright red blood, and that he appeared to be nursing a wound with his right hand.

Instinctively, Wendy leapt up and tried to chase after him, but it was hopeless. The crowd were in full patriotic mode, bellowing the last words of Jerusalem, arms interlocked and it only took seconds for her quarry to disappear into the melee. Typical, she thought, somebody always has to spoil the fun. But the fireworks had started, and she fought her way back to Catherine to share the enjoyment of the spectacle. The display was always good at the last night of the Castle Lofts Proms, and the clear sky this year made it spectacular. A plane was flying over, on its way into Stansted. Wendy wondered if they warned the pilots what they would encounter on their approach. She also wondered how they made sure they didn't collide with the spitfire that had been looping the loop earlier in the evening.

Catherine turned to her.

'What was that all about?'

'Heaven knows. I'm surprised louts like that come to this. Perhaps he didn't read the programme properly.' She laughed, 'you don't suppose Lloyd Evans is employing someone to destroy any bottles of White Zinfandel brought to the concerts, do you?'

'Now that's just being obsessional. Absolutely ridiculous! Anyway you didn't have to chase after him.'

'You know me, always on duty. And I'm sure he was injured. But yes, this is a night off. Let's enjoy the fireworks.'

*****

The marquees on the playing field at Bonhunt Academy had all been closed up for the night. Outside, the names of the various tents were displayed as they were every year. Robins, Sparrows, Chaffinches, Cuckoos, Swifts, Kestrels, Eagles.......this was Summer Bible Club. Started years ago by one of the small chapels, as a way of enticing children into its Sunday School, 'SBC' as it was known had grown into something resembling a small industry, with marquees for each of the different year groups, fifty plus children in each. Every year in August it was here, in Chipping Bonhunt.

John Davies stood outside the Swifts tent with Peter Lord. He was already finding it very heavy going. Security duty on the tents was a requirement of the insurance, but he was never quite certain as to what they would actually do if they were confronted with a drunken group of teenagers or the proverbial mad axe man on the rampage. And here he was, on the night shift, having given in and said 'yes' to joining the volunteer rota on the fifth time of being asked.

'I don't understand you' his wife Alice had said. 'We agreed you didn't have time to do it this year if we're also going to be running one of the tents. You're going to be up half the night and then you've got to set off first thing in the morning to open up the tent. Just be sensible!'

'There's a limit to the number of times you can say no. They're finding it really difficult this year.'

'Just don't blame me when you've got a sore head and can't get up in the morning.'

God give me strength he thought, realising that for once he probably really meant it. And so here he was, two hours still to go with Peter. He could never remember which of the small village chapels Peter came from, and he couldn't pin down exactly which strand of the judgemental side of the church it belonged to. Probably a fringe Baptist group John thought, one of what he referred to as the "anti everythings."

John decided this was all the result of some kind of wicked sense of humour on the part of the security team and the rota organisers, the Maitlands. Putting a Liberal

Democrat town councillor on duty with the most illiberal member of the SBC team.

They'd already had a serious falling out over one of his tent helpers. Rachel had been a stalwart in the preparation, lots of ideas as to how you can keep fifty five nine year olds entertained in between assemblies and lunch break. Everybody knew her marriage was on the rocks but, with the exception of Peter, nobody had taken much interest in her domestic arrangements. John still felt sore as a result of the conversation they'd had.

'We can't have her involved. It will send out completely the wrong message to the children.'

'Surely we're not saying that you can't be involved in SBC just because you're marriage is on the rocks?' John had replied.

'But she's living with somebody else, another....*woman.*'

'Oh come off it, just because they're sharing a house doesn't mean they're in a relationship and would it really matter if they were?'

'You need to understand that sin is unacceptable to God. We can't have Summer Bible Club looking as though we think it's alright to sin without showing any repentance.'

'Oh stop being so judgemental. If we apply those rules, there are a number of our young helpers that will also have to be banned - after all, we know a bit too much about what some of them are up to.'

'But that's different. They're still young. Rachel should know better.'

And so, the day before Summer Bible Club was due to start, Rachel had been banned.

John had thought of resigning, but felt it would have let too many people down. So instead he had diverted his anger into adding the words *"except Rachel"* every time they sang the chorus of *"Jesus never, never, never, turned anyone away."* A small but important gesture of defiance to the over-judgemental attitude that prevailed, he had thought.

They hadn't gone over the same ground now they were back for security duty. No point, thought John, as they'd never agree. Instead they were enjoying watching the fireworks at Castle Lofts. The one bonus for doing this particular Sunday night was the grandstand view.

There was a rustling sound in the distance and John thought he caught a glimpse of something moving out of the corner of his eye, a movement in the bushes along the edge of an old railway cutting, and he was certain he saw the flash of a torch.

'Did you see that?' he asked Peter, who was clearly looking in the same direction.

'Don't think it was anything, probably just a fox. You stay here and I'll check it out: I need a pee. If I don't come back, call the cavalry.'

'OK, sure you'll be alright on your own?'

'God protects his own!'

Peter disappeared into the darkness. Ten minutes later, John was certain he heard a noise coming from the Eagles tent. He ran across, but the front was well secured, the door flap tied firmly at the bottom. He started to run round the side but tripped on a guy rope and just missed smashing his head on a large metal tent peg.

'Damn' he cursed, thinking they were always stopping the children running down the sides of the tents to prevent exactly this happening.

'In a hurry?' said Peter as he appeared round the corner.

'I thought I heard something.'

'Your imagination is running away with you tonight. There was nothing over by the cutting and there's nothing here.'

'Let's just check the back of the tent.'

It was all tied up, but not quite as firmly as the front, thought John.

*****

It was chaos trying to get out of Castle Lofts Park. Wendy and Catherine were glad they had walked.

Wendy went over to one of the police constables on duty. 'What the hell's going on? I know it's always bad, but not like this.'

'High Street's closed and everything is backing up. Some sort of fire I'm told. We're changing the system – going to direct them out the other way, but we've got a whole lot who need to turn round and come back!'

'Well' said Wendy, 'Wonder where the fire is. Perhaps we'll lose that dreadful red shop front at the discount store. That might be an improvement.'

Wendy and Catherine cut across Castle Lofts Park and along Monastery Walk. As they passed the United Reformed Church, Wendy stopped. A thin figure was climbing up the scaffolding that surrounded the building.

'You there, come down.'

'Why the fuck should I?'

'Police – come down now or I'll make it official.'

Slowly the darkly clad figure climbed down.

'I might have known it would be you' said Catherine, recognising Daniel Morgan from one of her A level English groups. 'I thought you were supposed to be turning over a new leaf now you're going to be off to Uni. Wasn't that the deal?'

'Sorry Miss. You won't tell dad, will you?'

'We'll be putting you in the cells if it happens again' said Wendy, 'now off with you, don't be so bloody silly.'

Daniel sloped off, muttering 'fucking bitch' under his breath.

Wendy looked up at the scaffolding.

'How long has this been here? They must have been painting this church for months.'

'I think they've stripped so much paint off that the place is in danger of falling down!' replied Catherine, laughing.

'Well, I hope they take the scaffolding down soon, or somebody will have the lead off their roof.'

They walked down to the High Street. At the traffic lights it was chaos because the road going up to the war memorial was completely blocked by fire engines.

Wendy walked up a short way and recognised Steve Turner, the local brigade's station officer.

'Hi Steve, I see they've got you out on a Sunday night. What's the story?'

'It's your lot, Wendy. The Quakers - Friends Meeting House. You've been very lucky.'

'Lucky? Being burnt down on a Sunday night?'

'Well, it's all relative. It's got to be arson, three separate attempts to light fires. But we caught it very quickly. Someone walking home early from the concert saw the fire in the foyer before it really took hold. And we got through before all the concert traffic came out. We've got it under control – it'll be smoke damage mainly. Can't think why anyone would want to torch the Quakers.'

Wendy could think of several reasons, not least the row with other local churches about signing the new covenant. But surely nobody would go so far as to burn the place down, unless they really did believe they were exercising the wrath of God.

'That's going to upset Trevor,' said Catherine. 'He treasures that building. And his foyer he spent so long getting us to change – how's he going to cope with that?'

'Oh, he'll cope. Trevor always does. He'll probably use it as an opportunity to try and get us to open up the café he wants to start.'

Wendy was running through her mind as to who might have such a malicious grudge against the place that they'd actually torch it. Then suddenly she slipped into Inspector role. Stupid, stupid me, she thought, the arsonist often stays or returns to the scene to watch. She looked back to the cordon across the road. Concert goers were stopping to watch the fire, some lingering, some just giving it all a quick glance.

Scanning the crowd, Wendy saw a figure she recognised, leaning against the corner by Mound Street. Why was it familiar? Of course, she turned to Catherine.

'Look, the lout at the concert.'

Catherine followed her line of gaze. There he was, the same cropped hair and brown leather jacket. But he wasn't going to hang around. When he realised the two of them had eyeballed him, he moved slowly away and started to walk briskly in the other direction up the High Street.

Wendy was in pursuit.

'Stop – police,' she shouted.

One of the police constables on the cordon joined her as she started to run. They followed their quarry up past the Latte cafe, then into Empire Street. He was a long way ahead and already heading into the Market Square.

Fortunately Wendy heard it coming, engine on full throttle and the sound of a Jaguar accelerating rapidly. As she leapt to one side, the wing mirror clipped her right elbow. She felt a searing, jabbing pain go right through her arm.

The Jaguar continued on into the Market Square and she heard a scream followed by the dull sickening thud of a body falling to the ground. Her quarry was caught, but probably not much use to her now.

Catherine came running up. 'God that was close, he almost drove that thing over you.'

They ran along the road to the scene of the accident where Wendy and PC Smart moved the crowd back. A horribly deformed body lay in the middle of the road, lifeless with a trickle of blood running down from the mouth.

Wendy was certain the maroon Jaguar was familiar. Last time she'd seen it, the car was parked on Commonside, outside the home of Lloyd Evans.

*****

The Jaguar pulled off the road. The driver stopped, climbed out of the car and carefully closed the gate behind him before proceeding down a long bumpy bridleway. Eventually he arrived at the old Essex barn and he stopped in front of the main barn door. They were well out of sight of any road or neighbouring property. People didn't realise just how remote parts of the north Essex countryside really were. The locals might get upset about new housing development, but you could build thousands of new homes and most of the area would still be very rural.

The man climbed out of the car again, opened the door, and drove the Jaguar inside. Having closed the main door behind him, he made his way through a small side door into a workshop area.

In the corner of the workshop, two terrified eyes followed the man's every movement. Naked, gagged and tied firmly to an old wooden chair, there was nothing the victim could do as he watched the man place the large kilner jars on the workshop bench. Very slowly and very carefully, he started to unscrew the lid on the first jar. The smell of sulphuric acid spread rapidly through the air.

Monday

Tom Garroway was not his usual calm self. He couldn't work out why the police closing the Market Square would cause such chaos. They were late. He'd promised his wife Jean he would get her and the children to Bonhunt Academy for Summer Bible Club by eight thirty, and it was eight forty-five already.

The Garroways had a beautiful house just outside the village of Finchwinter, but sometimes it did feel just a bit too far out of town.

'If we'd left earlier, as we were supposed to do, we'd have had plenty of time' said their daughter Lucy.

'So why didn't we do that then Lucy?'

'Because my wonderful little brother Joshua was still in bed.'

'Oh yes, always my fault,' retorted Joshua. 'How long did it take you in the shower? I was waiting for a quarter of an hour.'

'For God's sake!' Jean raised her voice but just managed to avoid shouting.

'Isn't that what Summer Bible Club is all about?' asked Tom smugly.

'You're all impossible.'

As they crawled down Finchwinter Road, it became clear that the problem wasn't the Market Square but the traffic lights, which had failed again.

'Won't this be fun when they build all those new houses?' said Tom.

*****

In the Eagles tent, John and Alice were busy counting out felt pens and dividing them equally across the different tables.

Agnes Rogers from the Baptist Church was fussing in the corner, worried that not all the children's badges were in alphabetical order and Jane Dawson was trying for the third time to 'phone her son to ask him to check that the oven had been turned off after she'd heated up the croissants for breakfast.

'Just go and check. Make sure that it's off. Well, you'll just have to get yourself out of bed then, won't you?' Clearly third time lucky, thought John.

'Typical of Jean to be late, but I'm surprised about the others,' said Alice.

'Well, I don't think we should expect too much from Sarah and Lewis,' replied John. 'They're both fairly hard working, but getting here early in the morning has never been one of their strong points. Hey, I'm sure somebody's played around with the quiet area since we set it up yesterday. The screen's been moved and the cushions are all a mess.'

'Why would anyone do that?' asked Alice.

'Haven't a clue, but I thought the back of the tent had been messed around with last night. As long as nobody was using it for nefarious purposes.'

'I can think of better places for a clandestine tryst.'

'I'll tidy it up as soon as I get a spare moment,' Agnes said, 'it shouldn't take too long.'

'Thanks Agnes, that's really helpful,' said John.

'Morning all, sorry I'm late, the traffic's dreadful.' Jean had arrived. 'I bring you bags full of tissue paper, cardboard, and a large box of assorted tins. What's this I hear that Rachel isn't helping anymore?'

'Word gets round fast,' replied John, 'let's all gather round.'

The five of them sat down at one of the tables.

'Hi everyone, is my eye candy here yet?' Sarah Turner, aged eighteen and wearing a skirt so short that it looked as though its previous life had been as a pocket handkerchief, had arrived.

'Hello Sarah' said Agnes. 'Lewis not with you then, I assume that's who you're referring to?'

'He's probably got a hangover. Out with the lads last night. Did you see the fire at the Quakers?'

'Yes, we all know about it,' said John, 'but now we need to go through today's programme. I really do worry about the things you wear, Sarah. One day the top will come down so low it will meet the bottom coming up the other way!'

'Don't be cheeky. Got to look the best for my eye candy haven't I?'

John decided it was time to bring order to the proceedings.

'Let's start with a short moment of prayer.'

*****

It was nine o'clock and Catherine was walking through the gates into Bonhunt Academy. With the A level results due to be handed out on Thursday, it was time to start putting the school's support mechanisms into place, ready for eight am on the fateful morning.

It's agony for those who do really well, let alone those who don't get the grades they need, she thought. After two years of really hard work, it only takes one paper to hit them sideways, and that would almost certainly be chemistry this year. Without warning, the exam board had completely changed the way they asked the questions in one of the papers. Catherine had spent hours since the exam trying to reassure one of her "star" girls that she was sure her answers would be fine.

Offers for medicine at Cambridge are great, as long as the students holding them don't have a nervous breakdown before they get their results. She prayed that Lucy would get her A. She prayed that all her students would get the results they deserved. Wretched government, she thought, forever changing the system as the politicians played to the gallery. Why couldn't they leave the exam system alone and just let our kids succeed without devaluing the results of all their hard work?

But chemistry aside, most of her students would almost certainly get the grades they needed. Sitting down at her desk, she realised she was the first to arrive.

She wondered who had made such a mess of the sixth form office. Normally, after the end of term, it was given a really good clean. But today it seemed as though it had been used as the ring for a prize fight.

As she looked across towards the window she saw a ghastly, mangled mess on the carpet. It looked like a cat that had been run over, or possibly a dog. She ventured a bit closer: whatever it had been, it was definitely dead now. A body, four legs, but no head.

Suddenly she felt nauseous and she ran to the toilet. It was locked, still being refurbished. Feeling a combination of nausea and giddiness, with huge embarrassment she was sick all over the new carpet in the study centre.

Oh shit! What do you do in situations like this; phone 999?

She might share a house with a policewomen, but she realised she hadn't got a clue.

Phone 111? No, that's the NHS number that everybody says doesn't work.

Catherine collected herself. Of course, phone Wendy: use my own personal tame police inspector. She picked up her mobile.

'High Wendy, I really need your help, something ghastly has happened,' she sobbed.

'God, you sound upset. Look, I'm really up to my neck with the fire and the hit and run, but what's happened?'

'There's this ghastly dead thing in my office.'

'What sort of dead thing?'

'Well, I think it must have been an animal, but it's been so mangled up it could have been anything.'

'Look, I'll drop in on you as soon as I've finished here at the station.'

'Thanks Wendy, I really appreciate it.'

Just at that moment the Head walked in.

'What the hell's happened here?'

*****

Outside the Eagles tent, fifty-five ten year olds and their parents queued to get in. Packed lunches, anoraks, sweatshirts: all were being dragged across the grass.

'Callum mustn't have any dairy, absolutely no dairy. His food is in his lunchbox, but don't let him eat anyone else's food, he's done it a couple of times recently.'

'Have you put it down on the form?' asked Alice politely.

'No, I'm telling you.'

'Please, just put it down on the form, that's what we ask.'

Shrugged shoulders, parent looks daggers. Obviously it is an outrageous request to expect a parent to fill in a short form and bring it with them.

'I won't be collecting Nigel, his brother is helping in Sparrows and he'll bring him home.'

'Have you put it on the form?'

'No, do I have to?'

'Yes, you have to.'

'But I've got to get away; I'm already late for work.'

'Please, just fill in the form.'

And so the task of checking the details of fifty-five children on the first morning of Summer Bible Club was underway. And this was just one tent. Nine others were going through the same process; all arranged in a very large semi-circle on the Bonhunt Academy playing fields.

The routine was always the same. Confirm the child was at the right tent, check their parents had filled in the form and it was clear who was going to collect them, give them their badge, and sit them down at the right table.

'I want to be next to Philip.'

'Sorry, you're on the table over there.'

'I don't know anybody on that table. I want to sit next to Philip'

'You'll get to know the others very quickly.'

'I'm going to sit next to Philip.'

Alice looked around for assistance. 'Sarah, could you untangle yourself from Lewis for just a moment and take this young lad to the table over there? Thanks.'

Sarah, who'd been sitting on Lewis' lap, stood up and duly obliged.

Well, that's encouraging, thought Alice, perhaps John was being a bit too hard with his views about the young helpers.

The last children took their seats at their tables and John rang a ship's bell.

'We're all sailors at sea this week, so let me introduce myself as Captain John. I've got a merry crew with me, ho,ho,ho, and we hope you young sailors are going to have a great time. First of all, let me introduce the crew.'

John looked round: Alice, Jean, Jane, Sarah, Lewis but no Agnes. Of course, she'd offered to tidy up the quiet area. And Agnes was definitely behind the screen, because at that moment she let out an almighty scream.

The children all laughed, thinking this was part of the fun.

Agnes screamed again.

The children laughed again.

'Help, it's horrible.'

More laughter. By now, Alice had joined Agnes behind the screen. The previous tangle of blankets and cushions were all neatly folded in a pile, except for the last blanket which Agnes was holding in her hands. In the middle was a large fresh blood stain, and on the ground, beneath where it had lain, was the unmistakeable severed head of a sheep, looking uncannily as though it was staring directly at Agnes.

'John,' called Alice, 'you need to take the children outside.'

'Right me hearties, time for a quick game of Port and Starboard. Outside everyone. A prize for the first five in the middle of the field.'

John feared he would be trampled to death in the rush.

*****

Chief Superintendent Warren had always had a bit of a soft spot for Wendy Pepper. She had coped well with all the cases to which she had been assigned and she seemed to have an instinctive feel for detective work, spotting details that many of the team just didn't see or realise were important. She had a pleasant personality as well, a refreshing change from many of the other officers he was forced to work with.

So perhaps he thought, as they met at the divisional headquarters in Braintree, today was the exception that proved the rule. Why was she being so belligerent?

'Look, I know it was a nasty shock and being hit by the car has shaken you up, but that still doesn't excuse making accusations that we just cannot sustain.'

'But it was his car. Maroon Jaguar XJ with his personalised number plate. E5VNS. Always thought it was a bit poncy, a bit desperate to get something that looks like his name!'

'Well, we got him out of bed at three in the morning, examined the car with him and couldn't find a thing.'

'Must have cleaned it up,' said Wendy, with a touch of resignation in her voice.

'Look, you and I both know that if the car was going at the speed you say it was, and it slams into a pedestrian sending them flying over the bonnet, and then it reverses – that's what you tell me the witnesses say happened - and runs over the poor sod at speed leaving something that resembles…well, I don't need to say, but if a car did that, you'd find something on it. There's not even a scratch.'

'Must have had it re-sprayed,' said Wendy lamely

Warren laughed, and it broke the tension.

'You were in shock. Not your fault. Knowing you, you wanted it to be Evans because you can't stand the pompous little prick. And, if I'm honest, part of me would love to get him again. All high and mighty up at the Parish Church and best mates with the Police and Crime Commissioner – we've read his letters and we're all fed up with him having a go at us all the time. But it wasn't his car and I don't want to hear his name mentioned again unless there's some real evidence. What is it he does at the church that makes him so important?'

'Oh, he's a church warden, although the way he carries on you'd think he was the bloody rector.'

'Well, the Commissioner's already 'phoned, so let's tread carefully. Now what about the poor sod who got run over. Peterson, have we got anything?'

Detective Sergeant Ian Peterson was a year into his posting working with Wendy Pepper. A tall spindly young man, he had joined the police fresh out of Cambridge having completed a degree in history. He was a good advertisement for the graduate recruitment programme; clever and quick witted, he didn't wear his education on his sleeve and mucked in with the team. His only fault seemed to be his quiet diffidence: he wasn't one to volunteer for long conversations.

'Nothing definite Sir. No identity on him, no 'phone, no wallet. The autopsy may find something to help. And some of his clothes have labels we don't recognise.'

'Well, two things for you then Pepper. You and Peterson focus on finding the driver and identifying the victim. Was the driver drunk, was it an accident, or was it deliberate? And then there's the fire, I need you two to lead on the arson investigation at the Quakers – your spiritual home Pepper?'

'That might be putting it a bit strongly, sir. It's the place where I feel most comfortable, unlike all the other churches I could go to.'

'How the hell are we mere mortals supposed to know the difference between you all? I thought your number one enemy on Commonside was one of your own kind, but it seems to me he must be worshipping a completely different God!'

Wendy reddened and Warren recognised this wasn't a line of argument worth pursuing.

'Look, I can spare you a few uniforms, but unless there's any real evidence the hit and run was deliberate, we'll be closing that one down fairly quickly. The arson's the thing that will concern the Commissioner. He won't want his electors getting worried their homes are about to be torched. Any ideas?'

'Well yes,' said Wendy. 'There's been a little debate, shall we say, about our – that is, the Quakers - attitude to gay marriage. We've had a few threats from some fanatics in the town, so we'll start by checking them out.'

'Fanatics in Chipping Bonhunt. Surely not?'

'You read the papers as much as I do sir, it's a veritable cauldron of extremism,' replied Wendy, very much tongue in cheek.

'Keep me posted as always. I'll spare you the rare breed sheep rustling in Rickling Green.' And with that, he was gone.

Wendy looked across to Peterson. 'Rare breed sheep rustling? It's beginning to sound as though we both live in the Wild West.'

'Well, the way things are going, Chipping Bonhunt's starting to look like the crime capital of Essex. Shall we hot foot it back to the Friends' Meeting House? – I assume you want me to drive?'

'You're surprisingly eloquent today. Yes, you can drive, but first of all we're off to the secondary school. Something's come up that I need to deal with.'

*****

Peterson drove into the car park at Bonhunt Academy and pulled up outside the main entrance. Catherine was waiting in the reception area, eyes still looking red and clearly upset.

Wendy ran over to her.

'You look dreadful; it must have been quite a shock.'

'Thanks, that makes me feel really good.'

'I can't stop for long, we've got to get down to the Meeting House and look at the result of the arson attack, and there's also the poor bugger who got run over. I'll take a quick look round here and then we'll send somebody up as soon as we can to decide whether it's worth us trying to do any forensics. But it sounds to me as though it's just a silly prank. Anybody pissed off about their exams?'

'Not yet, as far as I know.'

Although Catherine could immediately think of three of the students who probably weren't looking forward to receiving results that would almost certainly confirm the outcome of their lack of effort for the past year. But none of them would do this, surely?

They walked through reception, up the stairs and into the sixth form study centre.

'Wow, this has all changed' said Wendy.

'Yes, the extension has doubled the size of the study area and we've bought all these fancy new computers.'

They walked down to the far end

'So this is the fancy new office to go with all the fancy computers. Very business like!'

'Complete with added animal intestines for that special little extra touch of "je ne sais quoi".' Catherine laughed, releasing the emotional tension that had built up inside her.

'Glad to see the usual Catherine's back. But what a bloody stupid thing to do. I don't suppose it could be our friend we ticked off for being up the scaffolding on the church?'

'I doubt it; this would take a bit too much organisation for Daniel Morgan.'

Peterson walked in. 'We're needed on the field, I think it's connected. Hysterical old lady found something nasty in the quiet corner at the kids' event.'

'Will we ever get to the Meeting House? Catherine, lock this room up if you can. I think we will need to come back. Leave everything as it is. Our forensic team will give it the once over after they've finished at the Friends' Meeting House.'

Wendy gave Catherine a hug. Peterson thought there was a hint of intimacy.

'Right Peterson. Off to the field and the joys of Summer Bible Club.'

*****

They were greeted by an anxious couple, Sylvia and Roger Maitland.

'Nothing like this has ever happened before,' said Sylvia, 'everybody works so hard to put this event on, and it's like somebody is just deliberately trying to spoil it.'

'So what are we here to see?' Wendy asked.

'There's a sheep's head been left in the Eagles tent. Poor Agnes Rogers found it and she's in a complete state of shock. It could have killed her. She's helped every year for the last twenty years, and to think she had to find this, poor woman.'

'I realise it's pretty nasty for all those involved, but it's probably just some kids being silly. A stupid prank that's gone too far. It will be the animal welfare side of this that will be our main concern. Stealing sheep and cruelty to animals.'

'But what about the children and Agnes?'

'They'll live, which is more than can be said for the poor sheep. Look, don't get me wrong, we'll try and get the so-and-so that did this and we appreciate the upset it's caused, but the serious offence is what's happened to the animal. Now, can we go and have a look please?'

They walked over to the Eagles tent. The children had been playing outside and were just setting off to the big marquee for the morning assembly.

John Davies turned to his wife. 'Alice, can you lead the way and I'll talk the police through what's happened? Thanks.' John turned back to Wendy.

'Bit of an unusual start to Summer Bible Club this year!'

'So show me the scene of the crime.'

John walked across to the quiet corner with Wendy, and she surveyed the scene. There was a pile of neatly folded blankets, with one blanket smeared in blood that had been dropped on top of the pile. There was also a pile of neatly stacked cushions, and of course the sheep's head, minus body, with eyes staring wide open. For some reason it reminded Wendy of the Peter Cook and Dudley Moore sketch about the Mona Lisa: the eyes follow you round the room.

'Has anybody moved anything?'

John replied. 'Yes, that's how we found the head. This area was all messed up when we arrived and so Agnes was tidying up. The head was under some of the blankets.'

Wendy put on some gloves and lifted the bloodstained blanket. Had it been used to move the head, or just placed on it? She lifted the next blanket. A sheet of A4 paper fell onto the grass.

The Arial typeface read:

"Beware of false prophets who come disguised as harmless sheep but are really vicious wolves"

Damn she muttered to herself.

'I'm afraid this is a bit more serious than we thought. I'm going to have to ask you to stay out of the tent and we probably need to search all the others as well.'

She radioed into headquarters. 'Hello, it's Inspector Pepper' A chorus of baa, baa, black sheep could be heard in the background. 'We're completely out of mint sauce at the moment, very sorry.'

She could never work out how news travelled quite so fast round the force.

'Very funny, but I don't think we're going to be laughing for much longer. We need some reinforcements.'

After a brief discussion with Chief Superintendent Warren, it was agreed to send five more police constables across to conduct a quick search of the other tents. And forensics would come up to the school as soon as they'd finished their initial investigations at the Meeting House and the hit and run site in the Market Square.

Wendy turned to Peterson 'God, what a start to the week. It's not eleven yet, and we've got an arson, a possible hit and run, a decapitated sheep and some nutter into biblical texts. Now I've got to ask this lot to move out of all the other tents for the rest of the morning.'

'Isn't that what this event is all about?'

'Nutters?'

'No, biblical texts!'

As they walked past the Swifts tent, they heard the children reciting:

"Trust in the Lord with all your heart
And lean not on your own understanding"

We're going to need some help from the Lord if we're going to understand this one, Wendy thought to herself.

*****

Trevor Sandling had gathered with some fellow Quakers to survey the damage. They weren't allowed into the three areas that had been fire bombed as the investigation was still continuing. Fortunately the taper on the bottle of petrol thrown through the Meeting Hall window at the back had extinguished itself before the fuel had ignited. So there was a pool of petrol on the hall floor, but little physical damage.

A second bottle that had been thrown through one of the front windows had landed in the gents' toilet. This had caused some serious fire damage to the partitions, but hadn't spread outside into the main circulation area.

It was the entrance foyer that had really suffered. A timber extension to the side of the building, it was now charred and roofless. But the local fire brigade had done a good job and for once nobody had left any of the fire doors propped open.

'You've no idea how difficult it is to get everybody to understand the importance of keeping all the doors closed,' Trevor was telling Steve Turner, the brigade's commander.

'Oh, don't tell me. We do our best to get the message across. Perhaps we should get everyone to look at this. Shows how fire doors really do work. They've reduced the spread significantly here. But you were lucky we were called out so quickly.'

The police forensic team were collecting up fragments of broken glass from the bottles. Apparently they were optimistic that the one thrown through the back window might produce some helpful results, even a fingerprint or two.

Trevor turned to George Balcombe, the convenor of the Meeting's Property group. 'How soon can the insurance loss adjustor get out here?'

'He's on his way, so I think it'll be anytime this morning. Now, are you happy if I tell him about our plans to open this up as a café?'

'As long as you don't think that'll look as though I was responsible for starting the fire in order to make it easier to go ahead.'

Steve Turner chuckled to himself. Nobody would ever believe Trevor was capable of something like that.

*****

In the Eagles tent, John was explaining the sequence of events that had taken place to a young police constable, Rowan Smart.

'Last night I did notice that while the opening flap at the front of the tent was really well tied up, the one at the back was pretty loose, tied by somebody in a hurry or who isn't very good at knots.'

'So did you check inside the tent?'

'No reason to really, I just assumed that the flap at the back had been done by one of our younger helpers, Sarah or Lewis, or perhaps one of their friends. They're our teenage helpers. It's great that they give up their time, but they often have their minds on other things.'

'What do you mean?'

'Each other!'

'Then this morning I noticed that the blankets and cushions were a mess in the quiet area, but again didn't really think much of it. Highly likely that some of the children had been mucking around in there. It was only when Agnes tidied up that we discovered the truth.'

'And what about these words on the piece of paper?'

'*Beware of false prophets who come disguised as harmless sheep but are really vicious Wolves*' read John. 'It comes from Matthew.'

'Matthew?'

'Yes, Matthew's gospel. You know, in the Bible? This is Summer Bible Club!'

'Oh, of course. Sorry, I didn't really pay much attention during RE at school.'

'I checked out the quote. It's Matthew Chapter 7 verse 15. Don't worry, I'm not one of those people who knows it all by heart, I have this handy little guide available whenever I'm here – it's my emergency rescue.'

John showed PC Sharp his battered copy of "The Bible Reader's Encyclopaedia and Concordance", which according to the cover included "15 Actual Views and 16 Coloured Maps." The constable read the label inside:

Bushey and Oxbey Methodist Sunday School
Presented To
John Davies
29th September 1968

'I was given this when I joined the Sunday School. Everyone else was given a Bible, but I already had a Bible. No wonder they all hated me, probably thought me a bit of a smart arse!'

'So you're saying this quote comes from the Bible and it's in Matthew?'

'Yes, but here's something to get your detective juices going. I think it's from a particular version of the bible. See here,' said John holding a bible, 'this is The New International Version. Its translation is:

"Watch out for false prophets. They come to you in sheep's clothing, but inwardly they are ferocious Wolves"

Then there's this, from the Revised English Version:

"Beware of false prophets, who come to you dressed up as sheep while underneath they are savage Wolves."

Or you could try this in the Good News Bible:

"Be on your guard against false prophets; they come to you looking like sheep on the outside, but on the inside they are really like wild Wolves".'

PC Smart looked confused. 'So what's the difference?'

'In one sense, there isn't a difference. They're all trying to say the same thing. But the New International Version and the Revised English Bible are both trying to be accurate translations, whereas the Good News Bible is more of a paraphrase, trying to be a modern retelling of the story rather than being too accurate.'

PC Smart still looked confused. 'Don't you all believe in the same thing then, why do you all have these different versions of the Bible?'

'Well, actually, you'll find that all of us here don't necessarily believe in the same thing, not at least in the detail. But don't let that confuse you. The version of the Bible used for that quote may help lead you to our sheep killer. It might be just chance, but it might also mean that they like to read a particular version of the Bible'

'Which version is that?'

'Well, I haven't checked this out, but I think you might find it's The Living Bible or something called the New Living Translation.'

'What type of person reads that, then?'

'I could offer several views on that one! But let's just say they're probably an evangelical, not a wishy-washy liberal like me.'

'So you're not too keen on this Living Bible you've described?'

'No, I find some of it unhelpful and I don't think it's a good translation.'

'So are you a Reverend or something. Do you do this all the time?'

'No, you could call it a hobby. I'm firmly a lay person, but the church I belong to has particular roles for lay people.'

'So, was there somebody else with you last night when you were doing the security?'

'Yes, there was a guy called Peter Lord.'

'Is he here?'

'No, I don't think he's helping during the day. But I'm sure the Maitlands can tell you. They're probably over there, in the Reception Tent.'

'So, what's he like?'

'Well, he's…' John thought for a moment. 'He's the type of person who reads The Living Bible. You'd better check if he's been decapitating any sheep.'

'Are you serious?'

'Not really!'

But John was thinking. He didn't really know a lot about Peter Lord; however what he did know suggested he might be right in the frame for this. However, that was something for the police to sort. No need to play the amateur detective.

*****

The police had set up an operations base from which to run the investigation at Chipping Bonhunt Police Station. The combination of the fire, the hit and run and the decapitated sheep had brought a demand from the Commissioner that something must be seen to be done.

Wendy had been put in charge, with Peterson assisting and PC Smart and several colleagues made available to do some of the donkey work.

'I think Warren meant "operations desk" rather than room. There's hardly room to swing a cat in here.'

'Or a dead sheep' chirped in PC Smart.

'Very funny, but that will do for jokes for the time being. Just remember, we're dealing with quite a lot of very upset people. That poor old lady who found the sheep's head looked absolutely white. I thought she was about to keel over.'

'She could hardly put two words together when I interviewed her,' said Peterson. 'Whoever did it must have thought it was very funny, but it was pretty sick if you ask me.'

'Right, let's gather round the board,' said Wendy.

A notice board, in front of the desk, had been pressed into service to display the various pieces of information that had been gathered so far.

'So, Peterson, what do we know about the hit and run?'

'Apart from the obvious, that the victim is dead, nothing. Post mortem hasn't shown anything other than injuries that you'd expect from being hit by a Jaguar at speed. They've taken some blood samples, but are not expecting to find anything.'

'Identification?'

'Nothing, so we're doing the usual. Dental records, finger prints. And we've contacted missing persons. But so far, we've drawn a blank. The only lead is the labels in a couple of his clothes. Most of them came from Primark, but his jacket was unusual. It has a brand label "LIVE IN HOPE" and we found the same label on the briefs he was wearing. Nobody's heard of it, so we're doing a bit more searching. But there's nothing on Google.'

'Nothing on Google! Since when did we rely on Google to do our detective work?'

'Didn't you read the e-mail?' asked Peterson, 'latest directive from on high. Don't waste precious detective time investigating facts you can find on Google.'

'They'll be telling us to do our research on Wikipedia next.'

'Actually they did, but the assistant who sent out the e-mail confused it with Wikileaks. We're all under strict instructions, on pain of being permanently put on parking enforcement, not to tell the press.'

'So we take this lot down, Google "*hit and run victim in Chipping Bonhunt*" and it does the job for us. Have you tried it?'

'Well, yes I have. First up are a bunch of no win, no fee solicitors. All the actual hit and runs it goes on to list are historic.'

'So we are going to have to do some real detective work?'

'Yes maam. We've got some posters out and appeals for information on TV and radio. Not much response, but we've got a couple of witnesses come forward. One of the PCs is out interviewing them.'

'So, let's move on to the arson. Three bottles of petrol thrown through three windows. Fortunately only one of them did any serious damage and that was caught by the fire brigade before it spread beyond the foyer. The only lead we seem to have at the moment is that our hit and run victim was watching the fire and decided to leg it when he realised I'd spotted him. And he was also the guy who kicked over my bottle of wine at Castle Lofts. Coincidence or something more? Perhaps he remembered me from the concert, or perhaps he had something to hide. Or it may be it was just a hit and run, but then on the other hand perhaps somebody really did want him dead. From what the witnesses say they saw, I think it was the latter. The driver of that Jaguar deliberately reversed back over the victim. Smart, anything we should know about our dead sheep?'

'Well, I've interviewed a lot of people up at the field and also your housemate Catherine. Not much to go on, except the guy who was running the Eagles tent, now what was his name,' Smart consulted his notebook, 'yes, John Davies, he came out with a lot of stuff about different versions of the bible. I never realised it was so complicated, but he reckoned the note that was left was a quote from a particular version.' Smart consulted his notebook again. 'He said it might be "*The Living Bible*" or "*The New Living Translation.*" He reckoned that might be an important clue.'

'So we've found our own answer to Miss Marple, have we?'

'No, I think he was trying to be helpful, although most of what he said went over my head.'

Most of what everyone says goes over your head, thought Wendy. He might not live up to his name and he would probably always be a police constable, but Smart was popular on the streets and the type of public face the force needed at the moment.

'Did he have any suggestions as to who it might put into the frame?'

'Yes, he suggested somebody who was on security duty with him, but I haven't been able to track the guy down yet. I'm going back up to the school tonight, because that's when he'll be there again.'

'No sheep rustling on the way,' joked Peterson.

*****

The drive home for the Garroways was as fraught as the one in that morning.

Tom had been late, and by the time he'd arrived, Lucy and Joshua were well and truly at each other's throats.

'You might at least have been on time for once,' said Jean, 'you know we've got to get both of these little darlings out again by seven. They're going into Cambridge with the Frosts for Nicola's Eighteenth.'

'I thought the party was next Saturday.'

'Yes it is, but today's her actual birthday and our two are the honoured guests so Nicola can do something to celebrate this evening. You know how precious she is. Ours are about the only children her mother will risk taking out with her.'

'You must be joking, the way they're tearing into each other at the moment, they'll make mince meet of poor little Nicola.'

'No we won't dad,' said Lucy, 'but please stop Joshua hitting me.'

'Well, it might help if you stopped pulling his hair,' said Tom.

'But he's always provoking me.'

'Will you stop it both of you,' said Jean, raising her voice. 'I really can't stand anymore of this. It's a hot day, we've all had a heavy time and we just need to get home.'

Suddenly Joshua perked up. 'Hey dad, guess what old Agnes found in the Eagles tent. It was very funny.'

'No it wasn't, it was really nasty,' Jean interrupted.

'Then why did all the kids laugh when it happened? My friend Tricia said it was very funny.'

'So, tell me what did poor old Agnes find then, Josh?' Tom asked.

'A sheep's head. It was all bloody round the neck and looking at her.'

Tom raised his eyes and looked quizzically at Jean.

'Well, that must have livened things up a bit. Perhaps I should take the week off and join you if you're sacrificing sheep. Is this part of an attempt to make SBC more appealing? My colleagues in marketing could always suggest some new angles. How about "*Get a head with Summer Bible Club*"?'

Jean gave him one of her daggers looks.

'Tom, you're really not helping. It's been a bloody awful day!'

*****

The Town Councillors were arriving in the Council Chamber. A long table filled the middle of the room and paintings of Mayors of yesteryear looked down on the assembled gathering. The Mayor focussed his attention on a painting that he thought always reminded him of one of the Ayatollahs. Put the right head gear on and yes, Councillor Ernest Smith, Chipping Bonhunt Mayor in 1932, could easily be running the Taliban.

This was the first meeting of the Mayor's new Town Centre Promotion Committee. Councillor Steven Hodgkiss had taken up the mayoralty in May and was already frustrated at the emptiness he found in the role. It was alright raising funds for his worthy cause, the inspiration play group, and he had plenty of engagements opening events, presenting badges and kissing elderly ladies (and not just elderly ladies if the chance presented itself), but he was finding it all a bit of a bore, a bit of a disappointment, and he wanted to DO something.

That something had become the Mayor's Town Centre Promotion Committee. It was time to do some moving and shaking.

'Still a few minutes to go,' said Councillor Hodgkiss 'bit of a lively night last night. I gather there's no news on the poor sod that got run over.'

'No,' said Councillor Dakin, 'I gave Lloyd Evans a call, 'cos he's usually up to speed, but this time I got a right earful. Apparently the police got him out of bed at three am and demanded to give his Jag a going over. Thought he was the one who'd run the guy down.'

'I bet that got him going,' said Councillor Hodgkiss, 'he's still smarting over that business last year. Don't know how he got away without being banned.'

'Got himself a clever lawyer who argued there was something wrong with the procedure. I reckon he pulled a few strings behind the scenes as well.'

'He's a modern day version of Mortimer Gadsby.'

'Mortimer Gadsby?' Councillor Thomas entered the room, 'who on earth is he, surely there's nobody can compete with our Lloyd!'

'You haven't heard of Mortimer Gadsby? Local magistrate who was notorious for sending allegedly honest working men down for being drunk, and then had to be wheeled home in a barrow from the Con club every Friday night because he was completely paralytic.'

'Wouldn't get away with it today!'

'Well some reckon old Lloyd is having a good try.'

'It's time we started,' Councillor Hodgkiss looked at his watch, 'I see we're waiting for Councillor Davies as usual. Typical Liberal, never on time.'

Councillor Thomas laughed, 'I think he's busy with all the God squad up at Bonhunt Academy. I can never work that guy out. Ridiculously liberal on every social issue and yet he's the only really religious person on the council.'

'That's not true, I go to church,' said the Mayor,

'Yes, Mayor making, Easter, Christmas and whenever you think there might be a photographer standing outside. I don't think that counts.'

The door opened and Councillor Davies arrived.

'Sorry I'm late. Bit of a heavy day. Don't expect to get sheep's heads in the tent at Summer Bible Club.'

'Haven't heard about that one,' said Councillor Thomas. 'Most of the town is full of the gossip about the hit and run and the fire at the Quakers.'

'Yes, I wondered if the Mayor was advancing his *"get the High Street alive"* campaign a bit too forcefully. You've been itching to get hold of that building for years, haven't you Councillor Hodgkiss?'

The Mayor scowled, 'I have my allies, but I don't like your tone.'

'Oh, come on, I was only joking, not even you would go so far as to burn the building down!'

'So what's this about a sheep's head?' Councillor Thomas interrupted, seeking to change the subject.

'Oh, one of our elderly helpers was tidying up our quiet corner and found it under a pile of blankets. Quite a shock, I was afraid she might have a heart attack. Of course the children thought it was hilarious.'

'So just the head?' asked Councillor Dakin.

'Yes, but they found the rest of the animal in the school. Police came round, did some interviews, but didn't come up with anything. There's a suggestion it might be connected to the fire.'

'Why's that?' asked Councillor Thomas.

'The guilty party left a quote from the Bible'

The Mayor coughed his "time to start" cough. 'Has anybody seen the Town Clerk?'

Right on cue, the Town Clerk entered the room.

'I've been going through the CCTV all afternoon with the Police; I hope this meeting isn't going to be too long.'

'As long as it needs to be,' replied the Mayor. 'Now, can you summarise the position so far. I hope we've had some response to the publicity the Council put out. Good article in one of the papers by the way, nice to see something positive for a change.'

The Town Clerk yawned, giving the impression he would rather be anywhere else than here in the council chamber.

'We've had a good response from most of the local traders we've spoken to, although the usual prima donnas are already being very negative. Everyone agrees we should be doing all we can to promote the town, build up trade and make it an attractive destination for visitors. But then we get into the tricky issue of parking. They all want it to be free, and if not free, to be much cheaper.'

The Mayor interrupted, 'But they know that's not really possible, and the District Council won't budge on it. Besides, there's plenty of free short stay parking all over the town.'

'I know, but they always reply by asking how they're supposed to compete against Tesco with the free out of town parking. And there's more to come with the development up Welsted Road.'

The meeting carried on. Councillor Davies felt his mind drifting off to the next day's programme at SBC. Why did he spend his time sitting through these hopeless meetings? Lots of hot air and never much to show for it. When the subject of toilets on the common was raised he wanted to scream. The Council had done that subject to death over the last few years. Death, an unfortunate thought given the poor soul who had been run down just outside the Town Hall in the Market Square. Somehow that event made the meeting seem even more pointless.

*****

Wendy and Peterson had decided they were in need of an outside case review. Outside meant not at the police station and review meant at least two pints of decent beer. So they had decamped to their favourite outside location, "The Great Eastern." The real Great Eastern, as in railway, had long since gone from Chipping Bonhunt, but the station building was still there. After many years as a large garage and car sales area, most of the old station site had been developed for housing. There were mixed views as to how it looked, but Peterson thought he had seen a lot worse. An attempt had been made to make the old station building look a bit like a real station again, and the combination of a bit of platform, canopy and lights worked. The pub across the road had clearly been built at the same time and was in the same style as the station building. Internally, it had been refurbished in a fake "traditional pub" sort of way. Normally Peterson didn't go for fake oldie, worldie interiors but here it worked, creating one open, pleasantly decorated bar area, broken down by the structure of the building into large spaces and more intimate smaller spaces to meet. Wendy and Peterson had placed themselves in their favourite snug area, out of sight of most of the pub in one of the corners.

'At least it's open again,' said Wendy, 'I was getting worried a couple of weeks ago when it suddenly closed. What was that all about?'

Peterson lived just round the corner from The Great Eastern, in what he referred to as his "digs" in one of the large Victorian houses located in More Road.

'Story is that the landlady handed back the keys and then thought better of it. It's a shame. Nobody seems to want to take the lease on, but it's a good pub and it certainly used to do a good trade.'

'The food was always pretty edible, better than most. A bit expensive perhaps, but always good for a lunch. Catherine and I slightly over did it at the last beer festival they held. They used to get some really good beers in. Couldn't believe it when they had some Front Street stuff from Binham. Normally only get that on our weekends in Norfolk.'

'Going away again soon?'

'October half term if the job permits. With Catherine's school work we can only do the school holidays. Twice the price of course.'

'Daylight robbery,' said Peterson.

'Yes, somebody should tell the Police. Anyway, what are you drinking?'

'Adnams please, if they've got it.'

Wendy made her way over to the bar. A small group of locals were sitting on the high stools. One of them was holding forth about how they could club together to buy the place.

'I'll help out. I'd serve behind the bar if it weren't for all my health problems.'

Health problems brought on by all the alcohol you consume, thought Wendy. Put you behind the bar and there'll be nothing left for anybody else to drink.

'Quiet in here this evening.'

'Always is nowadays.'

Wendy bought a couple of pints of Adnams and some crisps of indeterminate, but expensive, brand. Returning to the "snug" she noticed somebody she hadn't seen at The Great Eastern before, sitting at the end of a large table by the window. She thought he looked a bit like a lumberjack. At least, he looked like what she imagined a lumberjack might look like. But why a lumberjack? Probably from watching too much Monty Python, she told herself. After all, he could equally be a truck driver or a concert pianist for all she knew. She laughed at herself for analysing the poor guy without knowing a single thing about him, except that he clearly had a taste for rather loud check shirts.

'Hello, you're new around here aren't you?'

'Yes, came in from across the pond a few months ago.'

'So, what brings you to Chipping Bonhunt?'

'Let me guess, you're the policewoman they warned me about. Don't drink at the Great Eastern Henry, they said, unless you can cope with a police interrogation.'

'I didn't realise I had such a fearsome reputation.'

'Oh, I don't think it was that bad. Person who warned me said it was good to have the police taking an interest. Said you were good at stopping the young tearaways from running riot. Said the little bastards listened to you.'

'Well, we're supposed to do our bit working with the local community. Anyway, let me introduce myself properly. Inspector Wendy Pepper at your service. Not exactly Chipping Bonhunt's answer to Sherlock Holmes, but hopefully keeping the good folk of Essex safe and sound.'

'And the bad folk?'

'Oh, community service for them or even, very occasionally, prison if they've been very, very bad.'

'Back where I come from we lock 'em up and throw away the keys. That's if we don't fry them!'

'Fry them?'

'Yeh, the death penalty. We find it concentrates the minds! Where I come from, they fry.'

'Bit excessive for petty vandalism though, don't you think? So, as I said, I'm Wendy Pepper, who are you?'

'Henry Buske, at your service Maam. True redneck which means I'm what you think all us men from the States are, truly loutish and bigoted.'

'You're being a bit hard on yourself aren't you? Are you working over here?'

'Yeh, if you fancy some flying lessons, then I'm you're man. I like to get people nearer to God.'

No thank you, thought Wendy. Flying was something she had never been very keen on.

'Flying lessons. You involved in the new flying school at Castle Lofts International Airport?'

'Castle Lofts International what? You mean that strip of grass next to the school, you're kiddin me!'

'It's our little joke locally .The local Lord of the Manor owns the place – well, I say Lord of the Manor, but he doesn't own the manor anymore, death duties at the end of the war saw to that. However, he does still own the airfield and he always includes it on his letterhead: "Airport: Castle Lofts International".'

'Well, what ever it's called, yes, that's where I've started the flying school. I'm out again first thing tomorrow with one of the locals. We're getting a lot of interest.'

'I'd better get these pints back to my table before my poor sergeant dies of thirst, but its good to meet you Henry. I don't think I'll be wanting you to help me get nearer to God, in one of your planes I mean. I've never been particularly good with heights. See you again sometime.'

'Sure will.'

Wendy returned to the snug. Peterson had been reading the newspaper cuttings on the pub wall. He'd read them so many times he could almost recite them off by heart.

'You took your time. You know I can never work out why a pub called "The Great Eastern" has a framed newspaper front page featuring the Rolling Stones and some Mars Bars.'

'Great scandal at the time.'

'Well, I don't think it was illegal, and while I'm sure it was very messy, do we have to read about it?'

Wendy laughed. 'You know, you are a bit of a prude. I think it's time we got down to business. What have we got so far?'

'One victim of a hit and run. Still not clear if it was an accident which would be bad enough given the driver has disappeared off the face of the earth, or deliberate in which case it would clearly be murder. I've made some progress today on the clothes. Not sure what it will lead to, but it may help us in identifying the victim.'

'So, one victim, and then we have an arson attack on the Quakers. No obvious motive unless you count Trevor Sandling and his idea to open it up as a café.'

'You're not seriously saying that he'd…'

'No, of course I'm not,' said Wendy, 'but he's the only one who seems to be smiling following the fire. And then we have our sheep rustler. All a bit bizarre.'

'*"Beware of false prophets who come disguised as harmless sheep but are really vicious Wolves."* All very religious, but perhaps we shouldn't be surprised given it was at Summer Bible Club. How's the old lady who found the head?'

'Still a bit shocked when the lads in uniform left, but I think a few cups of tea restored some colour to her cheeks. Back then to the clothes. What was that label?'

'LIVE IN HOPE,' said Peterson, 'It's American, and not available generally in the UK. But PC Smart has lived up to his name and discovered that there's a trendy boutique in Cambridge selling it. I thought I'd go over tomorrow and see if they recognise our victim.'

'You're never one to miss an opportunity to visit the bright lights of the city, are you?' said Wendy. 'An opportunity for lunch with that budding student girlfriend of yours eh?'

'Well, as I'm there, a quick sandwich in a college bar is never to be missed.'

'But surely it's not term time in Cambridge?'

'No, she's gone back to do some work with a visiting professor. He needed somebody to do a bit of reading for him so he can write a book on some obscure area of the law.'

'Sounds a bit heavy, how's it going?'

'Oh, long hours, lots of cases to read up, complicated papers to write, and this guy's a right dinosaur. Some sort of chauvinist monster who hates undergraduates. She calls him the chauviraptor.'

'I thought you told me she liked the people at Jesus.'

'She does. This chap's not from the college, he's visiting from Oxford and seems to have something to prove.'

'So how's she coping?'

'Having a drink with me at every opportunity and then wearing her shortest skirt to distract him from reading her papers in too much detail.'

'And that works?'

'Seems to. Apparently last term he tore one of the other student's essays in half all because the guy didn't understand the law relating to a divorce settlement. It was meant to be some sort of visual illustration. Trudy said the poor guy was almost in tears.'

'You'd think that sort of thing would have stopped by now. Anyway, you go and give moral support to your Trude, and see what you can find out about those clothes. I'm going to do a tour of the churches: There's some sort of religious connection to all of this.'

*****

John Davies was back again at the Summer Bible Club site. After making a tour of the whole area, he was standing outside the Swifts tent with Peter Lord. It had been a rush up from his meeting at the Town Hall, but he had made it. However he was finding this late night duty a bit of a killer. He realised Alice had been right, he should have said no. Night duty at SBC was just one too many things to take on. He felt angry inside, it was the moral pressure he'd felt to help out that had made him say yes on the fifth occasion he was asked. He was angry with the pressure that other people in the churches put on him. It's no wonder so many professional people have deserted the church, he thought. Churches just don't understand the stress that professional working people are under. On top of that you only need a few creationists spouting their fairy tales and that's the credibility of the Christian message completely shot through for anyone who actually uses their brain.

And Peter Lord was exactly the type of creationist that John had in mind. It was all John needed, on top of everything else that had happened that Monday. Peter was determined to give John the full low-down on his new "dream box."

John had made the mistake of sounding interested.

'So what's a dream box?'

'It plugs into your television and you get satellite broadcasts from all the best Christian channels. Real evangelism, broadcast straight into your home. There are some fantastic American preachers on there, really great Christian teaching. We watch it all the time.'

'All the time?'

'Yeah, we've got one of those huge wide-screen tellies in our kitchen-diner, so we can watch it 24 hours a day if we want. Some mornings we're all late for work and school because we're watching it over breakfast.'

John groaned inside. What sort of example is that for the kids, he thought, more important to watch some egocentric American preacher than get to school on time?

'So don't you watch anything else?'

'Oh, we've got an older telly in the living room. The kids can watch stuff on there when their friends come round. But I watch the dream box. I can't get enough of it.'

Remind me not to drop in for tea, thought John, not that he was ever likely to do that. 'Let's do a round of the tents. And let's hope there won't be any more sheep.'

They were just setting off when a car drove on to the site.

'Looks like trouble,' said Peter, 'why would anyone drive up here at this time of night? I hope its not kids mucking around.'

'More likely the police. There was a constable said he'd come back. He wanted to interview you.'

'Why's that then? Why's he after me? I don't know, you give up your time and then they just hassle you. That's what it's like being a Christian.'

'It's hardly persecution. He just wants to check what you saw last night.'

'That's just the beginning. The state is too powerful, you'll see. All this equal opportunities and so-called political correctness, they've got it in for us. We Christians are under attack.'

'I can't help feeling you're over-reacting a bit.'

Over-reacting, thought John, this guy seems to have gone completely over the top. Anyone would think he really did have something to hide.

'Evening there,' said PC Smart. 'Are you Peter Lord?'

'Who's asking?'

John interrupted 'Well, judging by his uniform and the word "Police" on the side of that car there, I would say it was Her Majesty's forces of law and order.'

'But how do we know? It could be anybody.'

PC Smart pulled out a wallet. 'How about this? My I.D. PC Smart from Essex police. Nothing to worry about sir, unless you've been decapitating sheep. I just want to check some details having interviewed your friend here this morning.'

He's no friend of mine, thought John. Never met him before this week.

'So, first of all, can I check where you live?'

'Whylett End, near Sandean.'

'Oh yes, drive through it all the time, whereabouts are you, on the main road?'

'No, I'm tucked round the back. We've got one of the new properties that the housing association built.'

'I know where you mean. What number?'

'Seven.'

'Lucky for some.'

'We don't believe in all that pagan superstition.'

'So you're active in the church are you?'

'The important thing is that I'm a Christian. I take my orders from a higher authority.'

'Well, take me through what happened last night.'

'I was here with John doing night duty. Nothing much went on. There was the noise from the concert at Castle Lofts, and we thought we heard a fox or something.'

'Could it have been somebody else on the site, a young person for example?'

'Didn't see anything.'

'And you can both vouch for each other?'

So I'm in the frame as well, thought John.

'We were both here together for the whole shift.'

'Well, not quite,' said John.

'What do you mean?' asked PC Smart.

'Well, Peter went off to check out if we had a fox.'

'Don't remember that. I said we thought we heard a fox, didn't say I went looking for one.'

'You said you needed a pee as well,' said John. 'Sure you don't remember?'

'If you say so.'

'So there was a period when you weren't both in the same place?'

'About ten minutes,' said John helpfully.

'What time was this?'

'Around ten past ten I think.'

'And there was nothing else?'

'I can't think of anything,' said John. 'Can you?' He looked at Peter.

'No, nothing.'

'Why don't you both show me round the site.'

'We were just about to do a round when you arrived,' said John.

They set off towards the end of the row of marquees. Outside the first one was an area that had been carefully cordoned off with builder's fencing. It was occupied by plastic slides, a Wendy house and some space hoppers.

'I think I'm a bit too old for those,' said PC Smart.

'Robins,' said John. 'The youngest children start here'. All the tents had been carefully tied up by the site team, so one by one John opened them up. Peter seemed to stand back, almost as though he didn't want to get too close to PC Smart.

Each tent reflected the characteristics of the person in charge of the group using it. Some were very plain and one even had a "teacher's desk" at one end, recreating a feeling of a Victorian school room that was reinforced by biblical quotes displayed along the sides of the tent.

'This one looks heavy,' said PC Smart as he surveyed the well ordered layout of tables and carefully stacked chairs.

'This looks a bit more fun, I might survive here,' he said when surveying the apparent chaos of the next tent, half finished drawings hastily pegged to string straddling between the poles and a pile of incomplete cardboard model houses.

'I think they're doing the story of the invalid being lowered through the roof of the house.'

'Why on earth would anyone do that?'

'Sorry, forgot you're not familiar with your Bible. A group of people were trying to get their friend close to Jesus so he could heal them. The only way they could do it was by making a hole in the roof and lowering him down.'

'Remind me not to invite them round to my house!'

They continued the tour of the tents.

'Just two more to go,' said John. 'The next one's mine. Eagles, and then it's on to Seniors. Years gone by there used to be separate tents for boys and girls in Seniors, but we've moved on in the churches since then.'

As he undid the front flaps to the Eagles tent, John noticed that Peter seemed to be falling further behind. What is his problem? thought John, he clearly doesn't want to get too close to our friendly policeman here.

John and Constable Smart entered the Eagles tent, and John shone his torch around.

'What the…?' he didn't finish his sentence, as he felt his throat tighten with the fumes that seemed to fill the inside of the tent.

'PC Smart here, urgent assistance needed on the field at Bonhunt Academy. Get Inspector Pepper and a pathologist up here as quickly as you can.'

John would reflect on how calm and professional the young constable had been in the face of the awful sight that greeted them.

Strapped to the ladder they used for decorating the tent was the horribly twisted figure of a human being. Judging from its contorted position, this had been an agonising death. Horrible burns had discoloured the naked flesh, which was a multitude of shades of red, purple and black.

Pinned across the middle of the body, in a way that John thought was a mocking attempt at preserving the corpse's modesty, was a sheet of A4 paper.

It was the same Arial typeface as on the paper left with the sheep's head:

"Then the LORD rained down fire and burning sulphur from the sky on Sodom and Gomorrah. He utterly destroyed them, along with the other cities and villages of the plain, wiping out all the people and every bit of vegetation."

'Where's your colleague?' asked the constable

John realised that Peter Lord was nowhere to be seen.

*****

'Coffee?' asked Catherine

'Yes please, then I really must turn in, it's been a long, long day,' said Wendy.

'How was The Great Eastern?'

'Almost as dead as the railway itself. I really don't think it's going to last much longer. They're not even doing any proper food now.'

'Shame, it's one of the few decent pubs left in the town.'

Wendy's 'phone rang.

'Wendy Pepper,' she said stifling a yawn. She listened for a moment. 'I've had a few pints, but I can walk up there straight away. Make sure they get everything cordoned off. We're going to need forensics across the whole site.'

'So what's happened now?'

'This morning it was a dead sheep. Tonight it's a dead body. What on earth do they get up to at Summer Bible Club?'

Tuesday

It was seven in the morning and Wendy was back at the Summer Bible Club site on the school field. She'd had three hours sleep, but felt she needed to return to the crime scene early.

Chief Superintendent Warren had turned up in Chipping Bonhunt at two am and Wendy hadn't been able to get away until three.

'I'm putting you in charge of this Wendy. First proper murder case for you. We're short staffed as ever, and I think you've got the local knowledge we need on this one. I thought this place was an affluent commuter town, not the home of the Wicker Man.'

'Sir, I think they were pagans. This lot are Christians. It might not seem very different at the moment, but I can assure you it is an important distinction.'

'Both lots seem quite happy to burn their victims. Now, leave some constables on guard duty, get yourself home for some sleep, and start tomorrow morning bright eyed and bushy tailed. And don't tell me it's bloody Lloyd Evans unless you've got a signed witness statement from the deceased that they saw him do it.'

'No sir,' she'd said, detecting the wry smile on his face, 'thought hadn't even occurred to me. He's a Parish Church man and I don't think he'd go in for Old Testament retribution, but who knows.'

Constable Smart had dropped her off in Granary Lane.

And now she was back. Strong black coffee brewed by Catherine and as the Chief Super had commanded, she was endeavouring to be as bright eyed and bushy tailed as she could be.

Thanks to Catherine making some early morning 'phone calls to the school's site team they'd been able to set up an incident room in one of the classrooms. Apparently some clever IT man was going to come in so they could even use the school network to go on line.

Smart was back, and had been joined by three other constables. The forensics team were on their way back from Chelmsford. Not too pleased apparently, as they'd been dealing with the fire at the Quakers and the sheep's head incident all the previous day and had hoped for some time to collate their results.

But one member of the police team was absent: Peterson was nowhere to be found. His mobile was off and his landlady, not best pleased at being 'phoned at that time in the morning, said he appeared to have been out all night.

I bet he went into Cambridge after we left The Great Eastern, thought Wendy. Spent the night with his girlfriend in college with the intention of making a leisurely morning visit to some clothes shops followed by a relaxed lunch back at Jesus College.

'Right, listen up everybody,' Wendy gathered her troops together. 'We've got some serious work to do.'

Wendy felt as though she was just about to start teaching a class. The police constables were all sitting in a row and she was at the front, standing behind the teacher's desk.

'We need to do a thorough house to house. Larches Close, Eve's Court, Oldtown Road, Angle Way. What have people seen? Any unusual cars, vans, disturbances late at night? You know the stuff. The body must have been brought in after the tent was closed up, which happened about six thirty yesterday. There were people on duty on the site all the time. What did they see? Did they get distracted at any time, or did any of them bunk off? We also need to interview everybody involved with the Summer Bible Club. Good news is that they're all probably setting off to get here now. The bad news is there are almost one hundred of them, but at least that increases the odds of one of them having seen or heard something!'

'What are they doing about the club?' asked one of the constables, 'my son's going to it and nobody knows anything about what's happened yet.'

'We've got that all in hand.' said Wendy 'the school has agreed they can use the hall. The Summer Bible Club stewards will direct everyone when they arrive. I'm going to talk to the children later this morning and ask them to tell the adults if they think they saw anything unusual. But we're not giving them any details. We're just saying that something sad has happened. Somebody died and we're just trying to find out how it happened. No more details to be given to the public at this stage as it might also hamper our investigation and we don't want to upset all the children at SBC. Right, let's get going on the door to door – have you all got details of the roads you're doing?'

'Yes' came the unanimous reply.

'Well, get going then. You need to be quick if you're going to catch people before they leave for work.'

*****

It was pandemonium as usual in the Garroway household.

'Look, will you just get yourselves ready?' shouted Jean; uncertain as to exactly which member of her family to which she was directing her anger.

Tom was oozing calm. 'We've got half an hour before we need to leave, even if the traffic lights are still not working. I just want to finish rereading this instruction manual that Henry gave me.'

'Are you flying again today dad?' asked Joshua, who was showing no sign of changing out of the loungewear trousers that he now insisted on sleeping in every night.

'Yes, I get to drive this morning.'

'Drive? I thought you were flying?'

'You know what I mean!'

'Look Joshua, I know you've fallen in love with those American trousers your dad brought back from Arkansas, but please, please, get changed and get yourself ready.'

'I don't want to go to SBC. I only have to go because you're helping in one of the tents.'

'Josh, you're going and that's the end of it. Come on Lucy, I thought you said you were enjoying helping in Robins.'

'Yes mum,' Lucy yawned. 'I'm almost ready, but I'm really, really tired.'

'Well, perhaps you shouldn't have drunk so much when you were out with the Frosts last night.'

'You know it was Nicola's eighteenth, what was I supposed to do? Her dad kept buying us more drinks. It was really embarrassing.'

Jean gave up on Lucy and tried to catch her husband's eye. 'Tom, will you please put that thing away and just help. Honestly, I seem to be doing everything.'

Tom looked up. 'Just chill a bit, I don't see why the rest of us have to suffer just because you're all stressed.'

Lucy stood up. 'Please you two don't have a domestic. I really can't cope with that this morning. I'm the one who's supposed to be stressed with my results coming this Thursday.'

'You'll be fine Lucy,' said her mum. 'You've got all the grades you needed up to now.'

'Mum, please stop telling me I'll be fine. That chemistry exam was a pig and I just want you to be at least a bit worried as well. You know that if I don't get that A, Fitzwilliam won't let me in. I only just scraped that place in the pool and I don't know how I'm going to cope if I don't get the offer.'

'Just calm down will you.' Jean realised she was raising her voice again.

'You shouting is the last thing that will make me calm.'

'Right, all of you, let's get going,' said Tom.

Outside, Tom walked across what had been the farmyard to open up the door to the barn where the family kept their cars. If you didn't have a knowledge of what Folly Farm had looked like when it actually had been a farm, only the barns gave any hint about its past. Tom's job in the media had taken off over the last few years, and being the key representative of an American company in Britain was proving to be very lucrative. The farmyard was now a beautiful, professionally designed "contemporary" garden. Most of it was laid out in a grid, with a variety of low level boxed shaped hedges defining the squares, each with a different feature. Water, tiles, stone, expensive rare breed roses and bushes: all of these had been carefully orchestrated to leave the visitor in no doubt that the Garroway family were successful, and discerning, professionals.

Tom opened the barn door and reversed the BMW X5 out onto to the Yorkshire stone drive. He got out and closed the doors, casting a brief glance over the other car that had been very carefully covered with some dust sheets.

*****

A couple of Summer Bible Club stewards had managed to organise a practical route for the helpers arriving at Bonhunt Academy. Everyone was being diverted to the upper entrance and into the car parking at the top end of the school. There hadn't been time to ring round, so traffic was building up on Castle Lofts Road as explanations had to be offered to each new arrival.

In the school hall, chairs had been hastily laid out for the older children and helpers. Unfortunately all the smaller primary school chairs were stuck in the tents, which were all out of bounds. The younger children were all going to have sit on the hall floor at the front.

Just like Bushey Manor Primary School, thought John. He remembered Mrs Fox telling them all that they should be able to sit crossed legged for hours. Lucky if we get five minutes out of this lot this morning he thought.

Back on the field, the forensics examination was underway. The Eagles tent was the starting point. The body had now been laid out on a plastic sheet and was being examined by Dr Jane Frobisher.

Wendy Pepper was talking to the pathologist. 'This is a nasty one,' she tried to keep herself composed as she looked at the terrible burns across the body stretched out in front of her, 'that looks like a very painful death.'

'Yes, throwing sulphuric acid over the body is a particularly cruel way to kill somebody.'

'How long would death have taken?'

'Difficult to say at the moment. It certainly wasn't instantaneous. He was tied up and gagged before the acid was poured over him. Looking at how little damage has been done to the grass, I'd say this had to be done somewhere else and his body brought here afterwards. Mind you, there is some spillage over there and we've found one jar in which some acid was brought into the tent. Not nearly enough to do all this, so it seems the killer wanted to go for maximum effect. It's pretty sick.'

'How could somebody restrain someone and do this to them?'

'One for you, I think. But he may of course have been drugged. If he wasn't, he would have been screaming when this was done to him. I'll get some toxicology tests done as soon as I can.'

The forensic team were doing a painstakingly systematic search of the tent. One of the officers held up the jar in his gloved hand.

'This was what the acid was brought in. Of course, it's clean of prints.'

'Any ideas about the jar?'

'It's a kilner jar, a sealed jar made for storing food. Not so common nowadays but there are plenty around and I think somebody still makes them. It will almost certainly be impossible to trace where it came from.'

Wendy called Catherine on her mobile. 'Managed to fight your way through the crowds?'

'Yes, a bit of a nightmare out there, but I made it.'

'I need a bit of help, who do I talk to about the science labs and your chemical store?'

'You need to talk to Dr Dreyfus, I'll ask the Head to get him to come to your incident room if he's in school at the moment.'

'As soon as he can, I need to go over some things with him.'

*****

Peterson had enjoyed a leisurely morning having had a good night with Trudy at Jesus College. He had arrived at midnight, but he knew the porter on duty who'd let him in. Trudy had run across to meet him from L staircase as soon as he'd phoned her on his mobile from The Chimney, the long walled path that led from Jesus Lane up to the Porters' Lodge. They didn't often get the opportunity to spend time together. Trudy was very serious about her law degree, fully in the knowledge that a career with a leading city solicitor would require the best degree she could get. She'd achieved a high first in her Part One exams and even the chauviraptor had admitted that she had 'quite a good grasp of the law.' But Jesus was also a strong rowing college, and the temptation to take to the oars when such good facilities were at hand was something Trudy couldn't resist. Her visiting Oxford chauvinist didn't approve.

'Nobody who rows gets a first in law,' he'd said.

That was like a red rag to the bull for Trudy, and she was determined to prove him wrong. She'd already achieved the top grade in her first year and now she would need to continue working at the same level next term. However, vacation time meant no early morning on the river and this morning she had her Ian with her.

'Oh shit,' said Peterson 'my 'phone isn't charged up. If Pepper has been trying to get hold of me I'm in trouble.'

Trudy switched on the radio. The nine o'clock news was just starting.

"A body was found last night at a summer camp in Chipping Bonhunt. Police say it was found in one of the tents being used for the annual Summer Bible Club. The death is being treated as suspicious."

'Christ, I need to ring in. Trudy, can I borrow your 'phone?'

'Here you are, never a dull moment for my lover-boy!'

Peterson punched in Wendy Pepper's number. The 'phone connected and he heard it ring several times. Then Wendy's voice came on.

'Hello, who is this?'

'It's me, just heard the news.'

'Aah, the wandering detective! Hoped we might hear from you sometime this morning, but I didn't recognise the number.'

'Had to borrow Trudy's mobile, mine's flat.'

'So how is the beautiful Trude? – give her my love. No need to panic, everything's under control here. You go off on your shopping trip and see what you can find out about Hopeless Living.'

'LIVE IN HOPE,' corrected Peterson.

'Whatever, - don't we all? When you've visited the shop, get back here as quickly as you can.'

The 'phone went dead.

'Sorry, no time for breakfast. I'll try to get over here again at the weekend.'

'And I'll try and survive the rest of the week without being eaten by the chauviraptor.'

They kissed, and Peterson made his way down L staircase, across to First Court and out past the Porters' Lodge.

'Had a good night, did we sir?' the porter said with a broad smile on his face.

*****

Tom was edging the BMW up along Castle Lofts Road.

'I've never known it as slow as this,' said Jean. 'The whole town seems to be gridlocked. Must be some sort of accident.'

'Well, you're late for Summer Bible Club and I'm late for Henry and my flying lesson. We seem to be losing all round.'

'We could always turn round and go home,' said Joshua enthusiastically.

'You just pretend you don't like SBC,' Lucy replied, 'you can't be seen by your friends to enjoy it because it's not cool. You're just pathetic.'

'That's enough,' said Jean, 'we're almost there now. What's going on here? There seem to be police everywhere.'

Tom wound his window down to talk to the steward who was directing traffic as it entered the school site.

'What's up, chap?' he asked.

'Can't say too much, but the tents are all out of bounds this morning. Everybody needs to go to the hall, and if you need to park this thing you should go to the upper entrance.'

'I'm not staying. I'll drop this lot off and leave again.'

Tom followed the queue round the lower car park, dropped the family off and headed back to Castle Lofts Road.

'Well, this is different. I can't wait to find out what's going on.'

'Suddenly you're all enthusiastic Josh,' said Lucy, 'they've probably found a whole load more sheep!'

'I'm sure we'll find out what's happened when we get to the hall.' Jean was marching purposefully up to the main entrance. For somebody who always liked to know what was going on, she was feeling distinctly out of it. Surely someone could have 'phoned to warn us, she thought.

*****

Another person stuck in the gridlocked traffic that morning was Lloyd Evans. He was fuming. Today was supposed to be a good day out. Wine tasting at the Club in Pall Mall. It had taken a lot of careful lobbying and had cost a fortune in dinners to get himself on the wine committee and this was the first meeting he was due to attend. But being late was very bad form.

It had all been fine when he'd gone to eight o'clock Morning Prayer at the Parish Church. Should have got away by eight-thirty, just in time to drive to Castle Lofts station for the ten past nine train to London. The nine-forty would still be OK, but he was clearly going to miss that as well.

What do the police think they're doing? Another call needed to the Commissioner, he thought. If you have friends in high places then you should use them.

He tried to call the Club on the car 'phone. At least it was hands free, but he wouldn't put it past that annoying female detective to try and do him for using it.

'It's Lloyd Evans here. I need to get a message to the chair of the wine committee. Yes, the chair of the wine committee. Please can you apologise to him that because of a complete bloody traffic foul up I've missed my train and I'm going to be late.'

Some words at the other end were in such a strong accent that Lloyd couldn't understand anything that was being said. What was worse, it was clear the person at the Club didn't understand him either. What was the point of having had an empire if we didn't teach the natives to understand proper English?

'Look, just tell the chair of the wine committee that Lloyd Evans…OK, I'll spell that…. L, L, O, Y. D, Evans, that's E, V, A, N, S, apologises that he will be late. You understand?'

Despite the yes that came from the other end of the line, Lloyd wasn't at all certain that he had been understood.

*****

Tom Garroway arrived at the airfield. The Maule MT7 was already parked up at the end of the airstrip, and the main hanger door had been closed.

Tom walked over to the side door, and entered the hangar. It was dark, so he called out 'Henry.' There didn't seem to be anyone around. 'Henry' he called out again. Fumbling along the wall, he found the light switch. A series of fluorescent tubes flickered into life. There were three other light aeroplanes and a beautifully restored spitfire lined up with their tails facing the far wall. Still no sign of Henry.

Wouldn't blame him for giving up on me, thought Tom, but I'm only half an hour late.

Tom walked up to the spitfire. It was in fantastic condition, looking as though it was brand new.

'I thought all of these had gone to Duxford,' he said to himself quietly.

Tom heard a door slam at the back of the hanger where the locker and store rooms were located.

'Hi there Tom boy, ready for the flight?'

'You bet. Looking forward to taking the controls.'

'Let's get going then.'

They left the building and walked over to the Maule.

'Time for your pre-flight checks. You take us through the checklist, and remember, this isn't just about going through the motions.'

He followed the standard procedure starting at the left wingtip and moving round the aircraft clockwise. When he'd finished they both climbed inside the plane.

'Do I have to brief you as a passenger?'

'Tell me the flight plan.'

Tom outlined their proposed route, a triangle out into Cambridgeshire, across Suffolk and back into Essex. He went through the other checks: cabin doors closed, seats adjusted and locked, belts and harness secure, circuit breakers all ok, all switches off and brakes set and tested.

It was time to taxi, go through some more checks and then, finally after what seemed to be an age, set off down the airstrip.

It always amazed Tom that by accelerating down this slightly uneven strip of grass you could ever get air born. He felt the exhilaration as they took to the air, and he pulled the plane up to ensure it was well clear of the trees that a seemed menacingly close to the end of the airstrip when you took off. Get that one wrong and it would be a quick and nasty end to the flight. Despite the fact that he had carefully called the flight plan in before getting airborne, this first take-off under his control reminded him that there was no rescue service to come running if something went wrong. No on site fire brigade or ambulance, no on site police, in fact nobody but the plane crew. There was perhaps some comfort to be gained from the police presence at Summer Bible Club. He hoped Jean was praying for him as he flew over the Summer Bible Club site. There was still a queue down Castle Lofts Road and he could see various cars looking as though they were lost in the array of parking spaces at the school. On the main school field, only police could be seen among the tents.

It was all probably very exciting for the kids, but it must be a nightmare for the organisers.

*****

Ian Peterson was walking down Mill Road. It had been several years since he had visited this part of Cambridge and he realised how much it had changed. At some point the Council had put in a one-way system on the side streets and planted trees at key junctions. It had transformed the terraces of houses built for the working classes into a fashionable middle class and student enclave. And this was reflected in the shops. The Co-Op was still there, but now with its "new image" incorporating the latest light green signs, and a Tesco Express had somehow negotiated its way through the planning authorities. Peterson seemed to remember there had been a bit of a campaign to try and stop that one. There was a general change in the feel of the road. A lot of the shops were still rather bohemian or "alternative," what Chief Superintendent Warren would call "trendy leftie," but the whole road seemed to be going up market.

Peterson found the shop he was looking for. A strikingly modern steel frontage had been inserted into the otherwise traditional terrace of shop fronts. A large rectangular glass window was mounted between two strong vertical steel pillars. The glass ran the full height of the shop front and spanning between the two pillars was a sign made out of elegant deeply moulded steel letters "Apparel." On the glass, a large outline of an American Eagle surmounted the words "Fine American Clothing."

A door, in similar style, occupied a recess to the left of the window. Peterson entered.

'Can I help you Sir?'

'I hope so,' he replied, opening his warrant card.

'Police? We've got some fine New York cop uniforms you might want to try. Very popular for student parties at the moment.'

'Not today thank you,' but I might be back, he thought.

'So what have we done to attract the attention of the feds?'

'I'm interested in who's been buying clothing from a particular range you stock.'

'Which range is that?'

'LIVE IN HOPE.'

The assistant thought for a moment.

'How recently? We haven't really sold much. Bit of a disappointment if you ask me. It's supposed to be a unique brand from Arkansas. Hope, Arkansas actually – home of the great President Bill Clinton and a Republican guy called Mike Huckabee who tried and failed to become President.'

'So why is it disappointing?'

'Well, it's nothing special. They make it in Hope, and charge a premium for their allegedly high quality and unique product. There are other brands that are unique, but with “LIVE IN HOPE” you could probably stick the label on a cheap import and nobody would notice the difference.’

‘So who’s been buying it?’

‘A few students with more money than sense. The underwear sells better than the rest, and that is a bit different. I think it has a certain cachet: Impresses the ladies when you have your own very special and unique boxer shorts.’

‘Makes up for the contents not being particularly special or unique?’

The shop assistant laughed. ‘You’ve got a point there, never thought of it that way. Puts a whole new meaning on the “LIVE IN HOPE” label. I’ll avoid using that as a sales pitch!’

Peterson took out a photo of the hit and run victim. It didn’t look too pretty, but it was a clear picture of the victim’s face.

‘Has this person visited the shop?’

‘What happened to him? No, doesn’t look familiar. I don’t think he’s ever been in here.’

‘Does anybody else who has purchased this stuff stand out, anyone unusual?’

‘Well, there was one guy came in. Older, not the usual type to buy things like the “LIVE IN HOPE” range. I only remember him because he particularly wanted to buy their loungewear trousers. It’s the only pair we’ve sold, and frankly they’re rather gross.’

‘Was that all he bought?’

‘I really can’t remember. I can go through the records. If he paid on a card I can probably track down a name for you, but it will take me a little while.’

‘OK, here’s my card. Give me a ring if you find anything. It could be very important.’

Peterson left the shop and walked back up Mill Road. He was asking himself if he should have pushed the shop assistant a bit harder. Better to retain his goodwill, he thought.

He drove back into Chipping Bonhunt down Old Mill Hill. The traffic through the town was still dreadful.

*****

At the Friends' Meeting House, Trevor Sandling was showing the Mayor the damaged foyer area.

'Well, every cloud has a silver lining,' said Councillor Hodgkiss. 'You could do a lot with this entrance area.'

'Some of my colleagues may think I'm jumping the gun,' replied Trevor, 'but now we're probably going to have to rebuild the foyer it's a great opportunity to open the building up a bit. I see a thriving café where everyone is welcome during the day time. There's lots of lonely single people round the town, and then there are the mums with kids and not a lot to do. This could be a real community benefit, and it will increase the impact we have. Lots of people think all we do is sit in silence together.'

'Isn't that what you do?' asked Councillor Hodgkiss, rather proving Trevor Sandling's point. 'I'm with you on the café idea, but I'm not so keen on the single people and mums with lots of children. We don't want to encourage too much of that in the centre of town. I was thinking more of visitors, tourists. Get this right and you can help bring trade into the town.'

'I think our values are a bit different. We're more about trying to meet the needs of the local population. This might seem an affluent town, but with the changes in welfare and benefits, there are a lot of people really finding things very tough.'

The Mayor raised his eyes to heaven and sighed. How many times had he heard all this do-gooding stuff? It was like an epidemic in the town. Nobody has a vision for what we need to make the town successful he thought. They just want to hand out charity to the poor. He collected himself. Time for some diplomacy.

'You've got a lot of space here. Can't you use one of the rooms inside for all these very worthy things you want to do? Then you could use your new Foyer for something targeted more at visitors. With the right design, you could kill two birds with one stone. Why don't I ask that architect further down the High Street if he'd sketch out some ideas for you? I'm sure he'd do a bit of work at risk if there's a prospect of the job later on.'

Trevor thought for a moment.

'Well, we think it's important to try and work with the Town Council. Days gone by, a lot of Quakers were on the old Borough Council. I'll talk to meeting about your proposal and get back to you.'

'So that's a yes then?'

'It's not a no.'

*****

In the hall at Bonhunt Academy, the improvised Summer Bible Club arrangements were going quite well. They'd started in their tent groups, spread around the hall. The noise was deafening, but most of the tent leaders were coping with running their activities despite the general air of organised chaos. John and Alice had been doing the story of Jesus raising Lazarus from the dead.

Had Jesus really raised somebody who had been dead for four days back to life? Never put doubts into the minds of children, thought John. He had found it difficult trying to explain to one of the children why Jesus hadn't raised her father back to life after he had died six months ago. He remembered the story in the local newspaper. Popular local amateur football coach died of cancer after a brave fight.

He'd felt his reply to the child could have been better. 'God doesn't always give us what we want. Your father isn't with you now, but he is with God. I'm sure he's very happy, but missing you and I expect he's taking an interest in everything you do.'

'But it's not fair. Nobody else's dad has died like mine.'

'It's difficult for us to understand. Things often don't seem to be fair, but I'm sure God knows what he's doing.'

Most of the children had drawn pictures of Jesus raising Lazarus. Agnes had, to everyone's surprise, recovered from the shock of Monday and turned up for duty, reliable as ever. She was busy sorting the pictures that the children had drawn.

The children were now all taking part in Assembly in the big marquee, which the police had decided was no longer part of the crime scene. The two naughty school boys, a favourite sketch at Summer Bible Club, were back. There was something about adults dressing up as school boys with caps that were too small for them which always seemed to work, and the kids loved it. The naughty school boys had borrowed the school's vaulting horse from the gym and they were trying to persuade the town's popular Salvation Army Captain that there was something inside the box that she would like. All she had to do was climb in to see what it was.

'It's very special,' said one of the boys.

'Yes,' said the other, 'we made it specially for you.'

'Shall I climb in?' the Captain asked the children.

'NO' they all shouted back.

'Are you sure I shouldn't climb in?'

'YES'

'So that's yes, I should climb in?'

'NO' they shouted.

'I'm all confused now. I really want to see what these two naughty boys have made for me, so I'll climb in.'

As soon as she was in, the naughty boys dropped the top back on the vaulting box and sat on it.

'Got her! Isn't this fun. I bet she feels very silly now.'

Most of the children were laughing, although some of them seemed worried about what had happened to the Captain.

'Is she going to be alright?' a worried young girl asked John.

'I'm sure she'll be fine. I think those naughty boys won't be smiling for long.'

Agnes came up to John and handed him a picture.

'Don't know how children get these things into their minds. What on earth possessed a child to draw this?'

John looked at the picture and froze. It was crudely drawn, but unmistakeable.

An upright man was tied to a ladder, and a second figure was pouring something over him.

*****

Lloyd Evans was continuing to have a very bad day. As he had feared, he had missed the nine forty train and had to make do with the ten nineteen. He'd been half way through his well rehearsed tirade in the ticket office when he'd realised that he was shouting at the nice lady who went to the Baptist Church. As he went bright red, he'd managed to control his temper and apologise. She'd given him her pitiful look, called him by his first name making it clear that she recognised him and said how sorry she was that his day had been spoilt. Then, in her most cheerful voice, she had told him that they tried to please but sometimes didn't manage it, and that while running the trains was the responsibility of Greater Anglia, getting to the station on time wasn't.

That had all been bad enough, but now he was stuck at Waltham Cross. Not a scheduled stop for his train, but apparently a bus driver had decided to try and jump the level crossing at Enfield Lock and the bus had taken one of the barriers with it. Nobody hurt, but nobody knew when the trains would start up again. Lloyd Evans decided it was pointless trying to complete his journey; the wine committee would be well and truly finished by the time he got to his club and he probably wouldn't even be able to make it in time for lunch. Particularly disappointing, as the steward's choice of wines for the committee lunch were legendary and he'd been looking forward to some of the rarities to be found in the club's cellar.

On his mobile he was having the same difficulty he'd experienced earlier.

'L, L, O, Y, D, Evans, that's E, V, A, N, S, apologises that he won't be able to make it.'

He decided to give up the journey and go for a walk. Climbing up a stairway nearby to the Station he made his way along Eleanor Cross Road. If his memory wasn't playing tricks, he was certain that Waltham Abbey was this way. A visit to the Abbey Church would calm him down. When he'd left Chipping Bonhunt the weather had been fine, but now a mild drizzle was turning into heavier rain. He passed a closed pub and was relieved to find a McDonalds. Compared with the club dining room it was a bit of a desperate alternative, but it was dry and served food.

Lloyd entered the restaurant and looked at the garish menus displayed above the serving counter. He decided on a Quarterpounder with Cheese.

'Do you want the meal?'

Lloyd looked confused. 'I thought I was ordering a meal.'

'No, do you want the Quarterpounder with cheese meal?'

'Yes please,' he managed, not quite sure what he was ordering.

'Extra large?'

'Why not, you only live once.'

'Which drink would you like?'

'No chance of a glass of wine I suppose?'

The young girl behind the counter looked at him blankly.

'No, I thought not, Coffee please.'

'That'll be five ninety-nine then.'

Well, at least it's cheap, he thought.

He paid and sat down as far away from the other customers as possible. Outside, the rain was getting heavier. Inside a young mother was shouting at her child to eat the food that was being spread across the table, while a baby was crying at one of those ear piercingly high volumes that only babies can achieve. Everyone apart from Lloyd seemed to regard all of this as being perfectly normal. He wondered how long he was going to be stuck in this plastic hell-hole.

*****

Trudy was cycling down to the river near Grantchester. The chauviraptor had e-mailed (quite a surprise, she hadn't realised he could) to tell her that he didn't need her that morning. So she'd arranged to meet Sue, a postgraduate student who rented a room in the village. Sue was in the second year of her law PhD, researching the role of women in the development of family law. It was all very complicated, but according to Sue there seemed to be a correlation between the increased emphasis being put on the views of children and an increase in the numbers of women serving as judges in the family courts.

Although they were both lawyers, Trudy and Sue had actually met through Student Community Action. Trudy didn't have much time to give to anything beyond her studies and rowing, but usually managed a weekly session with Sue volunteering at Jimmy's Night Shelter. From this a friendship had grown, as they enjoyed debating legal issues and Sue had rowed for her college, Corpus Christi, as an undergraduate.

Trudy heard a light aeroplane flying over her and instinctively looked up. She couldn't see clearly, but was sure she saw something being thrown out of one of the windows. Perhaps it was a trick of the light, as she couldn't see anything falling and it was really too far away even for her excellent eyesight to be certain as to what she'd seen.

*****

Henry closed the small window on his side of the plane.

'Sorry about that,' he said to Tom. 'Bit of cloth that's been annoying me. Won't damage anyone if it lands on the sidewalk.'

Little chance of that, thought Tom, we're flying over open fields.

They continued on their flight north. The idea was to reach Ely and then turn towards Suffolk.

*****

All the children from the Eagles tent had been moved out of the hall and into a classroom. After Agnes had shown him the picture, John had gone straight to one of the police and explained what had been found.

Wendy had decided that they really needed to talk to all the children, but that they should get parental permission first.

'This is an important piece of evidence,' she said to John realising that she was stating the obvious, 'and whoever drew this is almost certainly an important witness. We mustn't put a step wrong; we're walking on eggshells when it comes to child witnesses in a situation like this.'

John had asked the children who had drawn the picture of the man tied to the ladder. Two children had claimed it was theirs. Nothing is ever simple, he'd thought, as he tried to explain the problem to Wendy.

'Neither of these two children is particularly truthful. They both have difficult family backgrounds. Chloe Gatiss can be very demanding and often doesn't tell the truth, but we think it's a problem at home. Dad's an alcoholic and mum often takes Chloe to her Nan's. She's very good and does her best, but she can't make up for the difficult situation back at home. Yesterday Chloe was seeking attention all day. Kicking one of the other girls and always needing the felt pen or scissors that one of the others was using. She could be claiming it's her picture just to get attention. David Bayliss is just dishonest and his parents always support him no matter what he does. He's very used to getting his own way and he's already pinched things out of the other children's lunchboxes. He went home yesterday with another boy's coat and it took my wife Alice over an hour of 'phone calls to sort it out.'

Wendy thought for a moment. 'I suppose you're not going to hazard a guess as to who's drawn the picture?'

'Well, normally I would say the rough drawing and lack of detail would suggest it was a boy, so that would be David Bayliss. It's not exactly a great work of art is it? Dashed off as quickly as possible. But Chloe doesn't have much of an attention span either, and it looks similar to another picture she drew yesterday. If you get her Nan in, she'll probably be able to get Chloe to tell the truth. She doesn't usually lie to her Nan.'

Two female constables were interviewing the children whose parents had arrived at the school. So far they'd talked to five and none of them had seen anything that seemed relevant to the inquiry.

'Its hard work' said PC Fletcher. John had thought she looked far too young to be a police constable, more like a sixth former in fancy dress. He kept his thoughts to himself.

Wendy decided it was time for a walk. The picture had been put in an evidence bag and sealed. She took it with her and went back to the classroom the police were using as their base.

As she walked round the school buildings she reflected on where the investigation was going. The key suspect had to be Peter Lord, who was nowhere to be seen. But it wasn't entirely straightforward. If he'd been with John Davies on the Sunday night, would he have had time to do a bit of sheep rustling and get back to the school to leave the animal's body in the sixth form office and the head in the Eagles tent? Possibly, but he'd have to have been very well organised.

*****

The rain had stopped in Waltham Abbey, and Lloyd Evans had made a hasty escape from McDonalds as soon as he felt it was safe to do so without getting soaked. He'd walked further down the road and arrived at the Abbey. It was a long time since he'd visited this unusual parish church, and he'd forgotten how impressive the grand Norman columns and arches were, just like a scaled down version of Durham Cathedral, he thought.

Henry VIII had particularly liked Waltham as a place to escape to and he'd enjoyed hunting with the Abbot; this probably explained why it was the last abbey to be dissolved. It had very nearly become a cathedral. Lloyd Evans pondered how different this small town (or was it a village?) would have been if this now humble parish church had been elevated to cathedral status. You could still walk round the Abbey grounds where you could see the foundations of all the buildings that had been demolished for their valuable stone. The nave of the old Abbey was the only part to survive, having always been the parish church.

Lloyd entered the Lady Chapel and studied the huge wall painting in front of him. The fine Doom painting had been discovered in 1905, and had survived the attentions of Cromwell because it was hidden behind a ceiling. Like all Doom paintings, it was a depiction of the Last Judgement, when Christ will come again to judge the living and the dead.

On the left were the jaws of Hell while Christ in Majesty was weighing souls in the middle. Lloyd pondered his own judgement. He might be a pillar of St Andrew's Parish Church, but did it really mean anything to him?

If attendance at Morning Prayer, not to mention services on Sunday, was important in the final judgement then his place at the heavenly banquet was guaranteed. But did he really believe any of it?

It's a pretty big ask, he thought, a man actually being the son of God, born of a virgin on Christmas Day; crucified on Good Friday; rose again on Easter Sunday. Lloyd Evans fell to his knees and in his mind he recited the words of the Apostles' Creed.

I believe in God, the Father Almighty,
the Maker of heaven and earth,
and in Jesus Christ, His only Son, our Lord:

Who was conceived by the Holy Ghost,
born of the virgin Mary,
suffered under Pontius Pilate,
was crucified, dead, and buried;

He descended into hell.

The third day He arose again from the dead;

He ascended into heaven,
and sitteth on the right hand of God the Father Almighty;
from thence he shall come to judge the quick and the dead.

I believe in the Holy Ghost;
the holy catholic church;
the communion of saints;
the forgiveness of sins;
the resurrection of the body;
and the life everlasting.

Amen.

Lloyd Evans realised he was crying. The tears flowed down his cheeks.

But I don't believe it, he thought.

Science tells us people don't come back from the dead.

I love the church, its ritual and the buildings.

I love the music, the position the church has in the town.

And I love my status in the church.

But I don't really believe, it's just something I do.

'Are you alright? Can I help?'

The sympathetic words caused him to jump. Rubbing his eyes and looking up, a young woman wearing a clerical collar met his gaze with a face that expressed sympathy and concern.

'Sorry, I wasn't sure if I should disturb you, but I couldn't help noticing you seemed to be upset.'

Lloyd Evans struggled to his feet.

'And kneeling in the middle of the aisle here wasn't very clever of me, was it? Sorry, just some old memories coming back. I'd forgotten how special the painting is.'

'A wonderful example of Doom painting. We're very fortunate to have it. Is there anything I can do to help? Would you like me to pray with you?'

'That's kind of you, but no thank you, I'm fine now. I need to get going.'

'Take care. God be with you.'

He made his way to the door and walked out into the fresh air. The sun had come out and he decided to take a walk around the Abbey ruins.

*****

Wendy Pepper and Peterson were using one of the school offices as an interview room. Chloe Gatiss' Nan had come up to the school as soon as they'd contacted her. She was a stalwart of one of the town's longstanding working families. Generations had lived in the area, working on the farms and serving in the larger houses. Nan Porter was part of the delicate economic balance that had kept the town working for decades. After her early years in service came to an end, her last job had been working at the outfitters on the High Street, where most of the local school children bought their school uniforms. So Nan knew most of the kids in the town, as well as their parents. It pained her to see the circumstances her granddaughter grew up in, but she was a wise soul. Her daughter's home was not the only dysfunctional family in the town, she knew far too many of them.

In her day, you worked hard, knew your place, and went to chapel on Sunday. It was still her philosophy of life, but nowadays the hard work was trying to keep her family on the straight and narrow. She had sleepless nights about Chloe, but she loved her granddaughter and she would be there for her for as long as she was able.

'Now Chloe, I want you to tell me straight, did you really draw this picture?'

'Yes Nan, I did.'

'You're not fibbing me, are you Chloe?'

'No Nan, I drew it.'

'There you are, Inspector Pepper. If she says to me she drew that picture, then draw that picture she did.'

'You're absolutely certain about that, are you Nan?' asked Wendy.

'Absolutely, I know our Chloe, and she's not lying.'

'Thank you. Now we'd like to ask Chloe some questions about what she saw and when she saw it. Is her mother aware you're here, and do you know if she's happy for us to question Chloe?'

'Her mum's said it's OK. I usually have to do the meetings at school if Chloe gets into trouble. Her mum's working at the care home. Has to take the work when she gets it – zero hours I think they call it. They expect her to work whenever they say so, but some weeks they don't give her any work at all. How's a mother supposed to look after her kids when she has to take work like that? Taking a liberty I call it.'

Diabolical liberty, thought Wendy, heaven knows how some of the local kids are going to grow up, but she didn't have time to get caught up in that debate.

Wendy turned to Chloe.

'We need to ask you some questions, Chloe. You're not in any trouble and nobody here is going to be cross with you. Sergeant Peterson and I need you to tell us about what you saw yesterday and when you saw it. We need you to remember everything you can. Do you understand?'

'Yes,' said Chloe, shifting awkwardly in her seat.

'So, Chloe, why don't you tell us what you saw.'

'I saw a car by the tent.'

'What sort of car?'

'It was big and red.'

'Anything else?'

'It was big and red and a man was driving it.'

'So what did you do?'

'I hid in the Robins tent.'

'Why did you hide?'

'Because I was frightened and scared I would get told off.'

'Why would you be told off?'

'Because it was late and I was playing on the field.'

'Playing on the field?'

'Oh, she's always doing that,' said Nan, 'she goes out on her own and nobody stops her. Her mum probably didn't even know she was out.'

'So you saw a big red car being driven by a man, and you hid in the Robins tent?'

'Yes'

'Where was the car?'

'It was up by that building on the field.'

'Do you mean the pavilion at the far end?'

'The building with the clock on it.'

'That's the cricket pavilion. So what happened next?'

'Another man got into the car.'

'Can you describe the men?'

'The man in the car had white hair.'

'And the man who got into the car?'

'He was very tall.'

'So what did you do next?'

'I hid in the Robins tent and waited for the car to go.'

Wendy was finding it very hard work. The trouble with interviewing children was that one wrong step meant you had the book thrown at you, but she also desperately needed to find out everything that Chloe knew.

After another 15 minutes, Peterson had noted:

- *stayed hidden in tent, frightened of being seen*
- *didn't see anymore of the men in car (not telling us everything? avoided eye contact)*
- *heard Coronation Street tune when she left home*
- *heard car leave and crawled in and out of other tents*
- *saw two people inspecting tents when she first got there. Didn't see them again (check who was on duty)*
- *looked into Eagles tent because entrance was open. Saw man pouring something on body in tent. Very frightened, ran home*
- *couldn't describe man she saw in Eagles tent. Might have been one of the men from the car, but not sure.*
- *didn't see anybody go in or out of Eagles tent*

'Right, we're going to stop there, Chloe,' said Wendy. 'We may need to talk to you again later, and if you remember anything else, you tell Nan and she'll let us know, won't you Nan?'

'Of course I will. Poor child. She's seen things no child should see.'

'You run along and enjoy yourself now, Chloe. You've been very helpful.'

Chloe and her Nan left the room.

'Has she?' asked Peterson

'Has she what?' replied Wendy

'Been helpful. I got the feeling there was something else she wasn't sharing about the man in the car. Surely she can remember something about the man she saw with the body in the Eagle's tent?'

'You may well be right, but we mustn't put any ideas into her head. It was a lot for her to cope with. She's given us some helpful things to go on for the time being. These are the things I think we should focus on.'

Peterson wrote some more notes:

- *who was in the car? Is the car on any of the CCTV footage?*
- *what time was Coronation Street on last night?*
- *who was on duty inspecting the tents when Chloe arrived? Why didn't Chloe see them again?*
- *what time exactly did John Davies and Peter Lord take over security duty?*
- *where is Peter Lord?*

'Get one of the constables to check out that pathetic CCTV again and see if there's anything on there. Check Coronation Street. I'll talk to the SBC leaders about the rota and see if any of them has any ideas about where Peter Lord might have disappeared to.'

'Are we going to bring the team together for a briefing?'

'Yes, let's say four o'clock in the classroom. We'll try and make sense of everything we've got.'

*****

Lucy Garroway had taken some time out from helping in the Robins tent. She'd been coping well, but the stress of waiting for her results was getting to her. Time for some sympathy from her favourite teacher.

Sitting in the sixth form office, Catherine was making them both a cup of tea.

'So does the school know yet?'

'The universities already have the results, but we don't get them until tomorrow, Wednesday. And you know we can't tell you until Thursday. Strictly verboten.'

'So I've really got to wait until eight am on Thursday? I'm just going to die!'

'Come-on. You've done really well so far. I'm sure it will be OK. There's no point in getting yourself worked up about it, you can't change anything now. Just try not to think about it.'

'Easy for you to say!'

Yes it is, thought Catherine, every year I trot out the same old lines to panicking students. Sometimes I'm right, and it turns out there's nothing to worry about. Other times I'm wrong and we have a disaster on our hands.

Fortunately, nine times out of ten Catherine was right, and she was pretty certain she was right about Lucy. She'd get her A* and two As and be off to read medicine at Cambridge. She deserves her place at Fitzwilliam College, thought Catherine. But even that had been fraught with tension and shattered nerves. Lucy had applied to Pembroke College only to be pooled. This meant, instead of receiving a letter saying yes or no, she'd had a letter saying she might be approached by another College. Two days later and a 'phone call had summoned Lucy for two more interviews. Eventually, after another anxious week of waiting, Fitzwilliam had finally made up their mind.

Please Oh please God, let it be an A in Chemistry, Catherine prayed to herself.

'So, what do you have planned for Thursday, surely you're not helping at SBC on results day?'

'No, I've been allowed off. I think having to help at SBC would be the last straw! Plan is that we come in, and if we've all got what we need, then the gang will go back to Gemma's for a champagne lunch. After that I think it's the Royal Sovereign in town, except of course I'm still underage until next week. I bet I get I-D'd, that would just be my luck. Happened last week when we all tried to get together. They wouldn't even let me have a lemonade!'

'So, nothing with your parents?'

'Oh, I think they've got something planned. Probably going out for a meal, but mum's not tempting fate by telling me yet. I heard her discussing it with dad when they didn't realise I could hear them. They, of course, are absolutely confident I will get my grades.'

'Well, they're never going to tell you if they're not. And they've been very supportive, haven't they?'

'Yes, I suppose so. But sometimes I feel I'm just having to do this for them. That "living your life through your kids" thing – you know.'

'I'm sure it can feel like that, but you want to go to Cambridge don't you? You're doing this for you.'

'I suppose so. But neither of them went to Oxbridge, and it's like I'm the one who's got to do it for all the family.'

'Look, just relax and don't let it all get to you. If the results are OK, you'll be off to Cambridge and the world will be yours. If it doesn't work out on Thursday morning, we'll find something that does. You've got great GCSEs, what was it, 11 A*s and a B?'

'Yes, a B in French. Bloody languages. Never could understand French or German.'

'Well, that's the least of your worries. It will be champagne on Thursday. Trust me!'

There was a knock on the door and Wendy Pepper's head appeared.

'Oh, sorry, didn't want to interrupt.'

'Don't worry, I'm just going,' said Lucy, 'thanks Catherine that was really helpful.'

'I'm not sure I did anything.'

'You listened, and that helped.'

'Good luck for Thursday morning.'

Lucy left the room and closed the door.

'Nervous student?'

'Yes, she shouldn't have anything to worry about really, but if I'm honest we are a bit concerned about chemistry this year. Exam board did one of those things where they change the type of question without warning. We've taken them through the last five year's papers so they go into the exam expecting one thing and then get something completely different. It means they really have to think on their feet, or in their seats, and it's probably a better test of their understanding of the subject, but of course it leaves them all thinking that they've failed.'

'So what happens if everybody's done badly? It must be the same at most schools.'

'Yes, it will be. I looked at the student room website and there are over a hundred posts on this exam. I expect the exam board will moderate the results, so they might get 100% in the module even if they couldn't do it all.'

'Sounds strange to me. You don't finish the paper, but you still get 100%?'

'I'm not even going to try and explain. How's the investigation going?'

'Painful. Our key witness is a nine year-old child of doubtful providence and our prime suspect is nowhere to be found.'

'So things are going well, then?' Catherine joked.

'That's just what I needed, your supportive and understanding friendship. Is this how you lift your students when they're stressed?'

'Come on, have a cup of tea. I've got some carrot cake here to go with it.'

'Now that sounds better, carrot cake might help get my brain cells working.'

While Catherine was pouring the tea, Wendy heard an aeroplane circle overhead.

*****

Tom Garroway had misjudged the approach into the airfield. He'd come in over Castle Lofts House, but Henry had told him to climb again because he hadn't descended fast enough to be sure of a safe landing. They were circling over the school while Henry took him through the process once more.

Tom had enjoyed the flight. He'd piloted the whole thing and was feeling pleased with himself until this final stage. He didn't like getting things wrong, but was concentrating on Henry's directions. The flight up to Ely had been very pleasant and it was the first time he'd seen the cathedral from the air. Then it had been off across to Suffolk and a great view of Ickworth House and another cathedral at Bury St Edmunds. Finally they had flown back to Chipping Bonhunt.

On his second attempt, Tom did a lot better, but the landing was still a bit bumpy and he braked late. Safely back on terra firma, he taxied back towards the hangar.

*****

It was four o'clock and it had been a frustrating day for the police with lots of house calls, lots of interviews and no real progress. Wendy was assembling the team in the classroom at the school they were using as an incident room. She'd talked to Dr Dreyfuss, the school's head of science and it was clear that the school had nothing like the quantity of sulphuric acid that would have been needed to inflict the burns on the victim. All the school's records in its chemistry store were in order, so that line of enquiry had hit the buffers. Three white boards had been lined up. The middle one was displaying some gruesome pictures of the body as it had been found in the Eagles tent.

There were also pictures of the sheep's head, sheep's body and copies of the biblical passages, together with a picture of the hit and run victim.

On the left hand board two names had been written:

John Davies and Peter Lord.

'Are these really our only two suspects?' asked Wendy.

'They're the only two who seem to have been around at the right time,' replied Peterson.

'Well, shall we add two persons unknown? The driver of the car that Chloe Gatiss saw, and the person who met him up by the cricket pavilion.'

Peterson wrote "car driver" and "car visitor" next to the two names.

'What about the security team that was on duty before John Davies and Peter Lord? Chloe said she heard them when she first arrived.'

'I think we can rule them out,' said Peterson.

'Why's that?'

'They're a bit embarrassed. They weren't really taking their security duties very seriously. It was a husband and wife team, Nigel and Mary Smith. They started their duty at seven, got fed up with it a little after eight and drove over to the Great Eastern for a pint. Barmaid remembers seeing them, and saw Mrs Smith rushing out at twenty to ten, which is when they left to get back in time to handover to John Davies and Peter Lord at ten.'

'She only saw Mrs Smith leave?'

'Yes, the barmaid had been down in the cellar to change over one of the beers. She just saw her leaving as she came up to the bar again. Thought Mrs Smith was probably following her husband out on the way to their car.'

'So is it normal for the volunteers to bunk off security duty at Summer Bible Club?'

'No, I think they're rather hoping we don't tell the organisers. Might well have breached the terms of the insurance for all the tents.'

'Relying on God to look after it for them, were they?'

'I didn't ask, but they seemed very "Christian" if you know what I mean and they looked very guilty, but hardly the sort of people that would tie someone up to a ladder after pouring sulphuric acid all over them.'

'And how would you describe the sort of person who WOULD tie someone up to a ladder after pouring sulphuric acid all over them?'

Peterson was silent.

'Put their names on that right hand side board. I expect you're right, but let's not rule them out completely at this stage. Now, where are we with the other suspects? John Davies?'

'Unlikely,' said Peterson, 'he'd have to be a very cool customer to face this down, given how much he's involved in SBC, including being on site all week. Why would you do this in the tent you're running? Unless the guy's really screwed up and gets some kick out of staging this and watching us investigate it under his nose, I don't think he fits the bill.'

'I'll buy that for now,' sad Wendy, 'but make sure we keep an eye on him. So, what have we on Peter Lord?'

'Not as much as we'd like. No previous but his views fit with the biblical quotes we've found on the body and by the sheep's head. And of course he's disappeared.'

'He can't have vanished completely.'

'He's not been home since his security shift with John Davies when the body was found. His wife is completely fazed by it, says he's never disappeared before. We've talked to a few people who know him from his church and also some neighbours. The picture is of somebody who has very judgemental views. He's very anti gay, thinks abortion is a terrible sin and won't let the family do anything other than go to church on Sunday.'

'So, your typical friendly and loving Christian then. Anything else?'

'Well, there's a suggestion he was behind some of the anti-Muslim stuff that was going on in the town last year. You remember? The campaign against Waitrose selling halal meat?'

'He wasn't the person who threw it on the floor in the shop?'

'No, that was somebody else, but people think that Lord was involved behind the scenes.'

'So where are we on tracking him down?'

'We've tried all the places his friends and family have suggested, but no trace of him. His car's gone, so we've put an alert out for it and we've circulated a description and picture to all the usual places. Should we go for a public appeal?'

'No, not yet. Let's see if we can track him down without too much melodrama. And let's not forget our two "persons unknown," have we found anything on the CCTV?'

'Just one camera has picked up a car in the distance.'

'Don't they have cameras on the main entrance?'

'No, apparently there's a school governor who's a libertarian. Doesn't like all the CCTV round the town, thinks it's a great intrusion on people's privacy, so they had a bit of a debate and agreed only to install cameras in places where they deterred break-ins to the building. Not to be used for wider surveillance.'

'I suppose nasty murders on the school field were never something that occurred to them. Have we got the footage?'

'Yes, it's set up on the screen here.'

The footage was a bit blurred, and the car wasn't completely in focus, but it clearly showed a Jaguar. A car that looked very familiar to Wendy.

'Can you enhance that shot there? We might just be able to improve the detailed view of the number plate.'

Peterson started working on enhancing the computer image and tried zooming in on the front of the car.

Part of the car was in dark shade, but the first part of the number plate was clear enough to read. E5V.

'E5VNS,' said Wendy calmly, 'there's somebody I want to talk to!'

*****

Lloyd Evans was in a 'phone box outside Waltham Cross Station. He was relieved he could find one that worked. A 'phone number was scribbled on a small sticker, above a crudely written message.

"Mandy's my name and 69's my game."

He wondered what sort of person took up the invitation. Fumbling in his trouser pocket, he found some pound coins. He didn't have a clue as to how much a call would cost. Infact, he wasn't sure he could remember how to even make a call. Who used phone boxes nowadays? Well, people who don't want their calls traced, he thought.

He punched the code into the small keyboard; followed by the number he had retrieved from his mobile. And he waited. After five rings, the 'phone at the other end picked up.

'Hello'

'It's me'

'Oh, I wondered when you'd be in touch. You don't usually call me here.'

'Can't explain now, but have the police seen you?'

'Not me, but they're all over the children at the Bible Club.'

'I don't want anyone to know.'

'Why's that, you dirty old sod. Might ruin your reputation with all your posh friends?'

'Our little arrangement has nothing to do with what the police are investigating.'

'And how do I know that you're telling me the truth? I don't know what the police are investigating. Perhaps it's dirty old men that have little secrets!'

'Look, I'm just asking for your discretion.' Lloyd Evans realised he was sweating, and he could feel his temper about to get the better of him.

'It's your little secret, not mine. If you want your secret to stay a fucking secret, then it's going to cost you.'

'Let's be reasonable…' he heard some pips. God, is that all the time you get? It's daylight robbery. He tried to find some more coins to insert.

'Just hold on a moment.'

'Look, I've got things to do. I think I'm due a few extra weeks payments for good behaviour.'

He hadn't found any more coins and the line went dead.

His mobile 'phone rang. Bloody stupid woman, the last thing I need is her calling me on this.

'Look, this is my private mobile; you know you shouldn't ring me on this.'

'Good afternoon, Mr Evans. I do apologise for disturbing you, but it's your friend Inspector Pepper here. I'd like to have a little chat with you. Where are you?'

Now he really was having difficulty controlling his temper. How had *she* got this number? And why hadn't he looked at his mobile before answering. Stupid, stupid, stupid, he thought, he would have seen it wasn't a number he knew.

'Sorry, Mr Evans, I can't hear you? Where are you?'

'Waltham Cross Station.'

Well, would you mind ever so much catching a train back to Castle Lofts? I'll send a car to meet you. Don't worry; we'll check the train times. We'll be waiting for the next train. I think you'll have to change at Broxbourne or Cheshunt.'

'Oh, they've all been disrupted this morning; I really don't think I can promise to get back quickly.' Buy myself some time, he thought.

'Don't worry, Sergeant Peterson here will check for me. We'll be waiting for the train. You won't be able to miss the car. It will have "POLICE" written on it in large blue letters.'

Lloyd switched his 'phone off.

'Bugger, bugger, bugger.'

*****

Jean Garroway was going spare. Lucy was nowhere to be seen. They'd searched all the school grounds that weren't sealed off by the police who'd told them that there was no way she could be in the area they were patrolling.

'We've got all that closed down, luv,' a young police constable had told her, 'we'd know if anyone was there.'

'Can we go home now?' asked Joshua, 'I've got some friends coming round.'

'Look, I'm really worried about Lucy,' Jean replied. 'She's been getting very stressed over her results. It may have got too much for her.'

'She's just attention seeking.'

'We've been searching for half an hour,' said Tom, 'and her mobile seems to be switched off. I suggest we go home and ring round her friends.'

Reluctantly, Jean agreed.

*****

In the Royal Sovereign, Councillor Hodgkiss was sitting in a corner on his own. He usually felt rather old when he drank here; surrounded by youngsters who he found it difficult to believe were old enough to drink alcohol. But today he actually felt young compared to most of the other customers. He wondered if they were doing a special offer on Harvey's Bristol Cream. He was waiting for Councillor Thomas to arrive. It was time to do some planning for the Mayor's town centre promotion initiative.

Councillor Thomas entered the building, looking hot, flushed and out of breath. With his portly frame and high blood pressure, he was not best pleased at having had to run down from the District Council car park.

'Sorry I'm late Steve, but if we don't do something soon about this flaming traffic there'll be absolutely no point in promoting the centre of town because nobody will be able to get to it.'

'Well Chris, just remember if we'd listened to the Liberals we wouldn't have any parking either. I seem to remember you were a bit wobbly on that one as well.'

'Goose Meadow? I still think it wasn't the right answer, but I towed the party line as I always do. It's half empty most of the time. I'd have put more cars on the common.'

'And as our learned Town Clerk is always telling us, we don't have the power to do that. The way he talks, somebody could still take us up before the courts and force us to get rid of the car park that's there at the moment.'

'I don't think he knows what he's talking about. Him and his beloved common. Nothing's impossible if you know how to go about it. Any way, I thought you were hoping to get the Fire Station redeveloped with some more parking?'

'Yes, but that will only happen if we get a major store on there, like a Marks & Spencer food shop.'

'Can't see Waitrose rolling over for that one!'

'Waitrose need to get on with their own plans. I get the feeling they're shilly-shallying around at the moment. Now, let's get down to business. This fire at the Quakers' place is a real opportunity, but we need to get some backbone into them. We all know they're really a bunch of yoghurt knitters.'

'Yoghurt knitters?' a puzzled Councillor Thomas interrupted.

'Yes, yoghurt knitters. That's what I call them. You know what I mean: save the whale, anti nukes, grow your own jumper brigade. Drive us all up the wall politically. If they're not supporting John Davies and all his silly Liberal party tosh then they're wasting their votes on the Greens. But at the moment they've got that guy Trevor Sandling and I think he's more on our side than he realises. Before they finish clearing up the damage we need to use him to encourage the other yoghurt-knitters to make something of that building. That top end of the High Street going up towards the war memorial is dead. There's a restaurant half way up on the other side and the fish and chip shop at the bottom, but nothing on this side beyond the pub we're sitting in, and I've lost count of how many times I've had to walk round the teenage sick on the pavement outside here on a Friday night. Not what we need at all.'

'So, what's your plan?'

'Well, my new American friend flew me across to France last week on one of his little jaunts from the airfield. I can't even remember the name of the place we went to, let alone pronounce it, but I gather it has great wines. Burgundy I think it was. Not sure if that was the wines or the region the place was in, might have been both. But my point is that this little French town was alive. It was heaving. Cafés, shops, market stalls everywhere and it had a great sense of community that lots of people think we're losing here in Chipping Bonhunt.'

'Now *you're* starting to sound like John Davies. Isn't that what he and his little gang of Liberals are always bleating on about? "No sense of community."'

'Yes, he bleats on, but he knows bugger all about what can be done to change it. Look, all his community stuff is upping their votes and we can't take this place for granted. We don't have a divine right to run the Town Council, you know.'

'Now that sounds just like one of his press releases. Guy at the Recorder said he's refusing to publish that phrase any more, John Davies puts it in at least two press statements every week!'

'And in a way he's right. We've got to be seen to do something. We can't get away with just being the natural party of power any more. The Con club has gone, our membership is down and we're starting to look out of touch. And all the time people are saying to me they're worried about the way the town is going. The traffic, more and more charity shops, all the new housing. We need a strong policy that shows we've got plans for this town. The Quaker building is the first step, and we do it right under John Davies' very nose, so he looks silly for not having thought of it himself.'

'So it's yoghurt knitters to the rescue, is it?'

'If you put it like that, yes it is. The real point of talking to you is to ask if you'd support giving them a grant in return for more public use of their new foyer area. We dress it up as including community groups and all that stuff, but the real prize is that in return for the grant we get them to open up a café and get them signed up to keeping it open during the day and early evening. We could even suggest they put some tables out on the pavement. It's wide enough, and if we get that far then we've created an attractive place half way down from the District Council to the traffic lights, and a nice little story to put in our leaflets come election time.'

'Now you've got my attention! Yes, the election. We need something we can say we've done. But surely poor Tom Dakin won't like it. Don't stir them up, he always says. Keep it low key and we'll all get back in.'

'Oh, I think Tom will be supporting this one.'

'You seem very certain.'

Councillor Hodgkiss smiled and said nothing.

'So are you planning to take this to group?'

'Yes, to next week's meeting. Are you with me?'

'Well, if you'll buy me a pint, I might be inclined to support you.'

Councillor Hodgkiss felt someone push sharply against the back of his chair.

'Hey there, be careful,' he said as he turned. But it was too late. A pint of lager was pouring over his best linen summer trousers, just in the most embarrassing place.

'What the hell are you doing?' he asked as he stood up. He realised that not everybody in the Royal Sovereign that afternoon was a pensioner and that this particular young lady was in trouble. At his feet, lying face down, Lucy Garroway had passed out.

It took twenty minutes for the ambulance to get through the traffic. By this time Lucy was conscious again, but clearly suffering from the affects of drinking a very large quantity of alcohol. The ambulance crew, who couldn't get any sense from her or her friends, decided the safest course of action was to take her into Addenbrooke's Hospital. No point in taking any unnecessary risk. They'd also asked a few questions of the bar staff as to just what age they thought this girl was.

'Another one,' said the ambulance driver, 'always a busy time of year, but we don't usually get them in the afternoon. I thought there was supposed to be a crack down on under age drinking.'

Councillor Hodgkiss set off home, having worked out the best way to hold his linen jacket in front of his trousers so as not to look as though he had wet himself. That would hardly be helpful in his quest to be seen as the Mayor who commanded authority and got things done.

*****

Lloyd Evans had caught the next train from Waltham Cross to Cheshunt and then changed there for Castle Lofts. His hopes that the earlier disruption might delay his return had been dashed. With uncharacteristic speed he thought, Greater Anglia had returned the service to its normal schedule. How typical, just when he didn't want the trains to be on time they were!

At least he wasn't on the fast service from Liverpool Street. Rather too many people he knew would be on that one. He had a nasty feeling that his arrival back at Castle Lofts wasn't something he would want a lot of people to witness. And so it proved.

As he walked across the footbridge he could see the large police car with a man in full uniform standing beside it. There was also a young chap, obviously plain clothes, standing next to him. Both were watching the passengers as they came down the bridge towards the exit. Should he try nipping into the newsagents on the pretext of buying one of their excellent, and very expensive, fine wines? He thought better of it. Difficult to believe that a station newsagent sold bottles of wine for £495, but as he knew himself, people did actually buy them. This was 'Castle

Lofts for Chipping Bonhunt' after all. He wished the police hadn't parked in such a prominent location.

'Lloyd Evans?' asked Peterson, 'Yes, that's me.'

'We're hoping you can help us with our enquiries. Please come with us.'

He was just climbing into the back of the car when he heard a familiar voice. 'Hello Lloyd,' said the rector from the Parish Church, giving him a broad smile and a cheery wave, 'hope you've been behaving yourself.'

Lloyd tried to pretend he hadn't seen him. 'Shit, shit, and shit' he mumbled under his breath.

*****

John Davies was looking forward to putting his feet up. A long and difficult day at Summer Bible Club was finally over and he was sitting down at the kitchen table with Alice.

'I feel absolutely whacked. I know we had no choice but to move into the hall, but wasn't it hard work!'

'I keep saying, don't look to me for sympathy. You've taken too much on. At least the police will be doing security tonight, so you don't have to do that.'

'Yes, I suppose there's a silver lining to having the body of a murder victim found in your tent! A bit drastic though, but at least it's a night in. Time for a bottle of wine me thinks. White or red?'

'Let's take a bottle of white into the garden.'

John went over to the wine rack and selected a screw top bottle. Should really put in the fridge first, he thought. But don't miss the moment. He picked up a couple of glasses and followed Alice down to the bottom of their garden where an old rustic bench was waiting,

'We don't get the opportunity to do this very often.'

'No,' said Alice. 'It's been a long time since we've both had time to stop and enjoy the garden.'

'Really must get the lawn cut this coming weekend.'

'I don't know, I think it's rather endearing: starting to look as though we're deliberately going for the wild look'

'Did you hear that?'

'What?'

'I thought it was a knock on the front door.'

'Oh, don't go. Probably just someone trying to sell tea towels again, or that man with the Betterware catalogue.'

'I didn't realise they were still going.'

'If it's not Betterware, it's something like it. I order stuff occasionally because I think he walks from the other side of town.'

'That was definitely another knock. I'll go and see who it is.'

'I'll stay and finish my glass. I'm going to enjoy the sun. You go and answer the door if you must.'

John walked back up the garden, through the French windows and made his way along the hall to the front door. Really must try and tidy this place up, he thought to himself.

He opened the front door. 'Can't you get a bell that works?' Peter Lord pushed straight past John and into the hall.

'What on earth are you doing here?' asked John. 'I thought the whole Essex Police force was looking for you.'

Peter stood in front of him. He was unwashed, unshaven and still wearing the same clothes as when John had last seen him the night before at the school. John looked into his tired bloodshot eyes and could feel his fear.

'I need your help. I can't go home, and the police won't understand.'

'What do you mean they won't understand? Just tell them what's happened and if you tell them the truth surely everything will be OK?'

'It won't be. I've got involved in something I don't understand. I thought it was what God wanted me to do. The man told me it was what God would want, how it was a chance for me to do my bit to bring about God's kingdom. But I realise I was wrong. It was the devil talking. I've been used by Satan. That's what the police won't understand. They don't see it, they don't understand the power of the devil, how he comes in so many ways and we don't recognise him.'

Peter Lord was crying, sobbing uncontrollably.

'Look,' said John. 'The police are looking for you and there's no point in running away from them. It just makes you look as though you've done something wrong, that you've got something to hide.'

Peter continued to sob, muttering 'Father forgive me' under his breath and what sounded to John like 'get behind me Satan.'

'I'll call the police and I'll come with you if they let me. I'm sure we can sort this out.'

'Who's so important that they've dragged you away from our bottle of wine?' asked Alice as she entered the hall. As John turned towards her, Peter panicked and fled back out through the front door, down the path and out on to Thomas Road.

'Come back,' called John, 'don't be a stupid fool.'

John heard a motorbike rev its engine. Afterwards he had difficulty recalling just how long it was between when he first heard the bike and when he heard the gun shot. But what he did remember was grabbing Alice and pulling her to the ground as the shot rang out. He needn't have worried, because it wasn't intended for either of them. Peter Lord lay half on the pavement and half in the road. A pool of fresh blood was slowly spreading out from under his head. One shot, right on target. It was the work of somebody who knew how to handle a gun.

*****

Wendy and Peterson were in the interview room at the police station in Mound Street. Lloyd Evans had been brought here because it was more private than the incident room that had been set up at the school. This was heavy duty.

Evans hadn't been charged and officially he was just helping the police with their enquiries but, thought Wendy, he's looking as guilty as hell and I really mustn't look as though I'm enjoying this.

Peterson showed him the pictures that had been downloaded from the school's CCTV.

'Is this your car?' asked Wendy

'I don't know,' Lloyd said

'It looks as though this is your registration. Always a bit of a mistake, personalised number plates if you ask my opinion.'

'Can I have a word with my client?' his solicitor asked

'OK, we'll leave you alone for five minutes. But don't waste our time. This is a murder enquiry and I'm in no mood for being mucked around.'

Five minutes later Wendy and Peterson were back in the interview room.

'My client has something he would like to say. Please listen to him carefully.'

'Well, Mr Evans, what is it you want to tell us?'

'This is a picture of my car and I was driving it. Judging from the picture that wall is the end of the cricket pavilion at the top of the school field, so I can see you want to know what I was doing there.'

'What you were doing there at about the same time as the body of some poor sod who had been murdered was taken into a tent within spitting distance of where your car was caught on camera.'

Lloyd Evans was looking white, tired and he was sweating profusely.

'I know you and I don't exactly see eye to eye, and we've had our misunderstandings. But you've got to believe me; I had nothing to do with that murder.'

'I haven't *got* to believe anything. If you're telling me you weren't on that field last night to commit murder, why were you there?'

'I went to meet somebody.'

'And who was that?'

'I don't know, I mean I don't know his name.'

'What did he look like, then?'

'I don't know.'

'This is beginning to get a bit tiresome. Why don't you know what this person you met looked like?'

'Because I didn't meet him.'

'You didn't meet him?'

'No, he didn't turn up.'

Wendy smiled as she went in for the kill. 'So what if I told you that we have a witness that not only saw somebody drive your Jaguar up by the pavilion, but also saw another man. A very tall man, climb into it?'

Lloyd Evans was silent and had started sweating again.

'Do you mind if I have another word with my client?' asked the solicitor.

'If you must, but you'd better come up with something good or I'll be charging Mr Evans here with murder when I come back. What is it you're hiding Mr Evans?'

Wendy and Peterson left the room again.

'But surely you can't rely on Chloe Gatiss to stand up in court against Lloyd Evans? She's hardly a reliable witness,' said Peterson as they stood outside in the corridor.

'Of course not, but Mr oh so grand I'm above the law Evans and his smart arse lawyer don't know that,' replied Wendy. 'He realises we know quite a lot, and he may decide that we know more than we really do. That way we might flush a bit more of this sorry tale out of him.'

PC Smart came running round the corner of the corridor.

'Here you are, glad I found you. All hell's broken loose. There's been a shooting and the chief super's on the 'phone demanding to speak to you immediately.'

Wendy went to the nearest office, picked up the 'phone and asked for the call to be put through to her.

'What the blazes is going on?' Warren sounded pretty angry. 'I put you in charge and it only takes two days before I get our beloved Commissioner on my back because he's had a garbled 'phone call from Lloyd Evans complaining of police harassment. Next thing I hear you've got him in the local nick being questioned when I specifically warned you to be careful with our dear church warden. Meanwhile mayhem seems to be breaking out on the streets of Bonhunt. What's this I've just heard about a shooting?'

'You've got the better of me there, sir. I've only just heard about it myself.' Thinking quickly, Wendy decided she'd better not admit she hadn't heard anything about it.

'Well, for God's sake get a grip of things. Are we going to need the armed unit?'

'I really don't know, it's more reassurance that's needed at the moment. More foot soldiers would help on the street, you know the sort of thing.'

'OK, I'll see what I can do. But please don't screw up on me Pepper. I've always thought you've got what it takes to go a long way in the force. But at the moment you seem to be turning that quiet little market town over there into the Bronx.'

'I'll sort this, Sir. We're making some progress but there's a link that we're not seeing yet.'

'Find it quick then or I'll have to put someone with more experience into oversee the investigation.' With that, the line went dead

'Bloody Hell' said Wendy, who was feeling uncharacteristically stressed.

*****

Also uncharacteristically showing the signs of stress was Tom Garroway. Jean and Tom arrived at the Addenbrooke's Accident and Emergency Department thirty minutes after they'd received the 'phone call. During the drive there they'd beaten themselves up over a litany of their own failings. They'd been too hard on Lucy; they hadn't given her enough time; they'd pushed her too hard; they'd ignored the signs.

'I need to rethink the job,' Tom had said as they ran through the entrance. 'It's supposed to let me work from home, but this is the first week in months I haven't had to fly to the States or travel to some godforsaken part of Britain on behalf of the company.'

'Tom, don't rush to any decisions before we see how she is. This may just be a one-off. It's the stress of finding out her results this Thursday. I'm amazed she's coped so well up till now. You know she's really worried about the place at Cambridge. Sometimes I wish she'd not got the offer. Nottingham or UEA would have been far less stressful for us all.'

At A&E they were directed to another ward and eventually arrived at a room with four beds. In the corner by the window was Lucy, sitting up and looking out at the view.

'Hello, mum. Hello dad. Sorry I over did it. Rachel, Jane and I just needed to chill out, and I wasn't thinking about how much I was drinking. I was amazed they served me at the Royal Sovereign.'

'Thank God you're alright,' said Jean. 'You really gave us a scare.'

'They say I can come home. I don't know what they gave me, but I feel a lot better. The ambulance only brought me here as a precaution.'

'Well, let's get out of here then,' said Tom. 'I'll go and find someone to tell us what we need to do.'

Forty minutes later, the Garroways were driving out of the car park having resolved to have a quiet evening in and to watch Lucy's choice of film together.

'Not sure what Josh is going to say about that,' said Jean.

'He can go and watch something on his own if he's unhappy,' replied Tom.

*****

Things would have been difficult enough around Thomas Road without the lorry driver who, seeing the queue of backed up traffic along Mount Ephraim Road, had tried to take his articulated lorry through the local streets only to become grounded while attempting to navigate over the old railway bridge in More Road before turning into Railway View. All three roads were now closed, with angry residents either unable to drive home or retrieve their parked cars.

In Thomas Road, Wendy Pepper was standing outside the police tent that had been hastily erected over Peter Lord's body. The forensic team were scouring the area.

Jane Frobisher finished her examination of the body and went outside to talk to Wendy. 'Whoever fired that knew what they were doing. One fatal shot straight into the brain. Bullet must be an exploding round. The guy never had a chance, there's not a lot left inside the remains of his skull.'

'Thanks for getting here so quickly, I think we've had more suspicious deaths in two days than this place normally has in two decades.'

'I'm getting to know the road up from Chelmsford pretty well. I'll examine the body thoroughly tomorrow morning in the lab, but I don't think there's anything else I can help you with about time and cause of death. This one looks pretty straightforward to me.'

'I wonder if you could do me a favour, Jane. That hit and run on Sunday. Just take a look at the victim again. We've had nobody come forward to report the poor sod missing, and we still don't know who he is. Anything we've missed?'

'I'll go over my notes. We were just confirming his injuries were consistent with a hit and run. Do you think his death might be connected with this?'

'Well, he was certainly hiding something and keen to get away from me. Any unexplained death in Chipping Bonhunt at the moment has got to be suspicious.'

They were interrupted by a local resident.

'Any chance of you reopening the road, we're meant to be driving to Cambridge this evening.'

'Sorry mate,' said Wendy, 'nothing moves until our forensics team have completed their search.' She looked along the road where a group of police officers were crawling on all fours, meticulously examining the tarmac and potholes, of which there seemed to be a huge number.

'Come on Peterson,' said Wendy, 'time to visit the widow.'

*****

Back at his home overlooking the common, Lloyd Evans was pouring himself a glass of one of his favourite clarets. His solicitor had advised him that it was best to come clean and he had. Now he wondered what Customs and Excise would do, and he realised just how stupid he had been in not checking out the identity of his supplier.

At the time it had all been too tempting. A very rare case of vintage Burgundy at a knock down price and no questions asked. But if he'd bought it direct himself then the tax almost certainly wouldn't have been payable. He could have gone out there and brought it back. To be consumed for personal pleasure or whatever they called it.

Instead, all this cloak and dagger stuff had him illegally importing alcohol, avoiding the tax and duty and, worse still, becoming a murder suspect thrown into the bargain as well.

He tried the number again. He recognised the Police Commissioner's wife's authoritative tone when it was answered.

'Good evening, can I help you?'

'Yes, hello Cecilia. It's Lloyd here. No chance of a word with George I suppose?'

'Good evening Lloyd, No I'm afraid he's tied up at the moment.'

'Later on then?'

'I'm not sure Lloyd. He is *very* busy at the moment. I'm sure he'll catch you at the golf club if he has time to play next week.'

'Please tell him I called.'

'Of course I will Lloyd, goodbye.'

The line went dead. Lloyd recognised the brush off. Cecilia was a pro, and there was no way he was going to get past her.

'Damn, damn, damn. What's happening to the world today?'

*****

Wendy and Peterson were standing outside a front door displaying the number seven. Definitely unlucky for some, thought Wendy. It was the first time she had visited this new development and she was struck by how unusual the properties looked. How would she describe them? "Different" she thought. Not unattractive, in fact they seemed to suit their location very well, but much of the exterior appeared to be some form of timber cladding, and the roofs were covered with large panels of photovoltaic cells. Everything seemed to be painted in varying shades of pastel green, and the fronts had what appeared to be double height conservatories, which would have looked very attractive but for all the junk that some of the residents had placed in them. Not how they would have looked on the architect's drawing, she thought.

The front door was opened by a small mousy looking woman. She looked anxious and had clearly been crying. As far as Wendy was aware, she hadn't been told the news, so things were about to get a lot worse.

'Mrs Lord?'

'Yes'

'Can we come in?'

'Is there any news about Peter?'

'Yes, we'd like to talk to you, inside if we may.'

Without further word, she turned and they followed her into the kitchen-dining room at the rear of the house. They could hear children playing a computer game noisily in the front room.

A large television dominated the space, but it was switched off.

'Peter hates those computer things, but I decided I had to do something to distract them. I think they're too young to understand that their dad hasn't come home. They keep asking me why he's hiding from us.'

Wendy was listening, but also trying not to show surprise at finding another person sitting at the kitchen table.

'Hello Luke,' said Wendy recalling his contribution the previous Sunday morning at the Friends' Meeting House, 'I don't often see you outside of meeting. I didn't realise you lived out here.'

'Oh, I don't,' said Luke Watson. 'I've just come over to support Abigail. We're old friends from school.'

'Luke's been very kind. He knows how worried I get.' Abigail Lord sniffed and started to sob quietly into a handkerchief

'Peterson, make us all a pot of tea will you, if that's alright by Mrs Lord here.'

'Yes, of course it is.'

'I'm afraid it's very bad news, Mrs Lord. Peter is dead.'

It sounded brutal, but Wendy knew you couldn't beat around the bush. "Dead" was definite and it was final; it offered no false hopes that somehow Peter might come back.

Abigail Lord started to wail uncontrollably. Wendy tried to calm her down and put her arm round her. 'Just take your time.'

Why do words always fail at moments like these? she asked herself. Every police officer she knew found this task the most difficult. It would be so much easier if you could just skip the bit when you told them, but you had to make sure the relatives understood what had happened.

'I'm very sorry, but he died earlier this evening.'

'How did it happen?'

'He was visiting somebody who lives in Thomas Road in Chipping Bonhunt. When he came out of the house, a gunman on a motorbike drove up and shot him.'

'I don't understand. Why would anyone do that?'

'Well we're going to find out. Do you know if there was anybody who he had fallen out with? Did he have any enemies?'

'I can't think of anybody.'

Clearly Abigail Lord was incapable of thinking about anything, but Wendy needed to try and find what might have made her husband a target.

'Look, I'm very sorry to have to press this at the moment. One of our family liaison officers will be here soon to help you sort things and help you deal with the media. But I do need to try and find out what the motive was. You see, it looks as though Peter was targeted, this was not an accident or a random shooting.'

Abigail managed to stop sobbing and thought for a moment. 'There was somebody at the chapel a few weeks ago. A new man, hadn't been before and hasn't returned since.'

'Why do you think he might be involved?'

'Well, he spent twenty minutes after the service talking to Peter. They went for a walk around Welsted together. I remember because I just wanted to get back here with the kids. I'd left the Sunday lunch in the oven and we were so late back it was ruined. Peter and I had a row, and he wouldn't tell me what he'd been talking to the man about.'

'Can you give us a description?'

'All I remember was that he was very tall.'

'Nothing else?'

'He didn't really speak to anyone except Peter. It was as though he'd come to chapel just to speak to him. I don't think even the pastor got much out of him.'

There was a ring of the doorbell. Luke Watson answered it and a young female constable introduced herself as coming from family liaison in Chelmsford. Wendy decided it was time to go.

'Mrs Lord. I'm really sorry about what's happened. Thank you for being so helpful. I'm going to leave you with this young lady here. If you remember anything else please tell her and she'll make sure we hear about it.'

Abigail Lord, Luke Watson and the young police woman were already in deep conversation. It appeared the constable went to a church that Luke knew.

As they left, Wendy heard somebody say 'Let's pray together about it.'

Outside Peterson said 'That's not the first time we've heard a description of somebody tall. Could it be the same person who met Lloyd Evans?'

'It could be or it could just be a coincidence. Tomorrow I want you to track down the pastor of the church that the Lords go to. See if he remembers anything about the mysterious visitor and his conversation with Peter Lord. If it's a small congregation, then it would be difficult for somebody not to talk to other people and get away without sharing something. Surely somebody asked him where he lived and why he was visiting.'

*****

John and Alice Davies had finally shown the last of the police officers out of their house. They'd both been interviewed three times. They'd lost count of how many people had 'phoned to find out what was going on and John had just politely despatched a local reporter with the words 'Please talk to the police.'

Thomas Road was still closed and it looked as though it would remain so for most of the next day. So, the immediate problem was how to get to SBC at the school on Wednesday morning. Normally this would be easy; it was fifteen minutes walk, no car needed. The problem was that Wednesday was scheduled to be Eagles' junk modelling day, and most of the junk was in the Davies' shed in the garden. Phone conversations with the other members of the tent team had led to the conclusion that it was going to be difficult to change things round, and all the children were looking forward to making the designs they'd been working on for their sailing boats. Besides, with all the children apart from the Eagles being allowed back into their tents, they would have the free run of the school hall. Just what they needed to get everyone in the Eagles team on an up again. Alice had suggested that they finish the day with a boat race along the whole length of the hall. There would be two winners, with a prize for the first to finish the race with a boat that was still intact and another for the boat that they thought was the best design.

After some discussion with the police and the Davies' neighbours at the bottom of their garden, it had been agreed that all the junk needed for modelling could be passed over the fence and collected from Mount Ephraim Road. Sarah and Lewis had come round to help.

'Look, you two, can you just untangle yourselves long enough to take all this cardboard out of my hands?'

John was at the top of a step ladder, looking down on the other side of the fence where the two lovebirds were enjoying a long smoochy kiss.

'Sorry John,' said Sarah as she extracted herself from the embrace. 'Come on Lewis, help me take this.'

Another pile of cardboard was added to the growing collection. A friend from John's church had brought his van to ferry the materials over to Bonhunt Academy. Two hours and three journeys later it was all stacked up inside the school hall.

*****

On the drive back from Sandean, Wendy and Peterson thought briefly about calling in at The Great Eastern for a quick drink, but it was a very brief thought. With Thomas Road still closed and the traffic chaos throughout town, they would just be looking for trouble by trying to get there, and Wendy didn't fancy endless questions about how the investigation was going.

'Not the place for a quiet drink this evening,' she'd said. 'Do you fancy a glass of wine back at Granary Lane?'

Peterson had accepted the offer and so they were now relaxing in the small but comfortable armchairs in the Granary Lane cottage, while Catherine was rustling up some cheese and biscuits and opening a bottle of wine.

'I was going to open some White Zinfandel,' said Catherine, 'but I thought you both deserved something weightier. How about a semi decent bottle of claret?'

'Sounds fine to me,' said Peterson.

'Aren't you going to drive home?' asked Wendy.

'No, I'll leave the car in Bartlow Road. Not too far to walk back to my digs, and I'll see how things are around Thomas Road on the way.'

'Ever the diligent copper. You are allowed to go off duty occasionally. What a day!'

'Well mine hasn't been without its dramas,' Catherine added.

'Tell us more?'

'As you saw Wendy, my star student came to see me all worried about the results on Thursday and I thought I did a pretty good job of calming her down, reassuring her it would all be OK and sent her off with a new spring in her step. Next thing I know and she's been rushed into

Addenbrooke's paralytic with the amount of booze she's hurled down herself.'

'Remind me not to come to you next time I need counselling,' said Wendy.

'That's a bit harsh,' Peterson exclaimed.

'Now, no taking sides,' laughed Wendy, 'otherwise it's the White Zinfandel for you and no mistake.'

'I'm not sure I'd mind too much. Some chilled sweet rosé would go down rather well.'

'That's you struck off Lloyd Evans' Christmas card list.'

'I'd be surprised if any of us are on it. That guy gets under my skin.'

'He's harmless really, just thinks he runs the country when actually he's a bit of a busted flush.'

'But it's his attitude. It's like he doesn't have to answer to anybody like the rest of us. Pillar of the parish church and so he thinks he's God.'

'Perhaps he is,' Catherine joked.

'Well, if that's the case, then that's me out!' Wendy said. 'I can just about cope with Friends' meeting at the moment, but if I was ever to think that God was like Lloyd Evans I'd be knocking on Satan's door at the earliest opportunity.'

'Knock, knock, knocking on Satan's door. Knock, knock knocking on Satan's door,' Peterson was singing in a parody of the Bob Dylan song.

'Now you're crucifying one of my favourite musicians. I don't know, you come here and drink my wine, accept my hospitality and then insult my music! Don't come to me for a reference when you're after your next promotion.'

'Well, I think leading a young sergeant astray with wine while he still might be on duty – am I still on duty? – could be a serious disciplinary offence.'

'Oh, then you're definitely on duty. I'm all for a bit of serious discipline.'

They all laughed.

'Changing the subject, have you heard anymore from your young Trude? I bet she's desperately texting you to find out how you're coping in the current murder capital of Britain.'

'She called once earlier this evening. Said she'd heard all the latest about it on the radio but she's having to work really hard at the moment. She wound me up by saying that the chauviraptor wanted to see more of her in her short summer skirt. Mind you, I wouldn't blame him if that was true.'

'You're very trusting.'

'Oh, he's harmless. It's all in his imagination.'

'So,' said Wendy focussing back on the case, 'where have we got to?'

'Some sort of bible fanatic murdering people he doesn't like.'

'Or somebody murdering people and making it look like they're a bible fanatic. Mind you, staying with the simplest explanation might be the right thing to do at this stage. So let's assume he, or for that matter she, is a bible fanatic. We've got a whole field full of them at the moment, running the Summer Bible Club at the school. It surely isn't a coincidence that all of this is happening this week, but what's the connection?'

'John Davies is an obvious one,' Peterson replied. 'He leads the tent where the body and the sheep's head were found and Peter Lord was murdered outside his house.'

'Yes, but unless he has Superman's ability to change clothes and move around, he couldn't have been both on the motorbike in Thomas Road firing the shot and standing on his front doorstep watching. Come on, use your brain Peterson!'

'You know I don't mean that, clearly he didn't shoot Peter Lord, but isn't he a connection of some sort? He may not even realise it and it may be nothing he himself is doing, but I think it might be more than a coincidence that he seems to be at the "scene of the crime" or "scenes of the crimes" as it were. And didn't he seem to think there was something in the particular version of the bible that the quotes came from?'

'You're right there. He does seem to be some sort of a link between events. Something he's done, or something he's said, even possibly something he believes. But what if the hit and run back in the Market Square is also part of this, there's no obvious connection to him. I have a growing sense in my gut that a hit and run death the same week we have an acid bath murder, a drive-by shooting and a decapitated sheep in Chipping Bonhunt is too much of a coincidence not all to be connected in some way.'

'Acid bath murder? That sounds rather Victorian!'

'Well, just thinking of my memoirs. Sounds better than "poor sod that was tied up and murdered by having acid chucked all over him" doesn't it? And a bit of melodrama in the press might help flush out some more information. If we feed this to one to the tabloids in the right way, we might just get some more leads.'

Catherine had been listening quietly to the conversation until now. Suddenly she looked up. 'This may be very silly, and I'm hardly the detective here, but I read a really interesting book about religion last year. I bought it when we spent that day at Blickling Hall. Do you remember that wonderful second hand book shop they have there?'

'Only too well,' said Wendy. 'I remember a beautiful sunny day when we were going to go round the gardens, take a tour round the Hall and finish with dinner at the Buckinghamshire Arms. I think I had to wait two hours pretending to look at their garden shop before I could prize you away from those books.' She turned to look at Peterson. 'Be warned, let her loose in a second hand book shop and time comes to an end, the planet stops revolving round the sun.'

She ducked just in time to avoid the cushion that came flying in her direction. Catherine was looking at their bookshelves. 'No, I'm serious. I'm trying to help you PC Plods with a piece of serious information. This might be a link you should consider.'

'This is like being back at school during GCSEs,' Peterson said unhelpfully. The cushion hit him full in the face.

'If you ask me, it's more like a pillow fight in the dorm,' Wendy replied.

'Well, now I know what type of school you went to, not like poor little Peterson here, humble grammar school lad.'

'Oh, don't give me that crap; I'd have swapped a dreary dark and damp third rate girl's school for your grammar any day.'

'Oh, stop it you two,' said Catherine, 'here's the book I meant. Take a look.'

Catherine handed Wendy the book.

She read the title: *'God's Own Country. Tales from the Bible Belt, by Stephen Bates.* Here you are Peterson, some bed time reading for you.'

'I was afraid that was going to happen.' Peterson started reading the back cover. 'This might be worth looking at more seriously. It's about how right-wing evangelical Christians are trying to dominate life in the States. Says it's a battle that sears America's soul and that what happens in the Bible Belt matters to us.' Peterson drew breath and looked round the room. Wendy had sat up and was listening intently.

'On second thoughts Peterson, I think I'd better read that. It might at least help me understand the mind of the killer, even if it's a bit far fetched to think the avenging angels of the Bible Belt have picked Chipping Bonhunt to launch their British crusade.'

'Well, if you're going to read the book, then I'm off home' said Peterson. 'All of a sudden my brain hurts and I need some clear fresh air. Thanks for the drink. Sleep tight both of you.'

'Cheeky sod,' said Wendy as she closed the front door behind him.

Wednesday

It was an early start for the Eagles team. In a 'phone call at seven, Sylvia Maitland, calling on behalf of the Summer Bible Club committee, had made it clear that they would fully understand if Alice and John felt unable to lead the tent today. In fact, there had been an emergency committee meeting late the night before that had discussed calling the whole thing off following what had happened to Peter Lord and the realisation that this year's event was going to be caught up in a continuing police investigation. But while some people thought cancelling the rest of the event would be an appropriate mark of respect, most felt it was more essential than ever that SBC carried on. The committee and assembly leaders were working on appropriate messages to use with the children.

Having listened to this explanation, it hadn't taken John long to agree with Alice that they would also carry on. They were both shaken by what they had witnessed outside their house in Thomas Road, but felt they themselves would feel better if they were continuing with the activities they'd planned and ensuring that the children had a good day. Having spent the previous evening ensuring everything would be ready for this morning they would see it through. John could hear the relief in Sylvia Maitland's voice when he 'phoned her back with their decision.

Now they were both in the school hall, where it felt as though they were waist deep in cardboard boxes, toilet rolls, plastic margarine containers and a seemingly endless quantity of every type of packaging known to humankind.

They weren't the only people making an extra effort. Agnes Rogers had also turned up early.

'Are you sure you're alright?' Alice asked her.

'I'm fine; I'm not going to let any of these dreadful events stop me from being here. I said I'd help and so I'm here to help. I'll get on with sorting this cardboard for the tables.'

'Well, it's very kind of you and I admire your spirit Agnes. A lot of people wouldn't have your determination.'

Alice turned and spoke quietly to John: 'Please God, don't let there be anymore nasty surprises.'

'Shouldn't be anything today, this lot was locked up in here until we arrived, and before that it was in our shed. Didn't see anything strange when we were moving it yesterday.'

'Well this is a bit odd,' said Agnes, 'look what I've found. Must be a piece of the children's artwork from last year.'

John went over and took the large piece of card that Agnes handed him.

The drawing was simple, but looked too ambitious to be drawn by a child. A large grey cloud on the left had formed into the shape of a face, which was clearly blowing as though it was creating the wind. On the right hand side small people and buildings were being caught up in a whirlwind that was channelling them into a large fire set in a huge furnace. John turned it over. He froze: a strip of white paper had been stuck across the back of the picture. Printed on it in Arial typeface were the words:

"Sinners blow away like chaff before the wind. They are not safe on Judgment Day; they shall not stand among the godly."

John cast Alice a quick look and she understood. He didn't have to say anything. He turned back to Agnes.

'Which pile was this in?' he asked.

'Oh, wait a minute. Now where was I? Yes, it was that one there.'

A pile of similar sized pieces of card to the one John was holding lay on the floor.

'Right, will you two be OK for ten minutes? I just need to go and see somebody. Could you just leave that pile as it is until I get back? It's important that nobody touches it.'

'Whatever you say John, although I can't see why you're so fussed about a pile of old card.'

*****

For once the traffic along Finchwinter Road was moving fairly well. Jean Garroway thought the reason might be that all the events of the previous day had put people off trying to drive through the town at all. Long may it continue, she caught herself thinking before realising quite how mercenary the thought was. Murder was serious, even if it did help sort the traffic problem.

Apart from Jean, there was only Joshua in the car this morning. Tom was at home looking after Lucy, who it had been agreed should stay in bed for at least the morning to ensure she gave her body time to recover from the previous day's excess.

'Why do I have to go if Lucy's skiving off?'

'Because, whatever you say, you're really enjoying it. I saw you with your friends yesterday and you seemed to be having a great time. You just like making a fuss.'

'Then Lucy should have to come as well. She's not sick. Just pretending that "everything's too much" for her. She's just a stupid girl wanting dad's attention.'

'Well, dad has been very busy recently and he hasn't been able to give Lucy as much time as he'd have liked. She doesn't complain. She's worked extremely hard this year and it's been very stressful for her. You just see when you're doing your GCSEs next year. Work, work, work: that'll be the order of the day.'

'Still think it's unfair that she gets the day off with dad while I have to spend another day at SBC. I bet they go riding this afternoon. When was the last time I got to go riding with dad?'

'You know he's promised that you can both go this weekend.'

'Until an important conference call comes up, or he suddenly has to fly to New York or somewhere.'

'Just give over Josh will you? I really have had enough.'

*****

Catherine had given the sixth form office a quick search before sitting down at her desk. Just to make sure no new decapitated animals had arrived. Fortunately, none had.

The A level results were in, but they were top secret before their release on Thursday morning. Fortunately most students didn't seem to realise that the schools get them in advance so they can be sorted. If they did, she would have to go into hiding until eight am the next day in order to avoid the anxious phone calls and other tricks her very able charges would doubtless attempt in order to prize the information out of her.

Overall, the results looked pretty impressive and they were at least as good as the previous year. There was always something very satisfying about watching good students who worked hard get the results that they deserved.

And Lucy would be going to Cambridge. Despite all the worry about the difficult chemistry paper, the students appeared to have coped with it pretty well. Probably factored it into the marking scheme, thought Catherine. But a good result, because it showed their students hadn't just learnt the stuff, but could apply it as well. She looked forward to handing Lucy the envelope and seeing her face when she realised she'd achieved not just an A, but an A* in Chemistry. She'd averaged 91% which was just over the 90% she needed on this year's A2 papers and well deserved it was too. So Lucy had achieved her A* in Chemistry, but she would probably be disappointed to have just missed an A* in Biology.

*****

Wendy Pepper and Peterson were engaged in conversation over a coffee when John Davies entered the classroom they were using as a base. PC Smart was writing something on one of the whiteboards, but turned it to one side so that John couldn't read it.

'Hello Mr Davies,' said Wendy. 'Have you brought us a present?'

'I think you should see this.'

'Well, this office is out of bounds really, so let's go into the room across the corridor.'

Wendy guided him politely out of the room and through the door opposite.

'So, what do we have here?'

John laid the card out on the table.

'Where was this?'

John explained how Agnes had found the drawing in a pile of cardboard.

'Right, leave this with us. You're in the hall; can I assume you don't need to use the area where the pile of cardboard is?'

'We can leave it free and move to the other end.'

'We've still got some of the forensic team on site, so I'll send one of them up right away. Leave this here. We're going to have to take all of your fingerprints for elimination purposes. Can we get that done now before the children arrive?'

'I suppose so, but you will need to be quick.'

Ten minutes later, John, Alice and Agnes were having their finger prints taken.

'That was really quite exciting,' said Agnes, 'just like on television.'

John laughed, 'not something you ever thought you'd do at SBC, eh? Mind you, in happier times we might be able to do something like that with all the seniors. I bet they'd enjoy playing detective.'

*****

Outside on the school field, the Summer Bible Club organisers were coping with an unannounced visit from the Mayor. Councillor Hodgkiss had decided that he needed to "show his support" at this difficult time and was processing round the tents, insisting on being introduced to all of the children.

'That's all we need, as if we hadn't got enough things to cope with,' one of the tent leaders had been heard to say. And, true enough; Councillor Hodgkiss had looked very disappointed when he'd learnt that none of the press was present.

'I'd have thought they'd have taken a bigger interest given what's happened. I mean, this is all terrible. A murder here at a summer camp for all these children. It should be a matter of national concern.'

'Actually, we asked them to stay away,' said Sylvia Maitland, 'and I think they've been very good. The police let them take some photographs yesterday when we weren't allowed on the field, and everybody agrees we have to do the best for the children.'

'But surely it's very dangerous? What if the killer is still lurking somewhere in the area?'

'There are so many police around the site that I think we're probably safe from that. Now, if you don't mind, I think it's time we moved on, don't you?'

*****

Tom checked Lucy's bedroom at Folly Farm. She was still fast asleep.

He went down stairs and started up his e-mail

From: *TGarroway@Intermed.com*
To: *FBrewster@Intermed.com*
Subject: Takeover of Anglia Media

Hi Francis

Not sure if you follow stories in the British press, but there's quite a big one here in little'ol Chipping Bonhunt at the moment. A couple of nasty murders.

Thought you'd be interested. Our concern about buying Anglia Media was that it would be too provincial; not a suitable fit for the overall ambitions of the Corporation. However, recent events move Anglia Media up a league. They've exploited events fully on their social media outlets, and their new start up paper in Cambridge is also showing strong signs of taking market share from the competition. I think we should move now. This could be a bargain, and their main shareholder wants to sell. It will give the Corporation the base it needs in the east of the UK. Is the boss up for this?

Call if you want to discuss.

Regards as ever,

Tom

Ten minutes later, Tom took a call on his mobile. It was the answer he was hoping for.

*****

Lewis was looking sheepishly at the forensic officer who was sifting through the pile of cardboard. The area of the hall around it was cordoned off with Police tape.

The children were split into groups, each starting work on their junk modelling designs. As Sylvia Maitland had said to John when she'd dropped by with the Mayor, 'It has a wonderful buzz of activity, and they all look as though they're having a fantastic time!'

'More like organised chaos,' John laughed, 'at least it channels their energy into something fun. But we haven't got to the stage when they're all fighting over the sellotape yet!'

The Mayor had looked on bemused. 'I thought they would all be sitting down studying the bible.'

'We try and find creative ways to get the children to engage with it. They're making ships today, and then we'll be talking about the story of Jesus walking on the water.'

'That's always fun,' said Agnes, 'we tell them that after lunch the leaders are going to walk on water, and there's a prize for anyone who can work out how we're going to do it.'

'So how do you do it?' asked Councillor Hodgkiss.

'Come back after lunch and we'll show you.'

The Mayor continued to look baffled as Sylvia Maitland moved him on.

John noticed that Lewis was being very quiet. 'Come on Lewis, what are you staring at? Something's clearly worrying you.'

'Well, it's not me,' said Sarah, 'he hasn't looked at me ever since we arrived.'

'I hope you won't fade away with the lack of attention,' John replied.

'You're just being nasty. But I expect a bit more attention from my babe here.'

'Babe? He's hardly in swaddling clothes!'

'You know what I mean.'

John turned to Lewis again. 'So what's the problem?'

*****

Ten minutes later John was back in the room the police were using for interviews. Peterson was accompanied by one of the female police constables.

'Right, Lewis, tell the police officer what you have to say.'

'I'm really sorry, it was only meant to be a joke for the tent team.'

'What was meant to be a joke?' asked Peterson.

'The drawing and the words on the card. I was doing some artwork for college when I got back from Summer Bible Club yesterday afternoon, and I thought I'd do this drawing, like I imagined the killer might do.'

'Why would you do that?' asked Peterson.

'We're supposed to be doing this project over the summer where we get into the mind of somebody famous or notorious. I thought this would work really well.'

'So how did the painting get into the hall?'

'Well, I wasn't very happy with it really. Thought I'd need to do it again, so I was about to throw it away and then Alice rang to ask if Sarah and I could go round and help with shifting all the junk we were going to use for today's modelling from their shed.'

'So you thought it would be funny to put your picture in amongst the cardboard?'

'Yes, it was just meant to be a joke. I was going to find it when we started making the models and pretend to be shocked before I let on that I'd painted the picture.'

'But the plan went wrong?'

'Yes, I should have realised that Agnes would probably find it first. She's always sorting everything and tidying up. I'm really sorry.'

'I'll talk to Inspector Pepper to see if we'll be taking any action, but at least you've confessed about the joke before we've wasted anymore time. You can go now.'

*****

Sylvia Maitland had finally navigated the Mayor back to the Reception tent and was looking forward to his departure. She was dismayed to see what was clearly a group of reporters and photographers standing outside.

'I hope you don't mind,' said Councillor Hodgkiss, 'but I thought it was important I reassured the press that everything was under control.'

Some very unchristian thoughts passed through Sylvia's mind, but she restricted her reply to saying 'It would have been nice if you'd asked us first.'

The Mayor probably didn't hear her reply as he marshalled the press pack.

'Gather round please. Thank you for coming this morning. As I'm sure you are aware, we are all shocked at the events of the last few days. These murders would be terrible events in any circumstances, but to find a body in a tent at a children's summer holiday club is one of the worst outrages that I can ever recall.'

'Actually it's a Bible Club, Councillor Hodgkiss,' Sylvia interrupted

'Pardon?'

'It's a Bible Club,' Sylvia repeated, and then added for good measure 'we run this every year to give the local children the opportunity to learn more about God and to explore the Bible. All the local churches come together to run it and everybody helping here is a volunteer. Despite these awful events, we've decided we owe it to the children to carry on and that is what we're doing. At a time like this, we think the gospel stories will help the children understand more about good and evil and I'd like to thank all the helpers and parents for supporting us so well.'

The Mayor was clearly irritated that Sylvia was now the centre of attention.

He coughed loudly. 'Of course we are very grateful to everybody who runs this event, but I thought it necessary that, as the Mayor of this town and its first citizen, I reassured you all that everything here is under control. I would also like to pledge our complete support for the Police. At a time when so many people no longer care about their community and fail to challenge the growing tide of immorality in society, we should not be surprised that terrible events like this occur. I have been saying for years that if we as a nation don't show stronger moral leadership and make sure there are tougher prison sentences for criminals then society as we know it will disintegrate.'

'Is it true that you are hoping to be the Conservative candidate at the next general election?' asked one of the reporters.

'More like UKIP,' came a reply from somebody that the Mayor could not identify.

Sensing a gap in the proceedings, Sylvia said:

'I'd just like to thank you all for your interest. I'm sure you'll understand why we've asked you not to bother the parents and children. At the end of the week you'd be all more than welcome to come and see all the things they've been doing and to join us for our Grand Finale which is at six pm on Friday evening. Please leave your details here at the Reception tent if you'd like to come.'

Councillor Hodgkiss couldn't think of anything further he could add.

*****

Wendy and Peterson were reviewing the information on the white boards.

One of their frustrations was that they still had no identifications for the hit and run victim or the victim of what the papers were now referring to as the "acid bath murder."

However, one lead had emerged with a report that two residents at Cambridge YMCA had disappeared. PC Smart was being despatched to check their identities and see if the staff there recognised the victims from the police photographs. In the case of the murder victim from the Eagles tent, it was agreed that they would be very careful who would be shown the photograph. There was one side profile of the head that might just be recognisable.

Wendy said to Peterson 'Sorry, no time to see your beloved today. I think Smart can handle the Cambridge visit. I need you to go and find the pastor from Peter Lord's chapel. Do we know who he is?'

'Yes, you have to laugh really, his name is Pastor Jeremiah.'

'Surely not his real name? You'd better check that out. Sounds as though the chapel must be a bundle of fun!'

'He lives in Welsted, so I'll head off there now.'

*****

The wine shop on Market Lane was one of Lloyd Evan's favourite haunts. Walking into town on the way to the Library, he'd often take a short diversion to stop by and see if this enterprising local trader had anything new he should consider purchasing. So good, he thought, to see someone making a success of a local business and also giving the big chains and supermarkets a run for their money. There was a lot of choice elsewhere, two supermarkets and a branch of a regional chain of trendy kitchen and wine shops. Then, of course, there was the extraordinary selection of wines at the station newsagents, but this place in Market Lane had a degree of passion about it. The owner seemed to search out interesting and different wines that were unique.

'Morning Mr Evans. How are you today? Are you looking for anything special?'

'Well, I've had a bit of a week. My daughter's coming round tomorrow with the grand children for lunch. I'm looking for something that would go well with a beef casserole I was going to cook. I think one of my clarets or the burgundy might be a bit too much for lunch.'

'Starting them early are you?'

'Sorry, I'm not with you.'

'The grandchildren. Giving them a taste for the good things in life?'

'Oh my God no, I see what you mean! They're only three and one. It will be fruit juice for the eldest and whatever my daughter's brought for the baby. No, this is for me to enjoy with my daughter if we manage a bit of peace and quiet once the baby goes to sleep.'

'So do you see them a lot?'

'Yes, I can't complain. She's been very good to me since my wife died. Comes round every fortnight without fail. Checks I've got the house in order, despite the fact she knows I've got a house keeper.'

'Well that's good. Nice that you keep in touch and still get on with each other. So many parents just seem to moan when their children partner up or get married. Mind you, there's a whole lot more moaning that their kids never seem to move out. I had the vicar here last week complaining that his eldest son had now been back from university for three years and was showing no signs of leaving.'

'Actually he's the team rector.'

'Team rector, vicar, I can never keep up with you lot in the churches. I call him the vicar and he never objects. Right, something to go with a beef casserole at lunch. Here we are, try this. Came in yesterday. It's a lovely smooth Californian Merlot. Pretty full bodied, but lovely on the palate and goes down a treat. It will cost you £24.99.'

'Sounds good to me. I'll take a couple. One for lunch and one for later.'

Lloyd Evans paid with his debit card and left the shop. As he turned onto the street he found himself face to face with Selwyn Roberts, a business acquaintance.

'Lloyd my dear chap, just the man I'm looking for. Have you got time for a quick chat? Perhaps a half at the DOY?'

'I was going to head off to the Library and then back to Commonside, but if it's a quick one. Something important?'

They were walking along Market Lane towards Mound Street.

'It's Anglia Media. I've just had word that Intermed are going to put forward a serious offer.'

'But I thought we all agreed we were going to keep the firm local.'

They turned into Silver Street.

'I know old chap, but that was before we knew a large multinational like Intermed would be prepared to offer a stack of wonga to buy the outfit.'

'Listen to yourself. "Stack of wonga", you're beginning to sound like one of those adverts off the TV. What do the senior team at Anglia think?'

'Well, James is on board. I think he rather fancies himself as a potential media baron, so he sees the idea of being bought out by Intermed as a great opportunity for him. Plus, of course, he owns 10% so he'll probably earn a few bob on the deal as well.'

They entered the Duke of York.

'What can I get you Lloyd?'

'Oh, a pint of whatever the best bitter is today. I lose track of what they sell here.'

Lloyd sat at one of the discrete tables raised at one side of the pub on a platform behind a pillar. Selwyn joined him holding a pint of IPA and a gin and tonic.

'So, if James is going with this, what about the others?'

'I think my brother's OK, Chris will certainly go for it; he always thought the strategy was all wrong and we should shift the company as soon as we could make a decent return. Then there's you, me and, of course, Catherine.'

'Ah, yes, Catherine. Our dear school teacher. Remind me why we got her involved and how on earth we ever thought that was a good idea.'

'One of the original aims was to piggy back this on the school, particularly with the reputation of its sixth form. The idea was that if we gave this an educational angle, students learning about journalism, young reporter of the year sort of thing, then it would reach a wider audience.'

'Well that was a great success, I don't think.'

'Better than you realise. But it never got the publicity we were hoping for. They do so much at that school that there was always a bigger story than this little venture of ours. Ironic when you think about it, successful media venture gets zero media coverage!'

'So, we're left with Catherine. Will she sell?'

'Catherine York. At the time we all thought how good it was of her to invest some money in the venture. Seem to recall it was some inheritance from her mother. Wanted to support a local initiative and was keen on the idea of working with the students. There was a bit of a fuss about whether it was a conflict of interest. Now we'll probably find she's a right pain.'

'Not "one of us" as it were?'

'You're right there. Goes to the Quakers or the "yogurt knitters" as old Hodgkiss calls them. Mind you, when she realises she's up for a few bob profit she might play ball.'

'And if she doesn't, surely we can out vote her?'

'Problem is the Americans. They're head guy in England lives out at Finchwinter. Tom Garroway, good chap who can see an opportunity. But he said his bosses at Intermed are nervous. Thought we were just a bunch of hicks in the sticks, you know the sort of thing. They're hungry to expand over here and give some of the other media giants a run for their money, but they want a united front at our end. Very sensitive about being seen as the big bad bullies from across the pond. Doesn't fit the caring image they're trying to foster over here.'

'Bollocks,' said Lloyd, 'they're as greedy as the rest of them, even more so if they're trying to compete with the big guns.'

'As ever, there's a subtle difference between what they say and what they do,'

'Subtle my arse! The investor column in my paper last week said they were one of the most avaricious media companies in the market.'

'Precisely, that's the image they don't want, so some idealistic Quaker teacher sounding off about how they're going to destroy a great little local start-up company might send them running a mile.'

'What's their alternative?'

'There's another company in Cambridge they might go for instead. Not without the potential for similar problems, but the guys at Intermed think Cambridge is a bit more "with it" than we yokels here in Bonhunt.'

'So why are they still interested in us?'

'Because James Thompson has done a very good job. Anglia Media is apparently the first port of call for the BBC and the other TV stations if they need anything researched in the eastern counties, including Cambridge. James may look an innocent, but he's very savvy at how it all works and he's built an unrivalled list of contacts, which are gold dust to Intermed. He probably knows more senior politicians than any journalist in Fleet Street, or Wapping or wherever they all operate out of nowadays.'

'I heard it was London Bridge, but that's probably not important. What's the offer going to be, then?'

When Selwyn told Lloyd the answer, he decided that his wine cellar would shortly be receiving a significant consignment of the latest release of en primeur from Bordeaux. In the mean time he settled for another pint of bitter while Selwyn Roberts moved on to his second G&T of the day.

*****

Peterson had parked his vehicle in the car park of the Maypole Hotel and was walking down Back Street in Welsted in search of Pastor Jeremiah. Eventually he found the number, a bit further out of the village than he'd anticipated. A fairly imposing house on the corner, with "The Manse" in modern letters painted on the smart white gate.

If the house hadn't been what Peterson was expecting, then neither had Pastor Jeremiah been the image he had anticipated on the doorstep.

'Well hello there,' said the very jolly, portly figure that opened the door in response to Peterson's pressing of the doorbell, 'how can I be of service?'

'Pastor Jeremiah?'

'That's the one, you win the prize. Come on in.'

Peterson entered into a light and airy hall, painted in a tasteful pastel yellow with lots of white gloss wood work. On the wall a poster of a large smiley immediately caught Peterson's attention. Underneath were the words "Smile, it's his birthday."

'I see you've caught my Christmas card there. Went down a treat with everyone I sent it to. The church doesn't have to be all boring and traditional you know. We should be putting a smile on people's faces.'

'I hope you don't mind me saying this, but you're not quite what I imagined. I thought that Jeremiah was a pretty miserable soul.'

'Glad to hear you use the word soul there. SOS, saving our souls, that's what we're all about at the chapel. But we don't have to be all miserable about it. Jeremiah isn't my real name. I'm Jeremy, Jeremy Hands.'

'So why Pastor Jeremiah?'

'Oh, that started as a joke among my friends at Bible College. I was always studying the book of Jeremiah and saying how wonderful it was that he stayed faithful despite everything the good Lord threw at him. My name's Jeremy, it didn't take the world's greatest intelligence to turn that into Jeremiah, and it's stuck ever since.'

'I see, well you're certainly a refreshing contrast to some of the Christians I've met.'

'Please don't be put off. Some of the faithful can get pretty serious. But as I always say, nobody likes a good party more than the Lord. And when He parties it's a real party, like no other you'll ever go to. But forgive me, I haven't asked you to introduce yourself.'

Peterson produced his warrant card.

'Sergeant Peterson from Essex Police. I'm here to ask if you can help identify somebody who came to your chapel a few weeks ago.'

'Apologies, this is about poor Peter Lord, isn't it. I visited his wife earlier today. We're supporting her best we can. But death is only the start of the final journey. Peter will be dining with the saints now. He was a true believer. So what is it you want to know?'

'When we talked to Abigail Lord she was obviously very distressed but she told us about a visitor that came to your chapel a few weeks ago. All she could remember was that he was a tall man. Hadn't been before and hasn't returned since.'

'So what's the interest?'

'Mrs Lord told us that after the service he had quite a long chat to Peter and that they went for a walk around Welsted together. Apparently she had a row with Peter as a result because they were late getting home for lunch. Did you talk to the stranger?'

'Well yes, at least I tried to. We're a very friendly lot and we usually get people to relax and join in. But he was a cold fish. Couldn't engage him at all. Spent the whole service at the back, didn't really join in and avoided all my questions afterwards. He was a master class in giving nothing away. Then he went off with Peter Lord, and I remember the argument with Abigail when he finally returned. Boy was she angry!'

'Is there anything you can say about him?'

'He had a bright check shirt. I can confirm he was very tall. And he was almost certainly American, definitely sounded like an American accent. He spoke very quietly, almost come to think of it as though he was trying not to be heard. But he definitely sounded like an American.'

*****

Wendy was sitting in the corner of the makeshift police office, looking out of the window across the field to the children who were enjoying their lunch break at Summer Bible Club. She chuckled to herself as she realised how, despite all the progress that had been made towards achieving equality between the sexes, it was almost exclusively boys playing football and girl's playing rounders. A young boy she knew from town was being wheeled round in his wheelchair by some of the other children. She was impressed how inclusive the event seemed to be.

Wendy and Catherine sometimes talked about what they would have done if they'd had children. Catherine had laughed. Knowing her luck she'd have had a boy and would have had to cope with soldiers, guns and nasty computer games, not to mention the mess behind the toilet every time the wretched child used it. But sadly there would be no boy or girl, as Catherine was not able to have children. She'd never told Wendy the details, and Wendy hadn't asked but she felt her housemate had an air of sadness about her whenever anybody asked if she had her own kids.

It's what made her a good teacher, she always replied, the fact she didn't have to take them home with her.

Wendy on the other hand wasn't so certain. She could have children if she wished, assuming all the technical side was working. But would she want to take time out of her career? Would she want the responsibility? At the moment, the answer was no. But later on in life, Wendy thought, she might miss not having a younger generation to bring together as a family. Being old might be very lonely if there were no children.

Time to set these thoughts aside. Wendy focused again on the book that Catherine had found the night before. She'd skim read quite a lot. All very interesting, but pretty far fetched surely in terms of a hit and run and two murders in North Essex. Wendy had reached a chapter titled *"Armageddon"* and had highlighted three short paragraphs in pink marker.

On reflection, she thought it would have been better to have underlined them in pencil, but too late now. Hopefully Catherine wouldn't mind. She went back to the first two paragraphs. They outlined how conservative white evangelicals in America were fermenting a split in the church, portraying Europe and Britain as being morally defunct, spiritually dead and overrun by Muslims.

Surely, she thought, those basically nice people out on the field weren't linked to the type of person the author of this book was writing about. This was all stuff that those crazy Americans believed, not the average church goer in Chipping Bonhunt. She moved on to the third paragraph that she had highlighted. It seemed the crazy evangelical Americans thought that Europe could not be trusted because it had lost its Christian faith, and they speculated gleefully as to when the UK would wake up and find Islam was the majority religion.

She got up, walked over to the whiteboards and looked at the photographs of the two unknown victims. Who were these bodies? Hopefully PC Smart would come back with some answers.

*****

Smart had dropped in at Parkside Police Station in Cambridge. Wendy had told him to introduce himself first and just make sure they knew what he was doing in Cambridge. PC Gwendolyn Makepeace had come down to the front desk.

'I bet you get teased with a name like that,' she said in her gentle welsh lilt. 'It's the same with my name; they all keep telling me I should make love not peace.'

'Sorry, I don't get it.'

'Surely you know the phrase, make love not war. It's a play on "make peace".'

'Oh, I see. Sorry, being a bit thick here.'

'So what do they call you?'

'It's usually "not so" which is supposed to be short for "not so smart".'

Gwendolyn thought she could understand where that one had come from.

'How unkind. You look bright as a button to me.'

Smart's face lit up. This young constable might be a bit flirty, but she'd made the trip to Cambridge worthwhile.

'Right,' said Gwendolyn, 'let's go for a little walk down Gonville Place. The YMCA isn't very far.'

As they walked along the pavement Smart was amazed how busy the large open area that spread out in front of the Police station seemed to be.

'Is Cambridge always this busy?'

'In the summer, yes. That's Parker's Piece. It seems to be full of language students at the moment. They're a nightmare on the bicycles. No idea how to ride safely and the language schools just give them out without any training. We're having a bit of a campaign about it at the moment.'

'Well you need one; I was almost mown down walking from the station. They seem to ride all over the pavement.'

'Yes,' Gwendolyn moved sideways to avoid a couple of erratic cyclists that perfectly illustrated the point, 'they've no idea about the highway code. Trouble is there's so many that we've given up stopping them, besides half of them pretend not to understand what you're saying anyway.'

They arrived at the YMCA. In reception, Gwendolyn made their introductions.

'Is there any chance of talking to the manager?'

The cheerful young man on reception raised his eyes to heaven. 'No chance of that, he's on leave this week. Doing his annual bible thing in Chipping Bonhunt.'

'What's his name?' asked Smart.

'John Davies,' came the reply, to which Smart tried not to show any reaction. 'He's run this place for about five years. Used to run a hostel in Bishop's Stortford before that.'

'Well, can we talk to somebody who might know the two missing residents?' asked Gwendolyn.

'Our housing officer might be able to help.'

Five minutes later they were sitting in a small claustrophobic office with a very large middle aged lady who looked hot and flustered and seemed to be wearing an excess of a very pungent perfume.

'We'll suffocate if we stay too long in here,' Smart whispered to Constable Makepeace, who giggled but quickly regained her composure.

'I really am terribly busy,' said the housing officer. 'We reported these two missing as a matter of good practice, but it often happens here in the summer. We get these foreigners and they go travelling around the country, decide to stay over somewhere and don't bother to call us and let us know. It happens all the time.'

'I'd like to show you a couple of photos if I may. First of all, this one.'

'Oh dear, how dreadful, what's happened to him?'

'I'm afraid he was hit by a car and didn't survive.'

'I think I do recognise his face, how awful. I'm sorry I was so short with you. Poor boy. Where did this happen?'

'Chipping Bonhunt. How long since you've seen him?'

'I'll go and check the signing in records. And I'll bring his file as well; we take a photo of all our residents so we can check the person staying is the person that's booked.'

'Could you bring the file for the other missing resident as well? It would be a real help and we can speed things up. If these are our victims I need to report this back ASAP.'

Five minutes later the housing officer had returned with two files, both open on the small office table. Smart realised how much he had welcomed the chance to breath in some air without the oppressive scent of that perfume.

Both Constable Makepeace and Constable Smart agreed that the hit and run victim was the missing resident. The photo on the file looked a bit like a prison mug shot, but there was no mistaking the similarity. The hair was identical, and the blue eyes were clear on both photos.

'I recognise that jacket as well,' said the housing officer. He was always wearing it. The last record we have of him signing out was on Sunday morning. Would you like me to check our CCTV?'

'Please just check he did sign out, but I'm pretty sure you won't find him coming back in.'

Sharp recorded some details in his note book:

Jake Kerry. 14 Cedar Drive, Hope, Arkansas, USA
Arrived at Cambridge YMCA three weeks ago.
Date of birth 16th July 1992. Aged 22

Smart took another folder out from the small wallet he was carrying.

'I'm afraid this one isn't very pretty.'

The housing officer winced when she looked at it.

'How horrible, what terrible injuries.'

'Yes, I'm afraid somebody really didn't like him.'

Between them they looked at the photo on the YMCA file and the photo of the murder victim. It wasn't conclusive, but they certainly could be the same person. Smart noted down some more details in his book.

Philip Frost. 98 Regan Way, Austin, Arkansas, USA
Arrived at Cambridge YMCA three weeks ago.
Date of birth 21st April 1991. Aged 23

'Clearly they knew each other,' said Gwendolyn. 'Arrived together, both roughly the same age and both from the same part of America.'

'Please make sure nobody enters their rooms, I think we'll need to search them. But that's a bit above my pay grade,' Smart said. 'Is there anything else that occurs to you about these two?'

'They were both very religious. You know that American type of Christian that thinks the rest of us are all damned or something. They found all of us a bit disappointing in our Christianity. Mind you, they probably got the wrong end of the stick about our name. We might be the Young Men's Christian Association, but the spiritual side isn't much to the fore nowadays.'

'After that song by The Village People, I thought YMCAs were better known for something else,' Smart joked. The Housing Officer scowled at him, definitely not appreciating the remark.

'Is there anything else you want to ask me? I really do have a stack of work to get on with.'

'Yes, did they meet anyone that you or other staff here can remember?'

'We have so many people coming thorough this building that I doubt anybody will remember any particular visitor. But we'll check the CCTV to see if anything shows up.'

'Thank you that would be really helpful. You can reach us on this number.'

Smart handed her a card.

'Now I need to make a call,' he said.

*****

Wendy took the call as soon as Smart 'phoned in.

'So let's just make sure we've got this straight. You're definite that one of the victims is a young American called Jake Kerry and the other is almost certain to be another American called Philip Frost. Anything else?'

Wendy listened carefully to Smart's summary.

'You say they were both very religious. Do you mean conservative evangelicals? Oh, never mind, I'll explain another time.'

Than Smart dropped his bombshell.

'You're telling me the manager there is John Davies. How on earth did we miss that one! Thanks then Smart. Get back here as soon as you can. Good work and well done.'

*****

Having made sure Lucy was still OK; Tom Garroway had left Folly Farm, taken a taxi to Castle Lofts station and caught a train down to London. Originally he'd intended to take his daughter out riding, but she wasn't keen. Probably still had an almighty hangover he thought and it meant he could spend some valuable time on the deal with Anglia Media. Now he was walking into the reception area of the splendidly refurbished Midland Hotel in front of St Pancras Station. He admired the way the old vehicular entrance had been transformed. His employers certainly didn't go economy class when it came to staying oversees.

It was fortunate the senior directors were in London. It meant that he could resolve the outstanding issues on the Anglia Media takeover quickly and make sure there were no misunderstandings. Personal contact was still the best he thought, even in these days of electronic communication.

He wasn't sure why so many of the senior Intermed team were over here. Normally he was in the loop on these things, but this was probably one of those "need to know" visits and clearly it had been decided he didn't "need to know." As a barometer of where he stood in the organisation, he felt a little disappointed. The only explanation he'd had was that they were here to do some important lobbying, which he understood to mean that they were trying to get some senior politicians on their side before they started taking on some of the competition. Rumour was that the boss was in town as well, but there was no evidence of him today.

Anglia Media looked almost pathetic in comparison to the battle-lines that might be drawing up, but Tom thought it had the potential to grow rapidly. They would be paying for James Thompson's expertise and contacts and in Tom's view that was expertise and contacts well worth paying for.

Hopefully the meeting wouldn't take more than a couple of hours, thought Tom. That would give him time to sort out some unfinished business back in Bonhunt. He'd promised Jean he wouldn't be too late as she didn't want to be on her own calming Lucy down the night before the results were out.

'High Tom,' a loud American voice echoed across the bar area, 'come and join us for a drink. Sounds as if we've got something to celebrate.'

*****

The Eagles were busy with the grand battle of the ships. The afternoon had seen a lively start as the leaders had demonstrated that they really could walk on water. Agnes had arranged for Waitrose to make an extra batch of the ice they used for their fish counter, and she'd collected it during the lunch break. Then they'd filled a small paddling pool with it while the children were out on the field. When the children had returned, each of the leaders had walked across the pool, "walking on water."

'That's cheating,' one of the more precocious girls had said. 'No it isn't,' John had replied. 'Water comes in three forms, liquid, steam and ice. We never said which type we were going to walk on!'

'That's cheating. I bet Jesus didn't walk on ice.'

'I expect you're right there. I doubt the Sea of Galilee was frozen. It's far too hot. But this was just a bit of fun.'

The walking on water trick had upped the anti among all of the children.

'They're all hyper now,' said Alice, 'I told you that would get them all over- excited.'

So it was agreed: It was time for the race between the five junk model ships that had been finished before the lunch break. John lined them up on the starting line. Each group had nominated two runners, who had to stand in their ships, front and back, holding them carefully so they didn't fall apart.

Supervising along the side of "the Aegean" as John was insisting on calling the main body of the school hall, Agnes, Jean, Jane Dawson, Sarah and Lewis were ready to stop any cheating. The crew for each boat could only walk or run forward if their ship was being held at waist line and was still intact. Otherwise they had to stop and make repairs. Alice was at the other end of the course, setting up the finishing line. She looked down the length of the hall. It was always a shame, she thought, that so much effort went in to making things like this when they'd be consigned to the rubbish bin by the end of the day. Some of the children might persuade parents that they could take their wonderful creations home, but she was pretty sure they wouldn't last long. How many people wanted a pile of LCD television and PC boxes, sellotaped and glued together with varying degrees of success, clogging up the living room? At least this helped burn off some of the kid's energy.

'Are we ready?' shouted John.

'Yes' came the reply.

'Are we steady?'

'Yes!' came the even louder reply.

'Then its,' he paused for effect, 'GO!'

A mad rush ensued and the volume of noise became almost unbearable.

One of the ships lasted barely two yards before it broke apart in the middle, with the child at the front having to come back so that running repairs could be made in sellotape.

A second ship lost all of its upper decks which had to be hastily re-assembled. And a third was crushed as the rear member of its crew tripped, creating a tangled pile of child and cardboard.

All of the children tried to run too quickly, with none of them remembering the truism that slow and steady wins the race.

None of the ships made it in one go, but after a brief stop for repairs, one that had been designed to look a bit like a cruise liner crossed the finishing line and was judged to be sufficiently in one piece to take the prize.

The award for best design went to a ship that had been lovingly constructed to include masts, sails and even had a few cannon on deck made out of toilet rolls. Unfortunately it was so intricate that it had disintegrated halfway down the course.

'That's not fair; they didn't even finish the race.'

'We said there would be a prize for the best design, and they deserve it. They put their effort into how it looks, not how quickly they could run with it in the race,' said John.

Sweets were handed out to the two winning teams.

'Can we talk please, Mr Davies?' said Wendy. John hadn't seen Peterson and Wendy enter the hall in the middle of all the excitement.

'Of course, shall we go over here?'

'No, we need you to come with us. We have some questions we need to ask,' said Peterson.

'I see, and you have to do this now?'

'Yes, we have to do this now.'

'Alice, can you hold the fort?'

She looked very worried. There was no way John was involved in the dreadful events that had taken place, but it seemed that the police were treating him as a suspect. She suppressed a feeling of growing panic inside her and managed to reply 'Yes, I think so.'

'Good, I'll get back as soon as I can. I'm sure the others will rally round.'

And he was gone. Not exactly marched out, but it was clear that the police were serious. This wasn't going to be a friendly chat outside in the corridor.

*****

Having made sure everything was ready for giving out the results the following morning, Catherine had returned to the cottage in Granary Lane. It was a beautiful afternoon, and she'd opened up the French windows on to the patio. The deep pink climbing rose was in full bloom, creating a richly coloured awning over the arbour. She sat on a light blue chair by a similarly coloured table in what she and Wendy both joked was a fashionable "distressed" look. This was more because of the number of times their garden furniture had been scratched over the years than a deliberate design statement. Still, it suited the small cottage garden and with the combination of the light blue furniture, the hot sun and the cheap bottle of white wine she had opened, Catherine pretended that she was in her own quiet corner of a Greek island. She was making notes to herself about her plan of action for the next morning.

There would be congratulations and wild ecstatic joy for some of her students. Lucy Garroway would certainly be celebrating, as would nearly all of Lucy's friends. But one of the group had come badly adrift on their music grade, and it didn't look good. It appeared as though something had gone wrong with the compositions this year and the music grades were down. Always difficult for those who miss their offers when nearly everyone else has done well. It seemed to be yet another case of a student failing to understand that the insurance choice she made, her second choice university if she missed the grades for her first, should require sufficiently lower grades to make it a meaningful choice. In this case the girl concerned had gone for too high an insurance offer, resulting in her missing that as well. It was going to be an emotional morning. One of her choices might take her if a lot of people had missed their offers, but they'd need to get started on ringing round quickly and give serious consideration to going for a place through clearing.

However, there would be some compensation. Another one of Catherine's girls had done surprisingly well, much better than she needed for her university offer, and it would be worth trying to get her on to a better course if she was interested. Oxford and Cambridge didn't offer extra places at this stage, but a lot of other good universities did.

The doorbell rang. Damn, thought Catherine, who on earth will be calling round now? Always the way when you're enjoying a bit of peace and quiet.

'Hello,' said the male Jehovah's Witness on the doorstep, 'we so enjoyed our last visit and we were just in the area.'

At moments like this Catherine felt she could kill Wendy, who had the bright idea of inviting this Jehovah couple in the last time they'd called. It had been pouring with rain, and Wendy had taken pity on them. Then it had taken two hours to get rid of them, and afterwards Wendy had just burst out laughing. Catherine remembered it was one of the few times they'd had a row.

'It's alright for you,' she'd said, 'but I'm due in school first thing and that's two hours of this evening's marking down the pan.'

And here they were again. She was frantically thinking of excuses to give for not having time to talk to them when help arrived from an unexpected source.

'Hello, Catherine, been meaning to drop by for a couple of weeks. But you look busy; perhaps I should come back again later?' Selwyn Roberts looked as though he had no intention of going.

'Oh, no, please stay.' She tried to sound as though she wasn't begging, but Selwyn had detected the sense of desperation in her voice.

'Actually, it would be good if we could talk now. There's something cropped up with AM.'

'AM?'

'Our little company.'

'Oh, yes of course,' Catherine turned to the Jehovah's witnesses and put on her best, broadest smile. 'I'm terribly sorry, it seems something's come up that I need to deal with. I'm sure you'll understand.'

'Yes,' they said. 'We'll just leave you this,' and a copy of the Watch Tower was thrust into her hand before they set off down the lane.

'Come in Selwyn. You are a life saver. I shall be eternally grateful.'

'You don't know what I've got to say yet.'

'Well, I'm all ears. Come outside and have a glass of wine. It's not what Lloyd would offer you, and given Wendy's attitude to him I'm surprised I'm still on your list of friends, but your timing today was just perfect.'

'Don't get sore about poor old Lloyd. He has never got used to the loss of the Empire, even though most of it had gone before he was out of short trousers. I always think he was born to wear a pith helmet and govern some obscure province in India.'

'He wouldn't like to hear you saying things like that about him.'

'Oh, I say them to his face. He was born too late to fulfil the destiny God gave him.'

They both laughed and moved back through the cottage and out on to the patio, where Catherine was quickly wiping down another "distressed" blue chair.

'Oh, how charming, how utterly charming.'

'On a day like today, I'm sure everywhere looks pretty good.'

'But this is so beautifully done. You've got it just right. Nothing overdone, just perfectly composed. Just right.'

'Well that's very kind of you to say so. Now, what can I do for you? I assume its Anglia Media you want to talk about?'

'Yes, I realise you've been out of the loop. We're all so busy and we should have got the directors together a couple of months ago, we really should. Anyway, cut to the chase. We've had an offer, a very good offer, and the other directors all think we should sell up our holdings.'

'Who's the offer from?'

'Do you know a chap called Tom Garroway? Children are at your school.'

'Yes, I was teaching Lucy, his daughter, all last year. A level results tomorrow. Big day. And Tom's wife is helping in one of the tents at Summer Bible Club. I think Wendy has bumped into her there with all the other things that have been going on.'

'Yes, pretty dreadful from what I've heard. Well, Tom is the British representative for a large international company called Intermed. He's destined for high things if their strategy for this country takes off, high things.'

'But they sound like yet another greedy American media conglomerate. Surely you're not saying we should sell out to a company like that?'

'I thought you wouldn't like the idea at first, but just think about it for a minute. James has really been making a name for the company. He's got AM boxing way above its weight, so at the moment the value is high. If we get out now, we all stand to make a great return. Think what you could do. Another investment, buy some more property, set up something new for the school.'

'It's the school bit that worries me. Anglia Media is doing some great work with students on our sixth form electives, and it's already helped several students make some really good career choices. I don't expect a huge American conglomerate is going to give that much of a priority.'

'They have an education arm, and they might think it worth looking at. But even if they don't, the money this will give you means you can set something up to replace that side of things. And I know James will want to keep something going, even if it has to be outside the firm.'

'I'm really a bit disappointed. Anglia Media was meant to be a local company doing some positive things here in the local community. We never intended it to be used by some dreadful Americans as their vehicle to move in on the British media industry.'

'Things change. You can't stand in the way of progress when it comes. No, you can't stand in the way. And I think you're over egging the dreadful Americans bit. Look how much of their television we watch. I seem to remember you telling me how you liked to watch Homeland on a Sunday evening.'

Catherine laughed. 'If I thought Anglia Media was going to get involved in making something like Homeland I'd probably be right with you, but this is very different. This is about controlling the news and what we know. And it's getting more and more difficult to keep the news and information about what's going on in this world available in a way that's objective.'

'Catherine, Catherine. You're getting very melodramatic. All I ask is that you think through the proposal. I'll get something e-mailed across to you when we have the details from Tom. I think you'll be surprised about how much Anglia Media might be worth to Intermed.'

'I'll promise to think about it for you. Now have another glass of wine and tell me about that holiday you had in Venice at Easter. Wendy and I keep saying we must go there, so I want to pick your brains about the best places to stay, although I don't think we can afford to travel on that luxury train you went on.'

*****

John Davies had been taken to the police station. He was sitting in the interview room with Wendy and Peterson.

'The problem we have,' Wendy was saying, 'is that you keep showing up at every turn in this investigation and we're having trouble understanding why.'

'Well, you surely can't think I shot poor Peter Lord.'

'Not you directly, but you could have planned it – paid somebody else. Pretty good alibi, watching it from your front door step. You see, I'm not sure I buy your laid back approach to all of this. Peterson here tells me you're very keen to paint a picture of yourself as the liberal Christian. You're cynical about the dogma and you seem to stand back from all the others at Summer Bible Club. Quietly aloof? Is that you?'

'That's a bit unkind, but yes, I do stand back from some of the things that other people at SBC say. I think we get too dogmatic, and sometimes that makes people very unkind.'

'So how do you explain our two dead bodies being your residents from the hostel at Cambridge?'

'First of all, we're not a hostel, and secondly, I can't explain it. I had no idea the victims were my residents.'

'So did you know them? Had you talked to them?'

'I certainly didn't know them. I might have talked to them, but I'm not hands on with the residents. That's not my role.'

'Well, let's go over the events so far. Sunday night, you're on security duty when somebody puts a sheep's head in the quiet corner of one of the tents. The tent you just happen to be leading. And, for good measure, the rest of the sheep gets left in the sixth form centre. I hear it rather spoilt their new carpet.'

'Later on,' she continued, 'after the concert at Castle Lofts, one of the residents from the YMCA that you manage in Cambridge gets run over in the Market Square.'

'So we get to Monday. During the day, nobody you know gets killed – at least, nobody we're aware of. But then, in the evening when you're back on security duty again, another of your residents cops it and turns up covered in the most awful acid burns. And where does he turn up? Once again in the tent you're leading. Finally, just to round off this saga of murder and mayhem we have another murder, this time a drive-by shooting, on your front door step.'

'I think there are three options here: either you're the coolest criminal living in Essex, or you're very, very unlucky, or somebody has really got it in for you.'

'Isn't this where I ask to see my lawyer?'

'You can if you want, but I'm beginning to think that you might be at risk yourself.'

'What do you mean?'

'Well, if it's not you responsible for all of this, and if you're not just very, very unlucky when it comes to coincidences, then I think you might be on our murderer's list as well.'

'Why would that be?'

'Well look at the facts. All our victims are connected to you and the link keeps coming back to the tent you lead. One victim might just be a coincidence, two I'm not buying and as for three – well, there's got be a link to you.'

'Surely the fact that two of the victims were staying in Cambridge could be coincidence? We get a lot of Americans coming over and we offer them a good deal.'

'But do you want to risk it? I think we need to get you and your wife some sort of protection.'

'So I'm not a suspect then?'

'Of course you're a suspect – I can't eliminate you at the moment. But I wouldn't put you top of my list. I don't see you as the cool calculating killer that you'd have to be to sit in front of me now and not give the tiniest hint of guilt.'

'I'm told I'm always too honest.'

'Well think then. Who might want to stitch you up? Why does all this seem to revolve around you when you seem not to have a clue what's going on?'

'I suppose I've upset a few people in the other local churches, possibly even my own,' said John. 'I find a lot of what other people in the churches say meaningless. It's as though they switch their brains off before they open their mouths. You know, the type of people who deny evolution and argue Darwinism isn't right? "The world is really only 5,000 years old" and all that kind of rubbish. I'm open with my opinions, and it upsets people.'

'So what do you believe in? Sounds to me that perhaps you shouldn't even bother going to church.'

John took in a deep breath and thought for a moment.

'Sometimes I ask myself that question. Do I just go to church because I always have done? But when I think things through, the idea of a creator God always makes more sense to me than this whole universe being some random act.'

'But who created God?' asked Peterson

'The million dollar question,' replied John. 'We just have to accept that he was, he is, and always will be.'

Peterson looked perplexed.

'Enough of the theology lesson,' said Wendy, 'we've got a killer to catch. I'll get one of the uniforms to stand guard. You've already got my card. If you think of anything relevant call me and please make sure you keep us informed about your movements. No disappearing from Chipping Bonhunt.'

'Message understood.'

'Well, you can go now. But think hard. If anybody who might have a grudge against you comes to mind, give us a call immediately.'

Wendy stood up, signalling John to leave the room. Peterson opened the door to let him out.

'So, what do you make of that?' Wendy asked.

'I don't think he's the killer or part of a wider plot,' Peterson replied, 'I just can't see him being the type. The state of that body we found in his tent. He was as shocked as everybody else.'

'I think you're right, but what is the connection? It's something linked to the local churches, or someone's trying to make it look as though it's connected to the churches. We're still no nearer to having a prime suspect.'

'Is it true the American Embassy is showing an interest? Heard they might be sending somebody up here to check out what's going on.'

'It's not surprising, two American nationals killed in this insignificant corner of the mother country. We'd better get a move on solving the murder before we have the FBI crawling all over us. I think you should spend what remains of the day talking to the Arkansas State Police. Find out if they know anything about Jake Kerry and Philip Frost and if they don't, can they put us in touch with anyone who does.'

'I'll get on to it right away'

'Better check the time first, any idea what time it is over there?'

'I haven't a clue, but I'm sure I can google it.'

'That'll keep the Police and Crime Commissioner happy. Make sure you tell him if and when he next visits.'

*****

Councillors Hodgkiss and Dakin were enjoying a late afternoon pint in the Great Eastern. It was quiet, with just a couple of other lonely drinkers sitting in isolation, tucked away in the various corners of the bar.

'This place needs an injection of something,' the Mayor was saying. 'It won't survive much longer unless it gets its act together. Ought to be a thriving community pub, but it's more like a morgue.'

'It is Wednesday afternoon; most of the locals will be at work.'

Dakin was looking tired and worried, trying to interrupt the flow of conversation coming from the Mayor.

'But what about the retirement homes around here – pensioners' lunches, afternoon deals, and dominoes – I don't know, I'm sure they could do something to attract the zimmer frame brigade.'

'Steven, there's something important I need to discuss with you. I need your help.'

'Whatever's the matter old boy? I thought you weren't looking too bright.'

'It's the bank, Steven. You know I borrowed the money to buy the old solicitors on the High Street, and the large house at the top?'

'Yes, and very helpful to me that's been. Good to know you're onside for boosting that end of the town. So what's the problem with the bank?'

'I'm having difficulty keeping up the repayments. By now I was hoping to have enlisted some development partners. Trouble is, everything's dead. The restaurant that was interested has pulled out and the wretched planners at District say they won't consider a change of use on the house. Can you help?'

'Got to be careful here. You know I can't afford to look as though I'm involved in any grubby business. Planning's all a bit sensitive with all the housing issues around the town; we have to keep our hands clean for the time being. That's not to say things might not change in a year or two's time, particularly if we review the town plan.'

'I'm not sure that's going to be quick enough to save my bacon. I was going to get that chap Tom Garroway to lease the old solicitor's building for his American company Intermed. He was keen at first, said he could do with a place in town. But then he said his bosses thought we were all a bit too parochial. No news worth bothering about and if they leased anything, it would be in Cambridge.'

'Word on the street is that they've got different fish to fry, sniffing around Anglia Media.'

Councillor Dakin's expression looked even more pained.

'I hadn't heard that, so all this news this week isn't going to change anything. I was hoping with Bonhunt being on the national media that I might persuade Intermed to think again. These Americans love a bit of rural English murder.'

'Next you'll be telling me it was you that tried to torch the Quakers' place. It wasn't you was it?'

Dakin sat silently and went red in the face.

'Well, if it was, thanks for kick starting the café plan. I think Trevor Sandling at the Meeting House is going to buy into it. You may have done yourself a favour if it gets things moving along a bit.'

'You surely don't think I did that.'

Councillor Dakin smiled at him and winked conspiratorially.

Neither of the councillors took any notice as a tall man in a check shirt took his glass to the bar and left.

'Of course it wasn't me that set fire to the Meeting House. I'm not that desperate, well not yet. But I need to do something to start getting a return on my two buildings. Otherwise I'll probably end up selling them at a loss.'

*****

Peterson took the 'phone call. It came from a pay phone and it was clear that the caller was trying to disguise their voice, which was being muffled by a handkerchief or something similar.

'First of all, please give me your name,' said Peterson.

'I've no time for that. You need to listen. I heard that Mayor chap and one of his mates talking about the fire on the High Street. The other one said he had some properties in the High Street and he was in some financial trouble, but the Mayor thought the fire would help – might get things moving along he said.'

'So where are you calling from. Where was this?'

The line went dead.

Peterson decided to give the Town Clerk a call. Perhaps he would know if any of the Mayor's mates owned property on the High Street.

*****

Back at their home in Thomas Road, Alice and John Davies were sitting in the garden enjoying a glass of white wine in the sun.

'You know, I think this might be the last year I do the Summer Bible Club,' said John.

'Well, I've been trying to tell you,' said Alice, 'it's one thing too many and with all the events this year I'm surprised your blood pressure hasn't gone through the roof.'

John sipped his wine and helped himself to some of his favourite vegetable crisps that Alice had thoughtfully provided.

'These are lovely, just what the doctor ordered. I'm trying not to let it get to me, but I have to admit I am actually getting a bit stressed this year, which is unlike me. But I suppose I'm also asking myself what it all achieves. We present this wonderful image of all the churches working together when in fact behind the scenes it's a very different story. I often think I'm worshipping a different God from most of the others.'

Alice laughed and poured out some more wine.

'Come on, I shouldn't encourage you to drink any more, but this evening I think you deserve it.'

*****

'Let's just run through this again,' said Wendy.

Councillors Hodgkiss and Dakin were sat at the dining table, facing Wendy and Peterson. They had agreed to meet immediately, and were both at the Mayor's house in a small upmarket development on the south of Chipping Bonhunt. Peterson had soon extracted the information he'd been seeking from the Town Clerk. The only town councillor who owned any property on the High Street was Councillor Dakin and yes, it was fairly well known that he was a bit strapped for cash and pretty desperate to see the Mayor's plans move forward.

Wendy had never liked this development. It felt a bit self important. Mock classical, she supposed, but all out of proportion. The builder clearly hadn't heard of the golden section and had achieved an unhappy blend of GRP columns, uPVC windows and doors that looked very grand but on closer examination were kitted out with cheap metal door knockers and letter box covers that were definitely not brass. If Wendy had stopped to think further about it she would probably have concluded that this was just the sort of house she would expect the Mayor to live in.

'On Sunday evening you were both at the concert at Castle Lofts. Mrs Hodgkiss was with you, but Mrs Dakin had decided not to go to the concert because she wanted to be at home in case there was any news about her mother who is in hospital. Afterwards you all came back here for a drink and then Councillor Dakin went home, so neither of you went near the High Street before the fire started. On Monday night you were both at the meeting in the Town Hall, and after that a group of you went for a drink and a meal at the Bonhunt Hotel, which means you couldn't have been at the school during the evening. Tuesday afternoon the Mayor here was having a drink with Councillor Thomas at The Royal Sovereign. But you, Councillor Dakin, don't have an alibi.'

'Not quite true,' said Councillor Hodgkiss, 'I recall you walking past the window and waving at us, or was I mistaking you for somebody else?'

'No, no, you weren't mistaken. I remember seeing you in the window seats,' Councillor Dakin stammered, 'gave you a bit of a wave I recall.'

'And he wasn't wearing motor cycle leathers?' asked Wendy.

'Certainly not,' replied Councillor Hodgkiss.

'One final question then, for Councillor Dakin here. Just how much do you stand to make if the plans for the High Street and the Meeting House go ahead?'

'Who knows? Probably not a lot the way things stand, but it might get the bank off my back. Funny really, when you think about it. The Quakers were the founding fathers of the banking industry here in Chipping Bonhunt. They might look all very green and leftie today, but they were very astute businessmen back in the past. Sold out at the top of the market and made a fortune. Not to mention the local brewing industry they established. Brewed a lot, but never drank a drop themselves. Now their Meeting House is one of the critical factors in me getting the bloody bank they helped found to give me a bit of slack. Get that Meeting House sorted out and thriving as some sort of café and it might help me attract a restaurant further up the hill.'

'Well that will do for now. Time for us to go, but we'll be checking out some of these alibis.'

Wendy and Peterson made for the hall. The flock wall paper really was over the top Wendy thought as she stepped through the uPVC replica Georgian front door. Why did these councillors always have to act as though they were far more important than they really were? Wendy cursed herself for being such a bitch. But all those digs at the Quakers – those councillors deserved a bit of their own medicine now and again.

'I really could do with a break,' said Wendy as they walked back towards the car. 'If I'd thought we had made any real progress I'd say let's go and show those councillors just how much a Quaker can really drink!'

*****

Folly Farm was in maximum stress mode. Lucy was sitting in the corner of the kitchen, sobbing quietly whilst Jean was trying to keep herself and everybody else calm.

'I really hope you get the grades,' Joshua was saying.

'That's nice of you, Josh,' said Jean, 'try and cheer your big sister up for us would you?'

'Well, if she doesn't get her place at Cambridge then I'm going to be stuck with her here at home for another year and I'm so looking forward to her going.'

'That's not so nice Josh; in fact we can do without that this evening, thank you very much.'

'That's just typical of you,' sobbed Lucy, 'stick the knife in just when I'm feeling down. You're just a horrible little pig. I really can't stand this waiting anymore.'

'Lucy, I know he's provoking but can you please watch your language. You've just got to get through to eight am tomorrow, and then the wait is over. Not long now.'

'Why isn't dad here? He's never here when we need him.'

'You know he's had to go down to London for an important business meeting. He'll be back later and he's absolutely promised that he will be in tomorrow evening.'

'It's going to be unbearably awful tomorrow. How can I go out celebrating if I don't get my grades? Everybody will want to hit the town and I just can't face it.'

'You'll have a great time with them all tomorrow. And I expect most of your friends will be going out with their families in the evening, just like us. It feels like we've all been through this together. Fingers crossed that we've all got something to celebrate tomorrow evening.'

'I doubt it.'

*****

In the workshop at the barn, the acid had been cleared away and the man had carefully laid out his equipment and materials on the table. He was nothing if not methodical. It had been relatively easy to obtain the C4 explosive. Just need to put together the detonator and everything would be ready to assemble. Nobody had an inkling as to who he really was, and that was how he liked it. God's work would soon be done.

*****

Wendy put down the 'phone. 'Damn!' she exclaimed.

'Me thinks Warren not a happy man?' asked Peterson.

'Too bloody right he's not. The Commissioner's demanding results and is desperately trying to suck up to the Americans. Sounds as though he's been watching too many American cop series and thinks the FBI is just what we need to, and I quote, "give our parochial plods a big kick up the proverbial". At least Warren is trying to hold him off and is still backing me, but basically we've got until Saturday before the Yanks fly in and start taking over the whole shooting match. Problem is that it's the first big opportunity for our Commissioner to throw his weight around and show everyone whose boss. Right, we need to get on. How are things with the Arkansas State Police – any progress?'

'Guy I spoke to was quite helpful. Gave me some other contacts. The ones I really need to get hold of are the sheriffs, or their officers in Hope and Austin. Unfortunately they're not available at the moment, I understand they're all out on a buddy fishing trip!'

'Buddy fishing trip?'

'Yes, it's just something they do, apparently. Raising money for charity. I've got some administrator in the Hope Sheriff's office trying hard for me. I had to give her my life history, but when I told her I went to Cambridge she just melted.'

'I knew it was supposed to open doors, but that's just ridiculous.'

'I've had to promise to visit her if ever I'm in the States!'

'I suspect your Trude might have something to say about that.'

'Does she need to know?'

'Keeping secrets and you're not even married yet. I think that's a bad sign. Well, I don't know about you, but I'm completely washed up. Let's finish here and go for one of our outside case reviews. I think we both need a drink.'

'Anything you say, boss'

*****

An assorted band of Summer Bible Club volunteers had gathered in the main marquee on the Bonhunt Academy playing fields. Wednesday night was prayer night and this year there were more gathered than anyone could remember ever attending before. It was an opportunity for everybody to come together and reflect on the week's extraordinary and dreadful events. A couple of the helpers had tears in their eyes and the mood was quiet and subdued.

Sylvia Maitland was running through the arrangements for the rest of the week.

'First of all, I just want to say thank you to everybody for coping so well, given all the dreadful events we've witnessed. I know it hasn't been easy for anybody. I can't imagine how Alice and John have managed to keep going; both of them will be back again tomorrow and I think we should pray hard for them. I know that some of you find John a bit too liberal – not just in his politics,' the mood lightened and there was some laughter, 'but he really sticks at things when he commits to them. I talked to him on the 'phone earlier this evening and he gave their apologies, so I told him the last thing we expected was that they should come out again this evening after the day he's had.

Now, one of the things the committee have been giving a lot of thought to is the Grand Finale on Friday evening. It would be a mistake to cancel it and by going ahead we can share with all the parents the positive things that have been going on here this week and also join together in prayer for the victims.

The rector has agreed to give a short talk that he's preparing very carefully in order to strike the right note, bearing in mind there will be a lot of children present.'

'What about the police?' asked one of the helpers.

'I was coming to that. They asked if they can talk to everybody, which we've agreed they can do at the beginning of the evening – so, Jeremy, please bear that in mind when you're leading the singing before the main event starts. I know that you enjoyed it last year, but please stop when we ask you because that's when the police will want to talk to everybody. They won't tell me anymore about what they're going to say apart from that they want to offer some reassurance.'

'Do we know if they're any nearer to catching the killer? If they're not, then isn't all of this going to be very dangerous, I mean he or she might strike again.'

'Definitely a he I think,' said Sylvia Maitland. 'I simply can't imagine a woman doing all these awful things.'

A couple of the men sucked their teeth, whilst there was some nervous laughter from the women.

'We've talked carefully to the police and they want to brief the stewards about keeping an eye out for anything suspicious. There will be a number of police present and some will also be in plain clothes mixing with the parents. I think one or two of them are actually parents with children here this week. They think we should be careful, but I get the impression that they think the killer is only after particular individuals. John Davies said he'd been assigned a police constable for protection because they think he might be at risk.'

'And knowing that, you're still going to let him come and run his tent tomorrow, surely that's downright irresponsible?'

'I think we should show our trust in the Lord on this one. If John feels up to it, then we should say to God, this is in your hands. As long as we're all sensible and watch out for anything suspicious, then I'm happy to go ahead.'

There was a general murmur of consent around the tent.

'Right, that's agreed then. Who's going to start us off in prayer?'

*****

Tom Garroway asked the taxi driver to drop him at the entrance to Folly Farm. He was a bit later than he'd intended. It had taken longer to complete the delicate task than he'd allowed for, and now he would have to face Jean who would doubtless be angry that he hadn't been back earlier to help calm Lucy's nerves. If he was honest, he was glad to have minimised his exposure to his daughter's tantrums. If she achieved the results she needed, she'd be off. He really couldn't wait.

As he approached the farm house, the front door opened.

'Where the hell have you been? I'd have thought that just this once you might have made the effort to get back at a reasonable time and help me calm things down. Lucy's been crying herself into a real state all day. I almost took the afternoon off at SBC but felt I couldn't because of everything that's been going on there.'

'I'm really sorry, but the meeting went on much longer than it was meant to. My American bosses are keen on this takeover, but they kept going over the financial projections. It's as though they don't trust me to add the figures up correctly. But I've bought these to make amends.'

Tom held up a bottle of claret and a bottle of champagne.

'Tom, whatever you do, don't show Lucy that bottle of champagne before she collects her results. She's under enough pressure already.'

'And the bottle of claret?'

'You can go and open that now. It will go well with the steak and kidney pie I've made.'

'My favourite,' he said, putting the bottles back in his bag. A streak of blood was running across the back of his right hand.

'Tom, what have you done there? You've cut yourself.'

'Oh, it's nothing. Just caught my hand on the door at the shop on Castle Lofts station.'

'I hope that's not one of their expensive wines – what was it, £495?'

'No, you're not worth it. This one was only fifty quid!'

'That's bad enough. Couldn't you have bought an ordinary bottle of Shiraz?'

'Ordinary is not my style, as you well know.'

That had worked, thought Tom. It usually did: an apology, a bottle of wine and a bit of smooth talk never failed to calm Jean down. He'd been doing it for years. They walked into the house.

'Hi dad,' said Joshua, 'thank God you're back. It's been stress city here. Lucy's in the living room crying again.'

'Well you just be nice to her, young man. It won't be long before you're going through all of this. I hope Lucy's nicer to you than you've been to her.'

'I hope she won't be here.'

'That's just nasty.'

'What I mean is, I hope she gets her grades and has gone off to uni, training to be a great doctor.'

'Good recovery there!'

'I do try.'

'Try, as in very trying, is the operative word. Right, where's my girl?'

'Hello dad, you're home at last. I've had a horrible day. Josh is being beastly and all mum does is tell me to stop worrying.'

'Sounds sensible advice to me.'

'But I can't stop worrying. I can't. I just want it all to be over but I don't want to open that envelope.'

'If you don't open the envelope, you won't know your results! It's the same for everybody. At least they don't post the results up in a list on the school notice board, that's how mum and I found out our results. I think you should just calm down, go and watch something on TV and try to forget about results until tomorrow morning.'

'Some chance of that.'

'I'm just trying to help. How about we drive into Cambridge and see a film. There's still time to catch something if you want to.'

'I just want to stay here. I'll find a DVD.'

*****

Wendy and Peterson entered the Great Eastern and headed across to their favourite corner.

'My round,' said Wendy 'I assume it's a pint of Adnams.'

'Yes please,' Peterson replied, 'and some crisps as well – salt and vinegar.'

The pub was busier than usual. A large group had taken over a couple of tables and were all intently writing out documents.

'Hi Rachel,' said Wendy, recognising one of the group as a fellow Quaker, 'you all seem hard at work.'

'Wendy, you should come and join us. It's our Amnesty group – you know, Amnesty International – we're writing letters on behalf of political prisoners to try and get them released or, at least in some cases, spared execution.'

'Does it work?'

'Yes, what we do is make sure that their governments are aware we know what they are doing. It stops them thinking "out of sight, out of mind" and they realise that people are concerned and taking an interest in the fate of their prisoners.'

'But do they worry about what we all think?'

'A lot of them are concerned that if they lose power they may find themselves in front of the international courts, charged with conspiracy to murder or war crimes. What we do is very effective.'

'Well, I can't help this evening – it's been a heavy day – but I might give it a go when things are a bit quieter.'

Wendy joined Peterson at their table in the snug.

'I need to clear my head on this one,' she said. 'I'm not certain we've made any real progress at all.'

'Well, hopefully we'll get something from the Americans tomorrow about Jake Kerry and Philip Frost. They were staying together at the YMCA in Cambridge and clearly there was a link between them.'

'So what brought them here to Chipping Bonhunt and why were they killed? Then there's Peter Lord and the mysterious man who met him at the chapel in Welsted. Have we got any leads there?'

'I went through that with the team this afternoon. We've interviewed everybody who was in the congregation at the church that Sunday morning. But nobody can add to the pastor's description of a very tall, softly spoken American wearing a bright check shirt. Perhaps that's the best way not to be noticed: be tall and wear a loud shirt – in other words be really conspicuous - but say nothing. Everybody will remember you but also everyone will forget you.'

'I think you're getting a bit philosophical there!'

'Philosophical or not, it worked. They all remember the man was there, but they can tell us nothing about him. We're left with just the obvious connection: like two of the victims, he's American.'

'But with no linguistic experts, nobody's going to be able to tell us if the accent places our anonymous enigma in Arkansas or if he's from some other part of the States. There's got to be a link though, it's too much of a coincidence otherwise. So, suspect number one: the mystery man from the States.'

'Suspect number two, then. Are we still including John Davies?'

'He's still on the list, but it doesn't make any sense. I can't see any motive that would justify three murders, and he'd have to have been working with somebody else in the case of Peter Lord, which means we're then looking for two murderers.'

'So still on the list, but low down.'

'I think so.'

'And we're fairly clear that we're ruling out the other town councillors.'

'The Mayor and his merry band. We should still check out the alibis, I find Councillor Dakin a bit of a slippery customer. Don't trust him, and he does seem to have something to lose. I think we should shake his tree a little more and see if anything falls out.'

'I've fixed to see the CCTV footage of the High Street first thing tomorrow, check whether he shows up walking past the Royal Sovereign. I felt they were improvising a bit with their story that Dakin walked past the pub window during their meeting and they just happened to see him.'

'Good thinking, I agree. They were definitely a bit shifty with that one. If he isn't on the CCTV, go round immediately and challenge him. I can't imagine that even he would be stupid enough to get mixed up in this, but I might be having a blind spot on that one. If he's lying, then we need to find out what he was really up to.'

'Anyone else on our list?'

'I've had to admit defeat on my good friend Lloyd Evans. Apart from a bit of dodgy wine importing, I reckon he's in the clear. We need to interview all the SBC leaders and volunteers again. See if there's anything we've missed. Set that up for tomorrow morning and we'll sift through everything again in the afternoon. We're looking for American connections and anyone who has a particularly reactionary set of religious opinions.'

'I'll get Constable Smart on the case and then join in after I've looked at the CCTV.'

'So, I don't suppose you've had much time to talk to Trude. How's she getting on with that dinosaur she's working for?'

'The chauviraptor? Apparently he's being a real bastard this week. He asked Trudy to read a whole series of complicated cases on some obscure point of European Law which she did. She made copious detailed notes and then when she met him to go through them he told her she'd made a mistake and read the wrong cases. But she just doesn't make mistakes like that. If it wasn't for the money he's paying her she said she'd have walked out there and then. At least thc college fellows understand the problem. One of them told Trudy that they're all looking forward to the chauviraptor going back to Oxford, but it was some complicated condition of a gift the university received that he was involved on the project that it funded.'

'Sounds heavy going to me. I expect she'd be better used on our case than reading obscure case law for an ungrateful Oxford don.'

'Well, I'll talk to her about it if you want. Normally I don't share details about our cases, because although I can trust her to keep it confidential, it's not good form.'

'With the way we're struggling, I'm not going to object if you ask her to apply her first class mind to our problem. She might just have read something in one of the cases she's studied: didn't she go to some lectures on American law?'

'Oh, that was just a bit of a sideshow. It wasn't part of the course, but they had some American lawyers over during her second term and she was invited to a couple of seminars. It put her off the idea of going to the States to practice, which was one good thing. I thought I might have a difficult choice to make.'

'Surely it's a bit early for her to plan out her career, she's hardly started her degree?'

'One year down. In law you need to start thinking about your options so you can apply for vacation placements and hopefully get yourself noticed.'

'It all sounds dreadfully competitive. Gone are the days of student innocence. Enjoy the degree and don't worry about what you're going to do next until you've finished it.'

'More like my approach. But because she applied to Cambridge late, she's several years older than most other undergraduates. She's worried about being left on the legal shelf, as she calls it. Squeezed out by the younger competition.'

'She shouldn't have to worry if she carries on getting Firsts.'

'I've tried telling her that, but she's a bit driven when it comes to pursuing her career, like she's making up for lost time. Anyway, before we lose any more time, do you fancy another drink?'

'I thought you'd never ask.'

*****

Councillor Dakin was back at the Mayor's house.

'I know you were trying to help, but you really might have dropped me in it.'

'You're not telling me you really were the drive-by assassin on the motor bike, are you? I think the police would have difficulty making that one stick. I bet you don't even know which way round you're meant to get on the thing!'

'It's not that, but they've only got to look at the CCTV from those wretched cameras you got put up in the High Street to see that neither of us was telling the truth. You know you didn't see me walk past the Royal Sovereign on Tuesday, which then begs the question of where I really was.'

'Well, I'll just say I was obviously mistaken. I must have waved at somebody else who waved back. Probably thought I was a bit of an idiot and decided the best policy was to wave in order to be kind to me.'

'It's not what you're going to say that matters. It's what I'm going to say if they question me again. I wasn't thinking fast enough, and I should have made it clear that it wasn't me. Now it looks as though I've got something to hide and that you were coming to my rescue. That's what the police will think, but if you stick to your story that you were mistaken they won't be able to have a go at you, even if they think you are lying. I'm the one who's going to get the third bloody degree.'

'But you'll be OK. Just tell them where you really were and that will sort everything. You are making it all very complicated.'

'It's where I really was that is the problem. It's going to make me a bit of a laughing stock and might not help us politically.'

Councillor Hodgkiss raised his eyes to heaven and then focussed his gaze closely on his colleague.

'You're not making much sense. I'm finding it difficulty to imagine where you could possibly have been that might cause us a problem politically, unless you've been molesting the choir boys or something, but I can't really see you doing anything as bad as that.'

'Not quite as bad as that. I was with Cheryl Gatiss in Huts Lane.'

There was silence. Councillor Hodgkiss looked slightly surprised and then let out a laugh so load that Councillor Dakin feared the whole road would hear.

'You were with Cheryl Gatiss, and that's what's worrying you?' He let out another roar of laughter. 'My dear old chap, as long as it was Cheryl and not her young daughter Chloe, I really don't know what your problem is. Half the town's been with Cheryl Gatiss. We used to call her the town bike, because she gave a ride to any lad that asked her.'

'But that doesn't make it any less embarrassing.'

'The only embarrassing thing for you is that you seem to have been so far down the queue!'

Councillor Dakin's face had gone completely puce. He couldn't find a comfortable position despite sitting in one of the Mayor's amply upholstered armchairs.

'You don't mean you know her as well, as it were?'

'Now that's a question you shouldn't ask and I'm not going to answer. If the police come around again, just tell them the truth and say you were too embarrassed to tell them in front of me. They'll understand. It's not as though you've broken the law.'

'But what about my wife?'

'I haven't noticed you showing much concern for her up to now. You've always treated poor Sybil pretty badly you know. You'll have to think a bit about what you're going to say if she finds out, that's if she hasn't worked out what you've been up to already. There's nothing that's going to cause us any problems here. You might just have to grow a thicker skin and put up with one or two people laughing behind your back.'

'But shouldn't we be worried about the Liberal Democrats? Won't they use this to have a go at us on the doorsteps at the next council elections?'

'They can hardly afford to have a go. I know John Davies is a bit "holier than thou," but their party has more sex scandals per member than the rest of the political classes put together. I don't think you've got anything to fear there.'

Councillor Dakin relaxed and looked as though a massive weight had been taken off his shoulders.

'Now you need something to build you up. Whisky or Brandy?'

'Have you still got any of that malt you offered me the other day?'

'I most certainly have. One malt whisky coming up.'

*****

Peterson had arrived back at his room in More Road. He always enjoyed the opportunity to have a drink with Inspector Pepper. Although she expected hard work and high standards, she was easy to get on with and often shared her thinking with him. At the back of his mind though there was the question as to whether he should move on, possibly to Cambridge where he could be nearer Trudy. However, there was something comfortable about his current arrangements. Chipping Bonhunt was a pleasant place to live and it was growing. He didn't share the antipathy that others had to the thousand or more homes being proposed on the edge of the town. Perhaps, he thought, being young made you see things differently. More houses meant more people and hopefully more facilities. It also meant that people like him might be able to buy somewhere of their own, particularly if he took advantage of one of the shared ownership schemes aimed at the police. Perhaps Trudy would settle down in a place like this, she could commute down to London if she got a job with a city law firm and then enjoy her weekends in rural Essex.

He looked around his room. It wasn't a bad size, and had a good view out of the front window. He needed to do something to improve the appearance. His cinema posters for *The Usual Suspects* and *The Godfather* were looking distinctly tired and dated. Some new pictures perhaps? When Trudy was next over they should visit a couple of the shops in town and choose something new. Update his image and reflect his confidence that he was beginning to take control of his life. He needed something that created a greater sense of permanency.

Time to ring Trudy, he thought. He picked up his mobile and selected her from the directory. She answered.

'High there Ian, I was hoping you would call, but I wasn't sure if you would still be on duty.'

'Well, I've finished for the day with the exception of one task on behalf of the boss.'

'Oh, what's that?'

'It's a long shot, but we just wondered if you could help us. When you were going to those seminars with the

Americans at the beginning of the year, did you look at any cases that had a religious motive behind them?'

'Umm, let me think. I don't think any of the cases did, but I remember having an interesting chat in the bar with one of the American lawyers. He'd been lecturing on the influence of the Bible belt on their legal system. He was a really engaging small town Democrat, who split his time between the University where he did some lecturing and his own practice. I got the impression it was all very laid back, the type of place where you take your dog into work with you and it sleeps in the corner of your office.'

'Sounds like a sensible pace of life to me.'

'His problem was that his dog was rather old and kept breaking wind when he had clients in the room.'

'Not the sort of problem you get with the average city law firm. What did he have to say about law and the Bible belt?'

'He was quite animated about it. Thought that they were basically corrupt. Used the justification that because they were working in God's name they could do just about anything. He said he'd heard about all sorts of cases where dreadful things had happened, but because there was this sort of Christian mafia in the local community - those were his words - it all got covered up. Everybody went to the same church and the pastor would tick a few people off, occasionally from the pulpit, but nobody ever got brought to justice. He said it was sometimes much more than a ticking off, and their so called justice could be very brutal, but it never went through the normal legal system.'

'So you wouldn't describe him as being enthusiastic about the church himself?'

'No, quite the opposite. Surprisingly he was very involved in his own church. I think he held some sort of position in it. But he explained that the churches over there make a big thing about their differences. His church was involved in something called "God is Still Speaking" which seemed to be mainly about attacking the churches that didn't welcome black or gay people and things like that.'

'Do they have churches that don't welcome black or gay people?'

'Yes, lots. Apparently some of the churches just make black people very uncomfortable, and as for being gay, that's an absolute no in many places, whatever the law says. They come down really heavily if they suspect any of their people of being in gay or in lesbian relationships. Just throw them out.'

'But his church was different?'

'Yes, they went out of their way to make everyone welcome. He said they were a church for people who didn't switch their brains off when they walked through the door on a Sunday. They'd picked up a lot of people who had been made to leave other churches and I think he was on a bit of a mission about it.'

'Would he be worth talking to about our investigation here?'

'I'm happy to try and call him for you. Is there anything specific I should ask? He said he kept a lot of information about what he called the "pernicious influence of the religious right".'

Peterson explained about the two American victims, their names, where they came from and also the elusive unknown American.

*****

Wendy arrived home at Granary Lane and collapsed into her favourite armchair.

'Have you got a suspect yet?' asked Catherine.

'Yes, but he seems to be a very elusive one. People remember seeing him, but nobody can give us a proper description. It's like he's hiding in plain sight.'

'Sometimes that's the best way not to be seen. I've got a few like that at school. You notice people by their absence and sometimes miss the obvious about those who are standing right in front of you. Do you remember when all those laptops kept going missing last term? We all thought it was somebody coming in after hours, so we clamped down on security, challenged everyone who came on site and reviewed hours and hours of CCTV footage. Nothing, absolutely nothing and not helped by the fact that the CCTV hasn't been put in the places where we really need it. Eventually we discovered it was one of the humanities staff, but it took ages to realise what he was doing. Took a laptop home with him every evening, but didn't bring it back the next morning.'

'So by the time you contacted us and we went round to his flat we found a bedroom full of laptops which he couldn't even sell. Some odd form of kleptomania which we never really understood.'

'Real pity too, because he was a good teacher and everybody liked him, including the students. But that's just the point: he was there, everyday, in front of us and nobody would have suspected him if it hadn't been for me catching him in the sixth form office, unplugging my laptop.'

'Remind me, what was his excuse?'

Catherine laughed.

'It really was pathetic. He said he'd heard of a problem that our laptops could overheat and might even catch fire if they were left on, so he was just making sure it would be safe. Even if that was plausible, he went such a bright red and stumbled over his words that I knew something must be wrong. And the Head of Sixth had lost her laptop the week before, so it seemed too much of a coincidence.'

'Didn't his union challenge his dismissal?'

'Yes. Ridiculous performance it was too. Sometimes they really do stretch their credibility. Despite the fact he'd been caught bang to rights, they said it wasn't certain he'd intended to steal the laptops. Some rubbish about he might have been trying to ensure they were placed in safe keeping. Mind you, not even their rep could keep a straight face when coming out with that one. It does make you wonder though. I mean, most of the time they do a good job, and somebody has to stand up to this government with all the changes they're making, but sometimes the dear old union seem to pick the wrong members of staff and issues to fight over.'

The two women sat quietly for a few minutes. Wendy scanned the bookshelves and thought they really did need a good dusting. Otherwise the room wasn't looking too bad. It had a homely feel from elegant but well worn furniture and walls painted in tasteful pastel colours.

'I fancy a drink,' said Wendy, 'it's a lovely warm night. What say you to glass of rosé on the patio?'

'I think that's just what I need, then an early night before the A level results tomorrow morning. White Zinfandel?'

'Nothing less will do!'

They both laughed.

Thursday

Folly Farm was not a good place to be. It was only five thirty in the morning, but Lucy was already up, showered and ready. She'd tried to sleep but had probably managed half an hour at the most. Joshua was complaining that she'd made so much noise he hadn't been able to sleep either and Jean was finding it really difficult to exercise self control in the situation. If it hadn't been Lucy's A-level results day then she'd probably have lost it already with both of them. She told herself, count to ten, take another deep breath and try and stay calm.

'Lucy, why don't you go back to your room and listen to some relaxing music? There's nothing else you can do and you really don't need to leave for the school until seven fifteen at the earliest.'

'OK mum.'

One minute later the sound of Metallica came out of Lucy's room, speakers at full volume and pounding through the house so that the bass notes were felt more than heard.

'For God's sake turn that bloody thing down,' shouted Tom, 'before the house self destructs.'

Tom came downstairs.

'I'm really sorry Jean, but I can't cope with this today. I've got an important conference call later and lots of other calls I need to make. What time is Lucy off?'

'I'm setting off at about twenty past seven. I'll get her to Bonhunt Academy at about ten to eight, so she can meet up with her friends. Then I'll wait in the car park and when she returns I'll either bring out the bottle of champagne or the box of tissues, depending on which is appropriate.'

'Good thinking. Look, I need to clear my head. I'm going out for a ride.'

'Surely you're not going across to the stables now?'

'No, a ride on the bike is what I mean.'

Tom went out through the front door and across to the barn. Ten minutes later the throaty roar of his Triumph motorbike echoed across the designer front garden and he was off down the drive.

'Why is everyone up so early?' asked Joshua as he walked into the kitchen. 'It's doing my head in.'

Another happy morning thought Jean.

*****

Despite the exhaustion of the murder investigation, Wendy had risen early to prepare Catherine her special "results day" breakfast. It had become a tradition that Wendy had started a few years before when they had first moved into Granary Lane. It was the only day of the year when they ate a "full English."

Build up your energy, Wendy had said the first year she had cooked the sizeable breakfast feast. Her mother had always prepared a similar meal whenever there was a particularly demanding day and this was Wendy's way of carrying on the tradition. Poor mum she thought, now living in a home and not aware of anything that was going on around her. A far cry from the imposing figure that had grown up in one of the terraced houses in Edmonton, north London, and had brought up three children on her own after Wendy's father had been killed in an industrial accident when she was just five.

Wendy's "full English" varied a bit from the ones she remembered that her mum had cooked. While Wendy couldn't recall all of the details, she very much doubted the eggs were free range, or the bacon from a farmers' market and the sausages weren't organic pork and herb from the specialist butcher in town. The hash browns were a concession to the convenience food industry, as were the baked beans, but the black pudding and mushrooms were 100% organically sourced and Wendy's own freshly baked wholemeal bread was to die for.

'What a wonderful smell,' said Catherine as she came into the kitchen.

'Would madam please take her seat, one plate full of heart attack coming up, as Michael Caine would say, or something like that anyway.'

'Mmmmm. This is absolutely fantastic. I think I can cope with just about anything after this.'

Wendy served up the meal and they both tucked in.

'So, many disappointments this year?'

'There are a few haven't made their offers, but only one that we really didn't expect. Problem with the Music grades this year, which we're probably going to challenge as we think they've marked the composition too harshly. A couple of others just didn't get down to the hard work and have blown some good university places. If they won't do the work now, then I expect they wouldn't do the work at uni, so it's probably for the best. But, on the other hand, there are some really good results with those who did put the hours in getting something to show for it.'

'Anyone you're particularly pleased about?'

'Lisa Simmonds has done really well, and I'm so pleased for her. She's always been very nervous and lacking in confidence, but she's really shone: two A*s and an A. I'm going to try and persuade her to go for UCAS Adjustment and see if she can get into one of the Russell Group universities. She'll be wasted on the course she's accepted at the moment.'

'So, just to make sure I understand the jargon you're using. UCAS is the body that handles applications to university?'

'Yes, the Universities and Colleges Admissions Service.'

'So what's UCAS Adjustment?'

'Oh, it's a fairly new thing where you can try and upgrade to a better course if your results are higher than you expected. Many top universities keep some places available to help students in that position enrol on their courses when they get their results. I have to admit that it's something the government has introduced that I actually agree with.'

'Well, there's a revelation! Shock horror, Catherine York agrees with Government. Hold the front page.'

'It was the last government, not this one!'

Wendy ducked as a chunk of wholemeal loaf missed her left ear.

'Attempted assault on a police officer, very serious offence: could result in a prison sentence. And after I've cooked this lovely breakfast.'

This time Wendy didn't duck fast enough.

*****

Peterson was another early riser. He'd not slept that well as he couldn't switch off from the details of the case. It was some of the things that Trudy had said about the churches in the States. The Summer Bible Club, the passages from the bible, the American link: There was something in all of these things that could reveal the killer. But why here, why in Chipping Bonhunt?

*****

John and Alice Davies sat round the table in the family room at the back of their house. It was another rushed early morning breakfast, because they wanted to get to the Eagles tent in plenty of time to set up the day's activities.

Police Constable Gordon Jones was sitting down with them.

'I'm not sure I should be doing this. I'm meant to be making sure you're protected and kept safe.'

'Oh, don't worry;' said John, 'I think this is a bit over the top as far as we are concerned. Why would anyone want to attack us?'

'Above my pay grade sir, but Inspector Pepper knows what she wants, and she's never been one to go over the top on things like this. She must be taking it seriously.'

The sound of glass shattering followed by a loud thud came from the front living room. PC Jones leapt from his seat, ran to the front door, opened it and reached the front gate just in time to see a motorcycle disappearing round the corner at the end of Thomas Road.

'Oh shit,' he said before he called in on his radio.

In the living room, Alice was surveying the broken glass that was spread across the brown leather sofa occupying the space inside the bay window. Nothing seemed to be broken apart from the window. On the floor she saw a brick, with a piece of paper tied round it. She stepped forward to pick it up.

'Don't touch it,' said John, 'let's leave it to the police.'

A siren could be heard in the distance.

'I don't know who we've upset,' said Alice, 'but I'm beginning to think I never want to set foot in Summer Bible Club again.'

*****

Catherine had decided to walk into the school. It was shaping up to be a beautiful morning and the walk was a good way of enjoying the calm before the storm of results day. Walking down Granary Lane she thought how pretty all the terraced houses were, many with window boxes and tubs of flowers and all watered and awash with colour in the morning sun.

Sadly, the Plough pub on the corner of the junction with Bartlow Road was looking a bit in need of some TLC. Another case of the brewery trying to close a local drinking hole in order to sell it off for housing development. They'd been thwarted, but the new owners didn't seem to know what they were doing with the place and now it just looked a mess. Poorly designed signs, paint peeling off and broken bottles and cans left outside from the night before. She could understand why Wendy and her sergeant preferred the Great Eastern. At least they still served up a decent pint there.

Catherine continued her walk along Bartlow Road towards the Common. She waved to Peterson as he drove past her towards Granary Lane. Another early start for Wendy. I hope they sort these murders out soon, she thought to herself, as it was clearly bearing down on Wendy.

One of the road's local characters was out already in her front garden, watering all of her beautiful borders.

'Morning Mrs Lilly, doesn't your garden look beautiful this year? I don't know where you find the energy.'

'Oh, thank you Miss York. I tries my best you know, and I always promised Jack that after he'd gone I'd look after his precious garden.'

'Well, you've certainly done that. He'd be proud of you.'

'Well, I hope he's looking down and smiling on us all, God rest his soul.'

Mrs Lilly was 92 and Jack had been dead at least twenty years. By all accounts he hadn't been a very nice piece of work, but time clearly heals and perhaps it was best that old Mrs Lilly only held on to her more positive memories.

Catherine continued her walk along Bartlow Road and reached Chipping Bonhunt Common, a large sloping area of grass just on the edge of the historic town centre. As she cut diagonally across the open space, she noticed a group of people at the top of the bank that went back up to Bartlow Road.

Large areas of the grass seemed to have been burnt or killed off and it looked as though something had been sprayed on to the common.

She stopped in order to try and work out what had happened. As she looked across the damaged grass, she realised that the dead areas were shaped in large capital letters:

"THE END IS NIGH"

Hoping this was not a prank by some of her sixth formers due to collect their results, Catherine decided to make a quick getaway. Crossing the common, she walked along Mound Street towards the High Street.

'Morning Catherine! '

It was the Head Teacher from the school, walking in the opposite direction.

'Oh, morning,' she replied, the surprise showing in her voice, 'you're not often in the town at this time in the morning.'

'Oh, no sooner had I arrived at the school than I had an angry town councillor in reception, demanding I do something about the vandalism my pupils had done to the common last night! So I thought I'd better come and see for myself, although it's typical that our students are always blamed whenever something like this happens. He had to admit he hadn't got a shred of evidence it was one of our pupils, but he was still adamant it must be somebody from Bonhunt Academy. Does it look bad?'

'Oh, I expect it will grow back pretty soon. Could be a sixth form prank for results day, although I'd have thought they all had other things to worry about. Anyway, you can't miss it – top of the common, letters about five foot high.'

'Thanks then, I'd better let you get on. I'll be back as soon as I can be to offer moral support. I trust we've identified the ones that will need help with 'phoning their universities or entering clearing?'

'Yes, not too many this year, but there are a couple we should encourage to upgrade their choices if we can. Some pretty impressive results, better than expected in some cases.'

'Good, that's what I like to hear.'

Catherine turned into the High Street and started walking up the hill. The Royal Sovereign was already doing a good trade in breakfast and she wondered if the place ever actually closed. Further up the hill, Catherine passed the slightly charred frontage of the Friends Meeting House. A large skip sat on the pavement outside, with bits of broken glass and charred wood ready to be taken away.

At the top of the hill Catherine noticed that there had been some more vandalism. Painted vertically in red on the war memorial were the words:

'I MUST PUNISH YOU"

Doubtless the school would get blamed for that as well, she thought. But this really was going too far, vandalising the war memorial. Catherine might be a Quaker and a pacifist, but she respected the town's memorial to those who had given up their lives. Is nothing respected in today's brutal world, she thought to herself.

Five more minutes along Castle Lofts Road and she arrived at the school. On the field, some of the tent leaders were opening up their marquees for Summer Bible Club. Catherine breathed in the fresh summer morning air. The site team had been out early with the grass cutters, and the smell was beautiful. She told herself it was going to be a good day.

*****

At the Davies' house in Thomas Road, the forensic team were already at work. They'd been staying in Bonhunt as there was a lot to follow up from the murders.

'No fingerprints I'm afraid,' said one of the officers to Wendy, 'but we've got ourselves another biblical text.'

PC Jones held up the by now familiar Arial print for examination by the Inspector.

"you are wretched and miserable and poor and blind and naked"

'Book of Revelation, probably chapter three and almost certainly The Living Bible.'

'Wow, that's impressive.'

'Not quite as clever as it sounds. It's a bit of a trend.'

'A brick through the window,' John paused and thought for a moment, 'at least it's not a murder attempt.'

'I can only apologise,' said Wendy, 'PC Jones really should have been keeping a better watch on what was going on.'

'It was our fault, I'm afraid we didn't think there was any reason for somebody to attack us. Didn't think we were in the firing line, as it were.'

'Well, our murderer, or murderers, clearly have you in their sights for something. We've talked about this before, but can you think of anybody you've upset in the churches over the last few months?'

'Quite a lot, probably. As I told you when you interviewed me yesterday, I don't have much truck with fundamentalists and I suppose I'm pretty damning about people who don't really think about their faith.'

'Sounds like quite a lot of people! Can you think of anybody in particular that you may have provoked?'

'Not really, although I disagree with a lot of people in my own church and others, I know them all pretty well. I think they go away and pray for me, rather than plot to kill me.'

'Pray for you?'

'Yes, goes back to my days at university. I remember somebody from the Christian Union telling me that they were praying I might become a real Christian.'

'Rather than a pretend one?'

'That's just about it. And the so called real Christians have been praying for me ever since. Problem is, I'm part of declining bread. Those who still call themselves Christians, but reject the simplistic certainty of the bible bashers.'

'It does seem a bit drastic to start killing people over it though.'

'People have been doing it for centuries. Think of Henry the Eighth. If you weren't on message, whatever the message was at any particular time in his reign, you could find yourself being on the receiving end of all sorts of nasty treatment followed by a particularly painful execution.'

'Hopefully we've moved on since then. This is Chipping Bonhunt in the 21st century.'

'I wouldn't be so sure. There's sometimes an almost primitive, primeval feel to the way some people express their religious beliefs, even in this outwardly pleasant and civilised part of the world.'

'Well, on the practical side, we're stepping up the surveillance. I wondered about telling you not to go to the Bible Club today, but I think it would probably be helpful if you did. Tell us immediately if you see anybody or anything suspicious. And if you can think of anybody you've particularly upset over the last few months, ring me immediately.'

'Will do, and good luck with the search.'

'I don't suppose I could ask you to pray for us?'

John shrugged his shoulders and laughed. 'Of course you can, and we will.'

*****

Catherine wasn't the first to arrive in the sixth form study centre and she was pleased to see that somebody had already arranged the tables.

They split the results envelopes across three tables, alphabetically A to H; I to P and Q to Z.

The easy bit was finding the correct envelope and handing it out to the student. The difficult bit was coping with the reaction that followed. Sometimes what initially sounded like a cry of pain turned out to be an uncontrolled scream of delight. But equally an initial cry of joy might be tempered when the reader realised that they'd misunderstood the piece of paper in front of them. The top grade might be for just one of the modules, not the whole subject.

The staff were assembling now. The leadership team were on envelope duty, the tutors ready to celebrate and commiserate and the rest of the team were ready to help access UCAS clearing or ring universities as necessary if there was any doubt about a student's place being confirmed. The countdown to eight am was well underway.

*****

It was finally time to leave for the school. Tom had returned and put the motorbike back in the barn. He'd decided to join the others when they drove into Chipping Bonhunt. Jean was calling Joshua to get in the car.

'Come on, we don't want to be late for Lucy's results. Have you got everything you need for SBC today?'

'Yes mum, but why do I have to go when Lucy gets to take the day off?'

'Because, dear Joshua, Lucy has a very special day today and she'll be off celebrating with her friends in town most of the morning. They've all worked extremely hard and they deserve some time off to celebrate their success.'

'Some chance of that,' Lucy interjected.

'Come on Lucy, be more positive. It'll be fine.'

'No it won't, I screwed up on Chemistry, I won't get the grades I need and I won't be going to med school in Cambridge or anywhere else.'

'That's what I like,' said Tom who had climbed into the passenger seat, 'a really good positive attitude.'

Joshua came running out of the farmhouse, rucksack trailing along the ground behind him.

'Josh, put it over you're shoulder for heaven's sake or you'll ruin it,' Jean shouted. 'Now climb in and we'll be off.'

They drove into Farm Lane and set off towards Chipping Bonhunt.

Lucy was trying to switch off from the impending results and was focussing on the passing hedgerows. Something caught her eye just before they turned into the main road.

'Mum,' said Lucy, 'somebody's been playing with the gate into Upper Field; I hope the horses are OK.'

'What do you mean?'

'Well, we never use the gate from Farm Lane, do we?'

'No, we always go the back way from behind the farm house.'

'It looks as though somebody's repaired the gate from the Lane. It used to be wedged in place and falling apart.'

'Perhaps somebody has been using the old bridleway up to the woods. We should have repaired it ourselves really; it's a public right of way. But it doesn't really go anywhere, only into Folly Wood. We'll check it out over the weekend.'

The journey to Chipping Bonhunt wasn't too bad, and at last the traffic lights at Finchwinter Road seemed to be working. It only took four minutes to get through.

The Garroways joined a steady line of cars driving into the main car park at Bonhunt Academy. Jean hadn't had time to pull into a parking space when Lucy opened her door and leapt out.

'Careful, I'm still…,' but Lucy was off and had disappeared into a crowd of friends heading off to the sixth form centre. At least Joshua waited until she had parked properly.

'Right, I'll leave you to hold the fort here while I walk into town,' said Tom. 'Give me a call as soon as you know.'

*****

Alice and John had arrived at the Eagles tent. Sarah and Lewis had already opened up and were putting out the badges, pens and paper.

'Well done you two,' said Alice. 'It's great not to have to do everything ourselves.'

'We've had a good look around,' said Sarah, 'and we haven't found any sheep's heads or anything else that's odd.'

'I should hope not,' said Agnes Rodgers who'd just walked in through the front of the tent, 'I've had quite enough excitement already this week.'

'With the security the police have put on this place I reckon only the Royal Marines could get in,' said Lewis, 'I didn't know there were so many police in Bonhunt.'

'I don't think there are,' said Alice, 'the rest of Essex is probably a police free zone at the moment.'

Agnes had sat down at her favourite table. 'I'm surprised they let us carry on with SBC this year, and even more surprised that they let us come back into this tent after the other night.'

'They say they've done what they need to do,' replied John, 'although I have to admit it feels a bit odd, doesn't it, to think that just two and a half days ago that body was found right here. We'll have to stop the children getting silly about it. The committee sent a letter home to all the parents and I understand only a couple of the children have been pulled out from the club.'

'Too exciting for most of them to even think about not coming!' said Agnes.

'Right,' said John, 'Jean is going to be a bit late because she's round the other side of the school with Lucy who's collecting her A-level results today. I suggest we start with a short prayer for Lucy and all the others collecting their results, and then let's sort out today's activities.'

*****

Lloyd Evans leant on his garden gate looking out from his front garden on Commonside over the road and across the Common. He could see a group gathered round the grass where some stupid vandals had been up to their tricks again. The town was going down hill he thought. Whole nation was going down hill what with Cameron and his silly coalition government.

Perhaps it was time to do something about it. But, if he was honest with himself, his doing something days were over. He'd rather fade away quietly with a few good cases of claret for company.

'Morning Lloyd,' said the rector as he walked along the path. 'Hope all's well.'

'It's just fine and dandy. That little incident at the station the other day, just a misunderstanding. Wrong place at the wrong time.'

'So nothing you need to talk about? I'm always here if you need me?'

That was the problem with Chipping Bonhunt's young and enthusiastic team rector, thought Lloyd. He's always here. In fact he's always everywhere, with a big smile on his face and doing all these modern things like encouraging the children to clap their hands in the services. It wasn't his type of church anymore.

'I'll let you know if I need any advice,' he said curtly.

'So will we be seeing you at the family communion next Sunday?'

Silly question, Lloyd thought. The rector knows the answer. He'd tried one of the new fangled family communions about six months ago and had survived up until the point where they shared the peace. It was then that the enormous Hildegard Brown had insisted on giving him such an all enveloping bear hug that he'd feared he would be swallowed up by her bosom. Family communion was definitely not for him.

'I'll see how it goes.'

'I'll take that as a no, then.'

The rector went off on his cheery way, leaving Lloyd ill at ease with himself. Why, he thought, did everything he cherished have to change? Gone were the days when you could turn up at the Parish Church and know that you would have a well-ordered, properly planned and, most importantly, familiar celebration of the sacrament of communion. Gone were the days when the children were seen and not heard. Next Sunday the place would probably be more like a farm than what Lloyd recognised as a church. Free range children everywhere, overexcited mothers singing happy-clappy choruses. Perhaps it really was time to sell up and leave his much cherished home over looking the common.

*****

Finally, and to the collective relief of students and staff, it was eight am. Lucy was tenth in line in her queue and was now completely oblivious to what anybody around her was doing. It seemed to take an age for the others to collect their envelopes but, at last, it was the moment.

Catherine handed her the envelope. Lucy didn't hear her say 'congratulations, well done.' She just grabbed it and ran to the corner of the room.

She tore the envelope open. Her hands were shaking so much she could hardly hold the piece of paper still enough to read what it said.

Maths was an A. Biology was an A.

A moment of panic went through her head. She needed two As and an A*. She'd banked on Biology being the A*.

Then, in stunned disbelief she read her Chemistry grade: A*

The subject she'd lost sleep over the whole summer was the one that had delivered. She read it again to make sure. She looked at the module grades. The really difficult paper, the one she thought she'd messed up, had scored a module mark of 98%. Unbelievable, but there it was, in black and white.

She burst into an uncontrollable fit of laughter, and felt all of her energy just drain away. It was as though the greatest moment of joy, of elation, in her life had combined with completing the London marathon, she was ecstatic and completely exhausted at the same time.

'Over here Lucy,' called Catherine, 'photo for the local paper. I'm sure you want to be in it.'

Lucy joined a happy line up of pupils with joyful smiles, waving sheets of results in the air and all experiencing the exhilaration that came from this sudden end to the months of agonised waiting for the outcome of their exams.

'Come on,' said the photographer, 'on the count of three I want all of you to smile and jump up in the air, waving your results above your head. 1; 2; 3 – yes that's it. One more time then.'

Catherine was pleased to see another smiling face walking towards her. Lisa Simmonds, who appeared to be reading, rereading and then reading again the sheet of paper with her results.

'Miss, I can't believe it. I was worried I wouldn't get the two Bs and a C I needed, I never dreamt I'd get two A*s and an A.'

'Congratulations Lisa. You so deserve those results, you know. I think you should try UCAS Adjustment and see if you can get one of the places on offer for applicants who do much better than they expected. There're some good places on offer at Bristol and Durham.'

'You really think I might get a place there?'

'You won't know if you don't try. Go on-line now and I'll come over and help in a few minutes. See what's available – you know, you'd just love Durham.'

Catherine turned to find Daniel Morgan standing right behind her.

'Miss, I just want to say thank-you.'

'Well, that's a first Dan. But really well done. Three Bs isn't it?'

'Yes, so I'm safely into Oxford Brookes. I realise I've been a bit stupid at times over the last year.'

'You certainly have, but you've also worked. I'm really pleased you got the grades. You'll have fun at Oxford Brookes. It's a great place to study.'

'Yeah, dad's told all his mates at work I'm going to Oxford. I don't think he understands that Brookes is a different university.'

'I'd leave him be. You are going to Oxford – just don't spend too much time giving people the details! Anyway, it is a very good university in its own right. Who knows, you might even end up teaching English one day!'

'Will you give me a reference?'

'Of course I will, but I'll be watching you. If you want a good one, you'll have to work hard when you're there.'

Catherine went in search of her student with the disappointing music result. Hopefully she'd secure a place through clearing, although they might want to try and persuade her current offer to hold until they knew the outcome of the challenge they were making to the result.

*****

Jean Garroway couldn't restrain herself any more. She'd been waiting in the car for 20 minutes and really needed to get to the Eagles tent to help set up. But she had to know. Surely Lucy would have rung by now? In her mind, she had conjured up a picture of Lucy missing her grades and behaving hysterically, surrounded by teachers desperately trying to comfort her. That's it, she thought, I'm going to ring her mobile.

'You have reached the voicemail service for Lucy Garroway….'

Oh come on Lucy; please answer the 'phone. She tried again and heard the same message.

Just as her stress level was hitting the roof, her mobile rang. It was Lucy. In her desperation to talk to her daughter she pressed the wrong button and terminated the call.

'Oh fuck,' she said out load, just as Sylvia Maitland walked past her open car window.

'Bit stressed this morning are we? I hope you don't use language like that in the Eagles tent!'

'Sorry, just cut my daughter off as she was calling to tell me her results.'

Jean's 'phone rang again.

'I'll leave you to it.'

This time Jean managed not to cut off her daughter. The minute she heard Lucy's voice she knew it was good news.

'Mum, I'm just sooooooo happy! I got an A* in Chemistry. I really thought it would be a B. Then A's in the others. Could have been better with the Biology, but who cares! A* in Chemistry and I'm off to Cambridge to do medicine.'

'Oh that's absolutely fantastic. Well done. Dad will be so pleased.'

'We're all going off into town before we go back to Gemma's for lunch.'

'Don't drink too much; remember you've got to get through the whole day. Dad's booking somewhere special for this evening and you need to be sober enough to enjoy it.'

'Don't worry; I think everybody's doing something with their families. And mum….thank you. I know I haven't been the best of company the last couple of weeks.'

'All forgiven now. You go and enjoy celebrating with your friends and remember I'm at SBC today. I can either take you home at lunchtime or after we finish at three-thirty.'

'Probably three-thirty. I'll text you if that changes.'

'OK. And congratulations again.'

Jean rang off and called Tom. A familiar 'you have reached the voicemail service of….' message answered.

Who an earth can he be on the 'phone to, she thought. Surely he would be keeping his mobile free for her call.

*****

Tom was sitting in his favourite sofa at the back of Costa. One of his ways of getting at his American masters was going to Costa whenever he could and avoiding using

Starbucks which was American owned and didn't seem to want to pay much tax in Britain. Just like his employers, he thought. Sitting with him were Selwyn Roberts, Lloyd Evans and James Thompson.

Tom was in the middle of a call on his mobile. 'Three of the key players are here with me now and we definitely have a deal.'

Tom turned from his 'phone and talked to Selwyn. 'Just write down what you think Catherine agreed so I can confirm it to them.'

'Yes, the tricky shareholder is Catherine York, the teacher.'

He listened for a moment

'No, socialist is a bit of an exaggeration. More an environmentalist and a bit left of centre.'

Another pause

'OK, you call her a socialist then. But Selwyn Lloyd has got her to agree the deal on the basis we make a large donation to the school. I think that would be a great PR move on our part. It's not so big here in the UK, giving to schools. It would get some good coverage and certainly oil the wheels.'

He listened again

'Oh, I think it would fund a new study centre. That's a library in old money, but with lots of flashy computers. They might even name it after the boss.'

He turned to the others.

'They're going for it. We've got a deal, and you are all each about one million quid richer.'

'I think this calls for something a bit more exciting than coffee,' said Lloyd Evans. 'Back to my place for a bit of champers?'

As soon as Tom Garroway finished the call, his phone rang again. 'Excuse me a moment, I need to take this. Important personal call.'

'So what's the news?'

He waited for the reply.

'That's fantastic. Is she OK for tonight? I've booked the Chop House in Cambridge. When I've finished here in town I'll walk up to the school and meet you there.'

Tom turned to the others. 'Another reason for that celebration drink, I think.'

*****

Wendy and Peterson were back at Chipping Bonhunt police station. Once again they were reviewing where they were with the investigation.

'Every time I think we're just about there, we find we've gone off in the wrong direction. This morning we've got graffiti daubed on the war memorial and words etched into the grass on the common. Is it all the same person, or kids mucking about, or what?'

Wendy was exasperated. Three murders, all with seemingly religious connections, arson at the Friends' Meeting House, and it would appear an American connection that they couldn't pin down.

'I can't understand why anybody would be killing people because of a difference of view about religion,' said Peterson.

'Oh come off it sergeant. The Middle East, Iraq, Israel and the Palestinians in Gaza. They're all supposed to believe in one God, yet they butcher each-other regardless. And that's not to mention the crusades – we're hardly angels ourselves, although at least we seem to have learnt from our mistakes. No. actually, we haven't. We thought we could sort Afghanistan and Iraq, and all we've done is make it worse. If we'd looked back in history we'd have realised that our getting involved in those countries would only have one outcome: it would end in tears.'

'Hey, you're getting on your high horse. I thought you had the religious thing as badly as some of these other guys we've been talking to at Summer Bible Club.'

'You just go carefully there, young Peterson. I'm not a Quaker for nothing you know. We don't believe in violence, we look for consensus and we abhor war. If you ask me, I'm on the militantly sensible wing as far as faith goes. It's about trying to put some common sense back into humanity.'

'So why on earth did you decide to join the police, I mean, we're not exactly the most progressive social force in this country?'

'I suppose I have some ideals, and I thought – in fact I still think – that I can do something positive by being one of the girls and boys in blue. The whole force doesn't have to be an over testosterone filled bunch of Neanderthals.'

'Ouch, that's a bit harsh,' said Peterson.

'One day I'll explain it to you. If you've been through some of the things I have, you might understand where I'm coming from. But let's return to our killer. How are we doing with your friend in the States?'

'I'm due a call. I'll chase them up later this afternoon – they're six hours behind us. Meanwhile, I think there's somebody else we need to look at. I was going through all the interviews and the name Tom Garroway came up. He works for an American company called Intermed and flies regularly to and from the States. We need to find out who he knows and what he does there. He's the only person we have identified with a direct American link. What's more, his wife's helping at Summer Bible Club and I just have an odd feeling about him.'

Wendy laughed. 'Be careful about odd feelings. They've got me into trouble before. Lloyd Evans being just one good example.'

'But you were right to be suspicious about Evans. Basically he's a crook. Clever lawyer got him off the hook on the drink-drive charge, but we all know he was as guilty as hell. Then he's been smuggling his precious wines into the country. Trouble is, he could have put them in the boot of his car and driven through Dover perfectly legally as long as he argued they were for personal consumption, and from the state of his red face, they probably were!'

Wendy looked hopeful. 'Yes, if we don't get him, his liver probably will. But back to Tom Garroway for a minute. I've met him a couple of times and if we look at what we know about him, he could well be a suspect. Although I have difficulty buying it, we can't ignore the facts in front of us. He could, with a little imagination, fit the description of the mystery man at the chapel in Welsted and am I imagining that he sometimes has a bit of an American accent, or at least an accent that somebody in this part of rural Essex could mistake for an American accent? It's probably rubbed off from the people he's been working with and visiting in the States.'

Peterson thought for a moment. 'I think you're right. If you are used to American accents, you'd realise he wasn't American. But if you're from around here, a bit parochial, and you've not met many Americans, you could think he was from the States.'

'So perhaps he is our mysterious stranger. Get over to that pastor and show him a photo of Garroway. See if he looks familiar. I think we need to start looking more closely at our friend Tom Garroway.'

'Should we bring him in for questioning?'

'Yes, let's do that. Let's see what he says when we dig a bit deeper into how he's been spending his time.'

PC Smart entered the room.

'I've had a call from the YMCA in Cambridge. Not a lot to tell us, but it might be helpful.'

'Well then?' asked Wendy.

'When they went back through the CCTV covering their reception area they found some footage of our two victims meeting a tall man. It sounds a similar description to the one we've had elsewhere.'

'Our tall American stranger.'

'They're going to try and download some of it and e-mail a copy over here. And there's something else. One of the staff there thinks the two victims came to Cambridge because there was somebody living in the area who had visited their church. But she can't remember anything else.'

'It fits the bigger picture we're getting. Ask them to be as quick as they can with the CCTV footage. Get them to fax us a frame from it or, if you have to, go over there and take a look.'

*****

Jean Garroway rushed into the Eagles tent. 'Sorry I'm late, just been offering moral support to Lucy as she collects her results.'

'How did they go?' asked Alice.

'Two A's and an A*, so she's off to Cambridge to read medicine. It was a close thing, and she got the A* in chemistry, which she really thought she'd screwed up. But she's got what she needed and I have one very happy daughter!'

'That's fantastic news, any celebrations planned for this evening?'

'If she's still sober enough, we're off to Cambridge for a meal. Tom has booked a restaurant we all like round the back of St. John's.'

The noise from the rest of the tent was deafening. John Davies had all the children playing Port and Starboard again.

'Funny how they love these old games when we use them,' said Jean.

'Yes,' said Alice. 'I think John remembers them from his days in the scouts. It certainly helps burn off some of the kids' energy.'

John had added some of his own ideas to the traditional game. 'I spy crocodiles,' he shouted. There was a mad rush while every child in the tent tried to find a chair to stand on.

'Some of you are a bit slow today; I reckon you're in danger of being eaten alive. Time to stop now and go back to your tables I think.'

There was a groan of disappointment around the tent.

'John, can I tell you something?' It was Chloe Gatiss, and John had that sinking feeling she was about to tell tales on one of the other children.

'What do you want to tell me Chloe?'

She started telling a complicated story about how she had been up early in the morning and decided to go for a walk.

'You really shouldn't leave home on your own you know,' said John, 'there are some nasty people about. Did your mum or Nan know where you were going?'

'Oh, I can look after myself. They don't mind.'

'Well I do mind, none of us want to see you hurting yourself. You need to be careful.'

'Don't you want to hear my story?'

'Of course I do, carry on, but just remember what I've said.'

Chloe told John how she had gone down to the Common, where she liked having the play equipment to herself.

'The roundabout is my favourite, but often the other children are mean to me and their parents tell me to go away.'

Typical of too many parents in the town, thought John. Chloe was a child they didn't want their children playing with. Very unfair really, because she wasn't a problem most of the time and it wasn't her fault her mother neglected her so much.

'So what happened when you were in the playground?'

'Someone drove a motorbike along the top.'

'Did they do anything else?'

'Yes they stopped, and got off.'

'And then?'

'They put something on the grass.'

'You're sure of this. You're not making this up because you saw the words on the Common?'

'No, I saw it, I saw it. I really did.'

'Thank you for telling me Chloe. I think there's somebody else who will want to talk to you as well.'

John went over to his jacket in the corner of the tent. He found his mobile 'phone. Now, where had he left that card with the contact number for Inspector Pepper, or would there be anybody in the classroom the police were using as their base in the school? He decided to leave the others in charge of the tent and walk over and see.

*****

Lucy and her friends had enjoyed posing for photos in the local papers. Everybody seemed very happy and the atmosphere at Bonhunt Academy had been really good. She had looked at her marks again. She'd needed 90% across this year's papers to get an A*. She realised she'd been very lucky. The mark on the Chemistry paper she thought she'd fouled up had been 98%. She realised it was only so high because the paper had been very difficult and the exam board had moderated the marks, pushing hers up because she must have scraped a few more marks than nearly all the other candidates. She'd only achieved 84% on the chemistry paper she hadn't been worried about but, because of the 98%, her overall average for this year's papers was 91%. It was her only A*, and a small drop in marks on her other Chemistry paper, or a difference in the moderation, would have meant she would have missed the grade. Biology was particularly disappointing as she'd missed the 90% needed for an A* by just 1%. She must have mucked up the essay questions. And as for Maths, well at least it was an A. She shuddered at the thought of how finely balanced it all was. Just a few lower marks and she wouldn't be going to Cambridge.

Time to put such thoughts aside she said to herself, as she and her friends set out for town. They were going to start with coffee before going on to her friend Gemma's for the planned champagne lunch. Their route took them into town along Castle Lofts Road, past the war memorial and down the High Street. Some fast work by the Town Council meant there were already a couple of workmen trying to clean the graffiti from the memorial. It was odd, thought Lucy. They'd all walked past it so many times without a blink of an eye. But now, with this graffiti, she and her friends shared the sense of outrage that anybody could desecrate the memorial in this way. She thought back to her memories of the history trip they'd all been on to the First World War trenches and the huge Menin Gate memorial. All those names - so many names and such a loss of young men. Their memory deserved better than this. Why, she asked herself, would anyone be so crass as to paint on the memorial, and what did the words *'I Must Punish You'* mean? Oh well, she thought, not her concern but she'd heard mum talking to dad about all the events that were happening at Summer Bible Club and in the town. There was definitely something strange going on.

As they walked past the skip outside the Friends' Meeting House, Lucy noticed yet more graffiti, daubed on the wall just below one of the charred windows.

'TURN FROM YOUR INDIFFERENCE"

It looked like the same red paint used on the war memorial, but it didn't show up very well against the red brick of the Meeting House. Clearly somebody was on a mission.

*****

When John Davies arrived at the incident room, the only person present was PC Smart, who was desperately trying to catch up on his interview notes.

'Can I help you?' he asked.

'Well, I think I may be able to help you.'

John retold the story that he had heard from Chloe Gatiss.

'A motorbike again. Seems to be a common theme, trouble is we've yet to get a decent description and I don't expect motorbikes are exactly Chloe Gatiss' specialist subject. Was there anything else she remembered?'

'Not really, but I thought you ought to know.'

'Yes, you did the right thing telling us. It might help make a connection and we'll see if anybody else recalls seeing our phantom motorcyclist out early this morning. Inspector Pepper will probably want to talk to Chloe to find out exactly what she remembers, but we'll need an adult to be with her, probably her Nan again I should think. Is she in your tent all day?'

'Yes, barring unforeseen events.'

'We'll come over when we're ready. In the mean time don't say anything more to Chloe.'

'OK.'

John left the room and set off back across the field to the Eagles tent.

*****

At Lloyd Evans' house on Commonside the small gathering had successfully downed a bottle of vintage champagne between them. Lloyd was threatening to open a second, but Tom decided it was time to move on. Lloyd looked a bit disappointed, but it would leave him more time to get ready to host his daughter and grandchildren for lunch.

'Thanks old chap;' he said, 'but I've had enough. I'm walking up to the Academy, but I'm driving later on and I'm not sure I've got such good friends in legal circles as you have!'

'Ouch,' said Lloyd recognising the reference to his near miss on the drink driving front, 'that was a bit uncalled for. Although he is very good, my lawyer.'

'If I ever need him, I'll be in touch. So we've agreed then. The formal signing takes place next week and then it's all done. I'll go back down to London tomorrow and finalise everything with the Americans. The great man himself is over here and he may want to be the person who signs on the dotted line.'

'You mean Robert Latimer? Surely he doesn't get involved in details like this?'

'Not normally, but I think this one's a bit special. He's very keen to get our British operation off the ground. He thinks the BBC is a bit on the rocks and it's a good time to expand. There may be new opportunities, and he's determined that a certain other well-known media mogul isn't going to have it all his own way.'

'So you're telling me we sold out at too low a price?'

'No, don't even think about trying to go back on what's been agreed. Latimer will pull out and that will be the end of it. He deals straight down the line, no messing. A deal's a deal, take it or leave it with Latimer.'

'I'll take your advice. Anyway, we're all making far more than we ever thought possible. I hope Catherine York realises just how fortunate she's been.'

'If she doesn't now, I'm sure she will when the money goes into her account. Bye all, see you at the signing next week.'

Tom shook hands with Lloyd and set off walking down beside the Common. He was due to meet Jean for lunch during the break at SBC, but first of all he had something else to do. From the Common, he cut through to the High Street via the Market Square and Empire Street.

'Hi there dad.'

Tom looked round. In the middle of the group of girls sitting outside the Latte café he saw Lucy, enjoying what looked like a pile of whipped cream perched precariously on top of something that was supposed be a drink.

'Lucy, congratulations, didn't realise you'd be here.'

He said hello to Lucy's friends.

'I think its celebrations all around. Can I buy you all another coffee or whatever that foul stuff is that you're drinking. All that cream on top can't be doing any of your figures much good.'

Tom took their orders, went inside and paid for them, asking the barista to take them out to the girls when they were ready.

'Cheers then Lucy. Congratulations to all of you. See you this evening Lucy, I'm off to meet mum at the school.'

As Tom walked up the High Street, he seemed to deliberately be looking in the opposite direction as he passed the Friends' Meeting House, and he chuckled to himself as he observed the ineffective efforts of the workmen who were trying to clean up the war memorial. He never had liked the design of that thing; perhaps if they couldn't clean it they'd replace it with something better.

He continued on into Castle Lofts Road. Rather than turn into Bonhunt Academy and the Summer Bible Club site, he carried on towards the airfield next door. Ten minutes later he was at the hanger. Quietly he slipped inside.

*****

After receiving PC Smart's call, Wendy had returned with Peterson to the incident room at Bonhunt Academy. There had also been some more news from the YMCA and it hadn't been good. After watching the CCTV tape it had been left on the shelf beside the recording equipment. A member of staff who hadn't realised its importance had wiped it and there was no longer any record of the meeting between the two victims and the mysterious tall man.

'We'll that's a fat lot of use. I'm tempted to try and charge them with criminal negligence,' Wendy said. 'At least we can have a go at interviewing Chloe Gatiss again, although I'm not sure there's anything more she can tell us from what I've heard so far. Peterson, try and set something up this afternoon. Get Chloe's Nan to come in if you can, she'll probably help us calm Chloe down and see what she can remember. I expect it's too much to hope she's got the registration number of the bike!'

'I'll get on to it as soon as we finish the meeting.'

'Now, aside from motorbikes, today's theme seems to be graffiti. At least our killer has taken to writing as an alternative to killing people, assuming this is all the work of the same person. So, on the common, we've got *"The End Is Nigh."* Is our killer some cranky end timer, do you think?'

'End timer?' asked Peterson.

'Oh come on, Peterson. Yes, end timer! There are always some of them hanging around on the fringes of the church community. Convinced that every earthquake or thunderstorm is a portent of the end of the world. Perhaps the murders are some kind of preparation. The end is nigh.'

Wendy paused for a moment's thought.

'Or it could be *"The End Is Nigh"* in the sense of meaning "I'm almost finished": the climax is about to be reached,' said Peterson.

'You may well be right, in which case our killer could be about to strike again. And it might even be both, the killer really does think the end is nigh, and his own plan is about to be completed.'

'Then we've got the graffiti on the war memorial,' continued Peterson. 'Red letters declaring *"I Must Punish You."* Why must he? It seems as though he's under some form of compulsion.'

"You are wretched and miserable and poor and blind and naked"

'That's a bit heavy going boss, if you don't mind me saying so.'

Wendy laughed. No, that was the message thrown through the Davies' window first thing this morning. And I had a call from poor Trevor. Yet more graffiti on the Meeting House in the High Street:

"Turn from your indifference"

Painted in the same red as used on the war memorial, but we all missed it because it doesn't show up very well on the red brick frontage of the Quakers. Do we have that bible lying around anywhere?'

'Several of them, which version do you want?'

'I have a hunch the answer will be in the Living Bible. Now this all started with the quotation that came with the sheep's head. Here it is:

"Beware of false prophets who come disguised as harmless sheep but are really vicious wolves"

'Matthew Chapter 7 verse 15'

'Oh very good! Mind you, I think you've had some help there. The next verse adds "You can detect them by the way they act, just as you can identify a tree by its fruit." Unless I've missed something, I don't think we've had anything that links to trees and fruit, but we have had fire and sulphur. Wendy read the quote that had been found in the Eagles tent with the body:

'Then the LORD rained down fire and burning sulphur from the sky on Sodom and Gomorrah. He utterly destroyed them, along with the other cities and villages of the plain, wiping out all the people and every bit of vegetation.'

'Heavy stuff!'

'Old Testament this time,' said Peterson just to make the point that he had been doing his homework, 'and taken a bit too literally given the state of the body.'

'Also it suggests a hang up about sexuality; it's pretty clear what our killer's hang up is about when he starts quoting Sodom and Gomorrah.'

'So what about today's quotes?'

Well, John Davies suggested the Book of Revelation, probably chapter three and it seems he was right. With the exception of "The End Is Nigh," today's quotes all come from the same chapter. Let me read it to you, from the Living Bible of course.'

Wendy read an extract from chapter three, emphasising the passages that had been quoted:

"This message is from the one
who stands firm, the faithful and
true witness of all that is or was or
evermore shall be, the primeval
source of God's creation:
"I know you well-you are
neither hot nor cold; I wish you

were one or the other, But since
you are merely lukewarm, I will spit
you out of my mouth!
"You say, 'I am rich, with
everything I want; I don't need a
thing!' And you don't realize that
spiritually ***you are wretched and***
miserable and poor and blind and
naked.
'My advice to you is to buy
pure gold from me, gold purified by
fire-only then will you truly be
rich. And to purchase from me white
garments, clean and pure, so you
won't be naked and ashamed; and
to get medicine from me to heal your
eyes and give you back your sight.
I continually discipline and punish
everyone I love; so ***I must punish***
you, *unless you* ***turn from your***
indifference *and become enthusiastic*
about the things of God.

'Seems he's being a bit selective,' said Peterson, 'you might say he was accentuating the negative and eliminating the positive.'

Wendy picked up another book. 'I've been looking again at the book we discussed on Tuesday night. *"God's own Country. Tales from the Bible Belt."* I found a quote from somebody in the States that the author said he had interviewed. It goes on about false teaching in England and how we don't believe in the supernatural, how the churches are dead and people compromise on biblical truth. Compromisers on biblical truth - I wonder if that could be at the heart of this.'

Wendy paused, waiting to see if Peterson would comment.

'But why would you murder somebody because you thought they were selling out on their faith. Surely that's a bit over the top?'

'Come on Peterson, we've already had that discussion once today: the Middle East, Iraq, Israel and the Palestinians in the Gaza. Yes, I suppose I thought the same as you at first. Then I started to think that if you take a very hard line and have a very judgemental faith, and if you really do believe that people who are in or who are associated with the church are undermining it, what would you do? If you were angry that they compromised on what you believe is the biblical truth, then you might just kill the compromisers to try and stop the rot.'

'A self appointed purveyor of the wrath of God on the unrighteous?'

'Yes, you could put it like that, a sort of purging of the church. But I still don't think we've uncovered the whole story. Some of it isn't making sense.'

'And it's difficult to see how Tom Garroway fits in, despite his American connections.'

'I was coming to our current number one suspect. But before I do, there are a couple of other details that bother me.'

'Such as?'

'Well, at least one of the victims, Peter Lord, was a pretty fundamentalist Christian. He and John Davies were on security duty together at Summer Bible Club. If I was purging the church of compromisers, John Davies would be one of my top targets for elimination not Peter Lord.'

'But two of our victims, Jake Kerry and Philip Frost, were staying at the hostel that John Davies managed. Coincidence, or a different way of getting at him: make him appear to be the murderer?'

'If that was the case, it didn't fool us for long. No, I'm not clear that the murderer knew the John Davies connection to where the two Americans were living in Cambridge. I think it's the way Philip Frost was killed that makes the connection: there must be something really driving the murderer to commit such a vicious act. It's clear he was making a statement with the text about Sodom and Gomorrah, suggesting he has some hang up about sexuality. The murder victim is found in John Davies' tent. John Davies is a Liberal Democrat Councillor and he also has "small l" liberal views in terms of his Christianity. The killer could be making a point because he thinks Davies is a false prophet, a wolf in sheep's clothing. It's like he's saying "I know what you are." So, moving on to Mr Garroway. Did you get to see the pastor in Welsted?'

'No, unfortunately Pastor Jeremiah appears to have gone away for a few days and can't be contacted. Not particularly helpful. We're doing some calls on members of his congregation to see if they recognise a photograph of Tom Garroway.'

'And we're still waiting for information to come back from the sheriff's office in Hope and anything your Trude might come up with from her friend in the States.'

'I'm going to call them all again this afternoon, after I've tracked down Tom Garroway. Right, let's see if I can find a contact number for him.'

*****

Catherine was finishing off in the sixth form centre. It had been a good day and by around three pm they had placed all but two of the students who wanted a place at university in September. She was particularly pleased that Lisa Simmonds had secured a place at Durham. Most of her students deserved their success, but there were one or two that Catherine felt particularly deserved to do well, and Lisa had been in that group. She'd had great difficulty getting Lisa's mother to understand why it was important for her daughter to try and upgrade her place following her excellent results. Despite all they did at the Academy to encourage their students to aim high, Catherine sometimes found it was the parents who lacked aspiration for their offspring. In the staff room they often discussed which were worse, parents with no aspiration or the "pushy" parents who failed to realise the limitations of their children.

'Hello Catherine, how's your day been then?'

It was Wendy, who'd decided to drop in after her meeting with Peterson.

'Really good. Some great results – I think the Head will be happy with how we compare with the other schools this year, and some of our individual students have excelled themselves, so I'm really pleased for them.'

'A good end to a good year then?'

'Yes, I think we should be very happy. So how's your day been, how's the investigation going?'

'I think we're getting closer, but we're still not there. We have some odd details that don't make sense at the moment.'

'You're looking exhausted. It's normally me that feels knackered on results day. It's like we've swapped roles.'

'Yes, it's been a very draining week, and I'm getting more pressure from the top.'

'I think I should take you and Peterson out for a drink this evening. Six thirty pm at the Great Eastern?'

'That'll do nicely. I'll see you then. Are they doing any food there at the moment?'

'I'm sure they can manage a pork pie and some pork scratchings if nothing else.'

'Pork pie it may have to be.'

*****

Peterson's mobile rang.

'Sergeant Peterson?'

'Yes'

'It's Marc Reynolds here.'

'Marc Reynolds?'

'Yes, from Apparel. You came to see me earlier in the week. You wanted to know who'd been buying some clothes.'

'Oh, yes, of course. You were going to check if you had a record of the person who'd bought the "LIVE IN HOPE" trousers.'

'You'll be pleased to know that I've found a name. It was a card purchase made by a Mr T Garroway. I hope the information is helpful.'

'Yes, indeed, that is very helpful. Thank you for letting me know.'

*****

In the Eagles tent, John Davies was just about to wind up the proceedings. The children were all sitting on the grass. Jean Garroway was leading some singing on her guitar. Most of the children were joining in with *"I'm special, because God loves me,"* but a few of the boys were more interested in tearing up bits of grass and throwing them at each other.

When Jean finished, John stepped in to the proceedings. 'Some of you are spoiling my carpet!' he said. The boys throwing grass at each other carried on, ignoring him. 'Nigel, Derek, Oliver, I'm talking to you!'

'What do you mean,' said Nigel, 'you always pick on me.'

'Well, if I'm picking on you, I'm picking on Derek and Oliver as well. That's my carpet you're pulling up and throwing at each other. So please stop it.'

Three sulky faced boys made one last half-hearted attempt at throwing the grass and then stopped. John was just about to sum up the day before the children's parents arrived, when Sylvia Maitland came into the tent.

'Jean will sing another song with you,' John said to the children as he turned to Sylvia. Most of the girl's jumped up enthusiastically, while most of the boys looked fed up and a couple of groans could be heard.

'John, sorry to interrupt,' Sylvia said quietly.

'Oh, that's OK. About time some of these charmers learnt a few good manners. What can I do for you?'

'I've just brought round some more flyers for the Grand Finale tomorrow evening.'

'We gave all the children in the tent one of these yesterday, and we've talked to as many of the parents as we can when they've been dropping off and collecting their children.'

'That's really helpful John. But we're a bit worried with all the events this week that people might stay away. We're planning a very special finale with a positive message for everybody to take away with them. We really need as many parents as possible to come.'

'Message understood. We'll plug it again with everybody collecting their kids this evening, and we'll try and catch the parents tomorrow morning.'

'Thanks John, I knew I could rely on you.'

With Sylvia gone, John turned back to selecting something to read to the children before they left. He picked up his bible, which had been in a pile of books on a table in the corner of the tent. As he flicked through it, a piece of paper fell out. He read the familiar typeface, and his heart sank

'I know you well - you are neither hot nor cold; I wish you were one or the other, but since you are merely lukewarm, I will spit you out of my mouth!"

'Are you alright John? You've gone very quiet,' said Alice.

'No, I'm not alright.' He showed Alice the piece of paper. 'Can you get Jean to finish for me? I need to go and visit the police again.'

*****

In the committee room at the Town Hall, the pre meeting talk was all about the vandalism on the Common. The third Thursday of the month meant that it was the Recreation and Playing Fields Committee. Cllr Derek Rogers was getting ready to chair the meeting, but was venting his anger about the words that had been burnt into the grass on the common.

'It's obvious to me. Some stupid pupils from Bonhunt Academy. They're always out on the Common this time of year and their A-level results were out today. What were the words they burnt into grass?'

'The End Is Nigh,' replied Councillor Thomas.

'Exactly,' said Councillor Rogers, 'the end is nigh – I'm getting my A level results today. Absolutely and definitely Academy pupils. Period!'

'I wouldn't be so sure,' said Cllr Hodgkiss. 'I'm the first to come down hard on our local youngsters when they do something silly, but we don't know who did this. I understand it was sulphuric acid that was used to burn the grass, and a considerable quantity of it. I don't think the pupils at Bonhunt Academy would get hold of a lot of that very easily.'

'Oh they'll have filched it during a science lesson. The Head Teacher there needs to get a grip.'

'Well, just be careful. If you say all that too loudly you'll end up looking foolish if it's nothing to do with the school.'

Councillor Rogers paused and drew breath. He looked around the room.

'I think its time we started the committee. First of all, apologies for absence.'

'Chair, Councillor Davies has given his apologies,' reported the Town Clerk.

'Still playing with the God Squad I suppose.'

'Don't be too hard;' said Councillor Dakin, 'I think he's had a bit of a week.'

'Well, let's see if that's changed his ever so liberal views on law and order,' said the chair. 'Now, the main business of the evening, play equipment on the common. Has everybody looked at the plans?'

'Yes,' replied Councillor Thomas, 'and I'm not happy. I thought we'd established that we couldn't expand the play area on to any more of the Common because it wasn't lawful. These plans show that the area will double.'

'Oh for heaven's sake, I thought we'd put that one to bed over a year ago,' said Councillor Rogers. He could see that as chair he was going to be in for a long night.

*****

Peterson and Wendy had just finished their meeting with Tom Garroway. When Peterson had called Tom on his mobile and asked him to come in to be interviewed, he'd discovered that he was at the airfield next to the school. Tom had readily agreed to come to the incident room and answer their questions.

'He had an answer for everything,' said Peterson.

'Yes, almost as though he had rehearsed the whole thing,' Wendy replied, 'but I find him a bit of an enigma. The evidence keeps pointing to him, but I'm getting the same feeling I had about John Davies. I can't quite see him as our killer.'

'I'm not sure I was convinced by his explanation about why he'd been around the school for so long. First of all he went to the hanger, but the instructor wasn't there. So after that he met his wife for lunch at Summer Bible Club and then he goes back. Claims he was trying to arrange some more flying lessons with the instructor. Meets up with him, does the business and then decides it's such a nice day he'll stay, sit on the school field and work on his tablet and his mobile.'

'It did all seem very convoluted. But then explaining some of the things I do would make me sound pretty irrational!'

'Did you buy the story about the "LIVE IN HOPE" stuff he bought in Cambridge?'

'It's plausible that he'd promised something for his son and forgot to get it when he was in New York. Rather than disappoint him, he bought it from a shop in Cambridge that he knew stocked unusual American clothes. It could be true.'

'So, time to set off for the Great Eastern?'

'If we get going now, we'll arrive before Catherine. That will stop her complaining that I'm always late!'

The door to the room opened and John Davies entered.

'I came across earlier, but you seemed to be very busy. I need to talk to you. I've found another Bible quote.'

*****

Catherine arrived at the Great Eastern on the dot of six thirty. She'd managed a couple of hours putting her feet up at home and had, for a moment at least, wished she hadn't been so rash as to offer to take Wendy and Peterson out for a drink. Of course, she thought, they're late. Five years of sharing a house with a police officer meant that Catherine was all too used to being kept waiting.

'Do you have any food on tonight?' she asked at the bar.

'We've got some pork pies and pickled eggs.'

'I don't suppose you have pork scratchings to go with them?'

'Haven't had those for years, but we've got a good selection of crisps.'

Catherine settled for a large glass of Chenin Blanc, a pork pie, pickled egg and a packet of sea salt and balsamic vinegar crisps. With that flavour description there was one thing that would be certain: they'd be expensive. She was shocked by how little change she got from her ten pound note. Taking her wine and food she walked over to the snug area that she knew Wendy and Peterson favoured.

Sitting on the other side of the pub, tucked in at the far end of the bar where it returned up against the wall, was a large silent figure, quietly drinking a pint of Adnams. He had slipped into the bar just before Catherine and was watching her carefully, not wanting to be observed. If she was here on her own, then others, almost certainly her friend Wendy Pepper and that other policeman she worked with, would probably be arriving fairly soon. So this was not a place to stay very long: time to think about making a quick and quiet exit. But there was something he should do before leaving.

'High there,' Wendy called across to Catherine as she arrived with Peterson, 'sorry we're late, but we had to sort something back at the school before we came over.'

'Careful,' said Peterson as somebody pushed past him on their way out of the pub. He turned and caught the rear view of a large, tall man in a check shirt walking through the outer door. 'Hey, Wendy, look.'

'What am I looking at?'

'The person who just pushed past me. Was that Tom Garroway?'

'Sorry, didn't catch sight of him. Does he normally drink here? I don't think I've ever seen him at the Great Eastern. He'd had to have been very quick to get here before us; we've only just interviewed him up at the school.'

Peterson heard the sound of a motorbike starting up on the street outside and then driving away.

'There's your answer: a motorbike yet again. He could have been down here in minutes once we'd finished talking to him.'

'So what was so important that you were delayed back at the school?' asked Catherine 'I'm usually the one that can't get away from the place.'

'We had to interview somebody and then there was yet another quote from the Bible. It seems we're very into the Book of Revelation at the moment.'

'Well, if it's the coming of the New Jerusalem then I suppose it could be a lot worse.'

'If only! Problem seems to be we're all lukewarm, wretched, poor and blind.'

'You forgot miserable and naked,' Peterson added helpfully.

'Speak for yourself' replied Wendy, laughing.

'If you're wretched and poor, then it's time I bought you both a drink. Wine or a pint, Wendy?'

'Definitely a pint.'

'And what about you Ian?'

'I'll join Wendy in a pint, thanks. And is there any food?'

'Only the best: pork pie, pickled eggs and a range of fancy titled and very expensive crisps. I'll get a selection.'

The pub was filling up, and Catherine had struggled to get served at the bar. She was saved by Peterson just as she thought she was about to drop one of the pint glasses she had somehow managed to hold along with two pork pies, four pickled eggs and three packets of assorted crisps.'

'It's a really pleasant evening, why don't we all find a table outside?' he said.

'Good idea, I'll call Wendy to follow.'

They settled in on one of the picnic tables in the pub garden. Wendy and Peterson tried not to look too tired as Catherine shared her excitement about the achievements of some of her students. Peterson decided he really couldn't keep track of her animated explanations about which were the best university courses and why various students had done so well to get into the vast array of places Catherine was listing so enthusiastically. He decided to try and push the conversation in a different direction.

'Do you really have so many students with pagan names?' he asked, 'so far we've had a Willow, a Rowan – not sure if that was a him or a her - a Hilary - I'm sure you said that was a boy - and I definitely heard you mention at least two Waynes.'

'Not sure I'd count Wayne as a pagan name, just two poor kids with fathers who worship Manchester United.'

'Now that really is a form of pagan religion,' said Wendy. 'Anyway, surely they're a bit too old to have been named after the footballer? But Ian's got a point. Pagan names are a sign of the times. We've become a secular nation.'

*****

At the Chop House in Cambridge, Jean Garroway was getting increasingly angry. She'd arrived with Lucy and Joshua at seven pm as agreed and Tom was nowhere to be seen. She knew she should never have agreed to him coming on his own, particularly as he'd struggled to come up with a reason as to why he needed to. It was ridiculous really, as it meant she'd had to drive the BMW into Cambridge with the children and he would be coming separately on the motorbike. So neither of them would be able to drink. Even getting through a bottle of champagne was going to be a challenge, although she and Tom ought to be able to manage one glass each.

By seven thirty pm, Jean had gone through two orange juices and she was losing count of the drinks Lucy and Josh had consumed. She decided to go ahead and order. Tom would just have to lump it if they were on the sweet course by the time he arrived.

Joshua insisted on ordering a venison steak, which Jean knew would be very good but worried he would find far too rich. Lucy, in sensible mode despite the excitement of the day, ordered a steak and kidney suet pudding. Jean decided she fancied the locally made sausages and mash.

'It's so typical of dad to be late. He really could have made the effort to be on time tonight,' said Lucy.

'I'm sure he'd have been here earlier if he could,' replied Jean, who had difficulty believing it herself.

'Why is it always our dad who never turns up?' asked Joshua.

'Well, I've turned up now.' None of them had noticed Tom quietly approaching the table behind them. 'Looks like you're struggling with your food there Josh. Shall I finish it off for you?'

'OK dad. I suppose mum was right, venison steak is a bit too rich for me.'

'So where on earth have you been, Tom? We said seven pm, not eight pm.'

'I'm sorry. It just took a bit longer than I anticipated sorting the details of our takeover of Anglia Media. I've parked it for this evening and I'll be going down to London early tomorrow.'

'Oh Tom, you know I need to be at Summer Bible Club first thing tomorrow. It's the last day, always a bit of a nightmare and I was late today because Lucy was collecting her results.'

'It's all right Jean. I'll take the motorbike down to Castle Lofts station, and then you won't need to worry about dropping me off and collecting me.'

'That doesn't make amends for what's happened today. Just for once I thought business could take a back seat. Lucy has done so well and we're supposed to be having a family celebration.'

'Mum,' said Lucy, 'let's just enjoy the meal now.'

'I'll go for that,' said Tom, 'first of all I'll order a bottle of champagne. You and Josh will have to drink most of it, because mum and I are both driving. Once we've opened the champagne, I suggest we look at the dessert menu. Personally, I fancy the Eton Mess. They do a really good one here.'

'There was a really good joke about that in the play I saw over Easter.'

'OK, Lucy, tell us the joke.' Jean was using her "if you must" voice. 'I hope it's not too crude!'

'Here goes: How do you make an Eton mess?'

'I don't know, how do you make an Eton mess?'

'You tell him he's going to Bristol.'

There were groans round the table.

'As somebody who went to Bristol university, I don't find that particularly funny,' Jean raised her eyes to heaven.

*****

The evening had passed quickly in the garden at the Great Eastern, and it was already ten thirty. It was warm, humid and the garden had been packed with a lively group of local residents enjoying the opportunity to sit outside on another very warm summer's night.

'Time to go,' said Wendy. 'Peterson, you and I have a lot of work to do tomorrow. I have this feeling we're on the verge of finding out what all this is really about.'

'So it's Peterson, not Ian. I always know how to recognise when you're on duty mam.'

'Cheeky sod! Just wait till you need a reference from me for the promotion board.'

'Now, now you two,' Catherine's words were a bit slurred following a single handed consumption of a bottle of Chenin Blanc, 'we don't want any falling out among our gallant boys and girls in blue.'

They made their way back into the pub and towards the front door. Peterson looked at the "specials" board which had been blank when they arrived.

'Oh shit,' he said, his body freezing.

'What on earth's the matter with you?' asked Catherine.

'I can see exactly what the matter with Ian is,' Wendy replied, 'look.'

She pointed to the board. On it, in crude chalked letters, were the words

'THE END IS NIGH"

Friday

It had been so hot and humid that Lloyd Evans, who was usually a very sound sleeper, had lain wide awake most of the night. He'd tried every angle he could on his supposedly finest quality cosseting mattress, but it hadn't worked. By five thirty he reckoned he'd had one hour's sleep at the most, and probably not even that. So he decided to make the best of a bad job and go for a walk.

Bounce, his lively and very excitable spaniel, seemed to be having the same problem, and as soon as Lloyd entered the kitchen, the dog was standing in front of him with his favourite ball.

'I suppose I'll have to take you with me. Let's head out for a walk. If I take the Jag then we could go out to that path near Finchwinter you like so much.'

My God, he thought, I must be losing the plot; I'm talking to my dog as though he's a human being. He continued with the task of making himself a quick cup of instant coffee (definitely not decaffeinated for the first one of the day) and put down some food for Bounce.

'There, I thought that would get you to drop the ball. Eat that up, get some energy and then we'll be off.'

Lloyd Evans opened his back door and went out to the garage. He was finding the two oak garage doors a bit heavy nowadays, but had resisted the idea of having them operated electronically, even though he could easily afford the expenditure involved. He wasn't going to give in and go soft quite yet. So having opened the doors with a bit of a struggle, he slowly reversed his Jaguar out into the drive. He climbed out and closed the doors, and then returned through the back door into the kitchen lobby. There he found the extending dog lead.

'Bounce, time to go,' he called. An excited dog came rushing round the corner and dropped the ball at his feet. He picked the ball up, walked back over to the Jaguar, opened the rear offside door and threw the ball in. Bounce didn't quite leap in quickly enough to catch it, but that had clearly been his aim. Anyway, he was safely in the back of the car now and, having closed and locked his back door; Lloyd Evans drove out on to Commonside and headed off in the direction of Finchwinter Road.

*****

Tom Garroway was also up very early. It had been quite a late night by the time they had all got back to Folly Farm, where they'd finished off the bottle of champagne that they'd brought back home with them from the restaurant. He hadn't slept well either. Too much alcohol late at night, and too hot. Not a good combination and he thought he really should have known better. But it was Lucy's big celebration night and he'd needed to join in, not least because he had to make sure Lucy realised just how proud he was of her.

It wasn't easy, being away in London and the States so much on business. He found he couldn't always be around when he wanted to be. Having dressed, drunk some coffee and grabbed a croissant that he quickly microwaved, Tom slipped upstairs and back to the bedroom.

'Bye Jean, hope all goes well today. I reckon you've got at least another hour and a half in bed – do you want me to set the alarm?'

'No thanks,' Jean groaned, 'I've hardly slept a wink. I'll get up in a moment. Take care.'

'Love you!'

'Love you too,' Jean replied so quietly that Tom didn't hear.

Once outside, he walked through the boxed shaped hedges, cutting across the fine tiles and stone paving, catching himself on one of the exquisite rare breed roses as he made his way to the barn. There he ignored the two cars and lifted his motorcycle leathers off the shelf. Ten minutes, and he'd be on his way to Castle Lofts Station.

*****

Lloyd Evans turned into Farm Lane on the outskirts of Finchwinter. As he expected, his favourite parking spot was completely free at this time in the morning. Bounce was leaping about in the back of the Jaguar, having difficulty containing his excitement at the prospect of an early morning walk. He put the lead on Bounce, locked the car and walked along the road to a gateway to the old bridleway that ran across Upper Field. He heard the roar of a motorbike approaching and stood close to the hedge, holding fast on to Bounce as the rider flew past. He's in a bit of a hurry he thought. Lloyd Evans opened the gate, and let Bounce off the lead once he'd closed it again. As he repeatedly threw the ball for the dog to fetch, he wondered just how many times Bounce would bring it back before he became tired of the game. So far, the maximum Lloyd had ever managed was thirty two times and it always ended up with him having to stop because he was more tired than the dog. Gradually they made their way across the field towards Folly Wood.

As they approached the edge of the trees, Lloyd could have sworn he felt as though somebody was watching them. He studied the woods very carefully but all he could see were the branches moving gently in the pleasant breeze that was cooling the temperature on what was otherwise going to be another scorching hot day.

Bounce dropped the ball at his feet once again. He bent with difficulty and threw the ball as far as he could. He let go slightly earlier than he'd intended, and the ball flew into the woods.

'Damn,' he said to himself, 'the dog will be off among those trees now. I hope I don't lose him.'

Lloyd Evans could hear Bounce chasing through the undergrowth around the bottom of the trees, barking excitedly. But gradually the barking seemed to come from further away.

This is going to be fun, he thought, as he followed the old bridleway into Folly Wood. In the distance he could hear Bounce barking, but the dog refused to come back no matter how hard he called or whistled.

'Damn dog, just thought we'd have our usual walk. Now I'm having to fight my way down this overgrown path.'

There were tyre tracks along the bridleway, but the tall grass was wet with the early morning dew and Lloyd Evans was realising he hadn't come dressed for this type of walk. Gradually his summer trousers were becoming soaked as a result of the wet grass brushing against them.

'Bounce, Bounce, come here you wretched dog. I'm fed up with this game.'

He realised he'd ventured further into the wood than he'd done before. The dog's barking was louder, but where was it coming from? He looked around unable to discern the direction from which the sound was coming, and then, close by but almost completely hidden from view by the low level growth under the trees, he could see some form of outbuilding. He made his way over to it.

'Bounce,' Lloyd Evans called out as he pushed open the large door, 'Bounce, where are you? Well you've certainly found something haven't you? I'd never realised this huge old barn was here.'

Bounce barked loudly, and Lloyd wondered why he wasn't running over to him like he normally did. Then he realised that the dog had been tethered by a rope, one end round his collar and the other tied crudely around a rusty hook on the barn's ancient timber frame. Suddenly he felt very frightened.

'Hello, is anybody here?'

Without warning the barn door slammed shut behind him and the whole barn was plunged into darkness. Bounce started barking loudly again, but Lloyd stood motionless. He couldn't recall afterwards how long he had stood still, but his army training had suddenly come back to him. He had to do nothing that would give his position away in case the other person was still in the barn. Images flashed through his mind of wild men with knives, of scythes flashing through the air, of heavy hammers coming bearing down. But there was nothing. He was certain. Only he and the dog remained in the barn.

Once his eyes had acclimatised to the dark he started to look round. The main body of the building was empty, but there was a small side door, slightly ajar. Quietly he walked over to it. Bounce's loud barking should hide any noise he made as he moved. Very slowly and very gently he pushed the door wide open. An old wooden chair stood in the middle of what looked like a small workshop, and four empty jars were placed on the floor beside it.

He walked back into the main barn area and over to the dog, who had been getting more and more excited.

'Time to untie you and for us to find a way out of here. This wasn't the day to leave the mobile at home!'

*****

Jean Garroway had decided it would be hopeless trying to get Lucy to join her and Joshua at Summer Bible Club, even though she was supposed to be helping. She'd left her in bed at Folly Farm and set off with a very unhappy Joshua in the BMW, driving down Farm Lane. First of all she saw the Jaguar with the bonnet up, and then she saw the man waving wildly at her, obviously wanting her to stop. Then she heard the dog barking loudly. She pulled up beside the Jaguar.

'Can I help you?'

'I hope so, I've had the most terrible morning, you really won't believe it, but I must get to the police station.' Lloyd Evans took a deep breath and gathered his thoughts. 'I really am so sorry, I'm being terribly rude and I haven't introduced myself. Lloyd Evans, I live on Commonside in Chipping Bonhunt.'

'Jean Garroway, I think you know my husband Tom. We live back down the lane at Folly Farm.'

'Oh, Tom Garroway, yes of course. He works for Intermed. I was drinking champagne with him only yesterday celebrating our deal.'

'Yes, he told me about it. He was late for dinner last night because of it, so I'm not the happiest wife around.'

'Last night? I wonder what he was doing then. I thought we concluded it all in the morning. Mind you, some papers had to be prepared so perhaps that's what he was working on.'

'So what's happened to you?'

Lloyd Evans told Jean about his experience during his walk with Bounce in Folly Wood. When he'd tried to get out of the barn he'd found that it had been barred from the outside. He'd managed to climb through a window in the workshop, followed by Bounce who'd then insisted on jumping back in as though it was a game. He'd opened the door so that he could put the lead on the dog and then they'd made their way back from Folly Wood across the field. When he'd arrived back at his car he found that somebody had forced open the bonnet and vandalised the electrics.

'Clearly they didn't want me to get away from here too quickly.'

*****

Tom Garroway drove his motorbike round to a small patch of land that accessed a footpath to the Cambridge platform at Castle Lofts station. It was a convenient place to park because it avoided the congestion over the foot bridge and out of the main entrance when returning from London. He was surprised more people didn't use it, although there was always the risk of the bike being vandalised. He took off his bike leathers, placed them in the pannier on the bike, retrieved his blazer and brushed down his fashionably smart but casual trousers. Looking at his watch, he realised he had ten minutes to buy his ticket. First class today, he thought. Only the best. And time to buy a coffee from the newsagent as well.

*****

Eagles were coping with another rushed morning. John had put Sarah and Lewis on duty lobbying parents about the Grand Finale that evening. This had the double advantage that it enabled the other members of the team to get on with organising all the children as they finished off their craft work and drawings from the rest of the week, whilst also making it impossible for Sarah to spend the first part of the day sitting on Lewis' lap.

John was preparing his opening remarks for the children, before they joined all the other groups in the big tent for morning assembly. As he opened his bible he said a silent prayer.

‘Please God, don’t let there be another one of those quotes.’

He was just collecting his thoughts when Sarah came rushing up very excited.

‘Most of the parents say they’re coming. I think everybody wants to support us.’

‘That’s great; it’ll mean we end on a bit of a high if we have a good turnout.’

‘One of the parents even gave me £50 towards the costs. They said it was wonderful the way the churches all work together to put this on.’

‘Well, I suppose they’re right. It is wonderful isn’t it? Make sure you take that £50 over to the Reception tent.’

‘Surely you trust me.’

John laughed loudly.

*****

Lloyd Evans had been waiting for around three quarters of an hour in the small reception area at Chipping Bonhunt Police Station. Jean Garroway had kindly dropped him there on her way to Summer Bible Club. He thought the police might have treated his visit with a bit more urgency, but apparently they didn’t officially open the reception counter until nine thirty, so he was lucky they had let him in at all. Still, there was a limit to the number of times you could read the posters and various leaflets that were on display.

Eventually PC Smart opened the door and ushered him through to an empty interview room.

‘This makes me feel more like a criminal than a victim,’ Lloyd said.

‘Oh, please don’t let this put you off, sir. I’m afraid we only have a limited number of rooms here at the station, and it’s not as though we’re putting you in one of the cells.’

'No matter how much you'd like to!'

'Sorry sir, I'm not following you.'

'Is Inspector Pepper in the building?'

'Yes, she is. Very busy at the moment, as I'm sure you'll understand.'

'Well, ask her what I mean. She knows what I'm talking about.'

'I'll do that. But in the mean time, please tell me what it was you wanted to share with us. I'm sure it's important.'

Constable Smart had been trying to sound both civil and interested. At first he wondered where this story about not sleeping and taking a dog out for an early morning walk was going to end. Lloyd Evans was elaborating things so much that he found it difficult to follow. Smart wondered if the whole thing had been imagined.

'Are you sure somebody closed the door, rather than it just being blown shut by the breeze?'

'I'm absolutely certain it was deliberate. The breeze wasn't strong enough. And how do you explain Bounce being tied up with a length of rope?'

'You have a point there, certainly.'

It started to dawn on PC Smart that something odd had definitely taken place, and when Lloyd Evans described the damage to his Jaguar, it was clear that there had certainly been a case of criminal damage, and possibly a lot more.

'Did you notice anything else? I know you said you felt that you were being watched. But did you actually see anyone on your drive there or as you were setting out for your walk?'

'Yes, just after I parked the car. A maniac on a motorbike almost ran me over. I had to stand hard into the side of the road holding on to Bounce as he went flying past. He was going at quite a speed.'

'Did you see where he was heading?'

'I assume he was heading into town.'

'Could he have stopped and come back?'

'I would have thought I'd have heard the bike again. But I suppose he could have come back, particularly when I was throwing the ball for Bounce. That dog makes quite a noise when he barks and we were walking into the middle of the field away from the road, so I might not have noticed the bike if the rider came back.'

Smart realised that this was all far more important than he'd previously thought.

'Wait here a minute, sir, if you would. I think your friend the Inspector might want to talk to you about this. She'll want to follow up some of the information you've just given us.'

A few minutes later, Wendy and Peterson were sitting across the table from Lloyd Evans.

'I know we've had our differences, but what you've told us this morning could be very important. You said that Jean Garroway rescued you and Bounce – are we looking after the dog, by the way?'

'Yes,' said PC Smart, 'he's out the back with one of the other constables. Plenty of water to drink and attention from PC Jones.'

'Good, so it was Jean Garroway that picked you up. Were you close to where the Garroways live?'

'I think so, I'm pretty certain that Folly Farm is just a bit further down Farm Lane. You know Farm Lane? It's a no through road that turns off Finchwinter Road a little way before you get to the village.'

'Yes, I know where you mean, but I don't think I've ever been down there. Look, I know this is asking a big favour, but would you come with Constable Smart and myself now and show us the barn where you were locked in?'

'Always happy to help. Perhaps we can build some bridges between us as well.'

Not if you keep drinking and driving, and then calling in hot shot lawyers, thought Wendy. She turned to Peterson and took him to one side to have a quick conversation.

'I need you to stay here and try and get a response from your American contact. We need to know if there is anything that connects Garroway to the American victims. I know you didn't get anywhere with them yesterday, but this is now very urgent. Get them out of bed if you have to!'

*****

Tom Garroway didn't usually worry about dress codes. His style was modern, an open necked shirt with a casual jacket if one was needed. He didn't go in for suits, feeling they were outdated, over fussy and too pretentiously English.

Today, however, he wondered if he'd dressed slightly too casually. It was apparently very rare for somebody in his position to get a one to one meeting with Robert Latimer when he was travelling abroad. If you were a president, royalty, prime minister or in government then you would be on the list. But simply being the company rep in the UK wouldn't normally make the grade. Despite his good relationship with Latimer during meetings, Tom would normally expect to be dealing with Latimer's flunkies, the team that shielded him from the more sordid operational side of the business. Tom knew that Latimer himself always dressed fairly casually, so he was pretty certain he had got it right. It came as quite a shock when they met in the foyer of the Savoy and his host was wearing a kilt and black tie. Latimer instantly recognised his discomfort.

'Hi there Tom, don't worry about this get up, I'm off to a lunch with fellow trustees of the Society for Aiding

Impoverished Scots. We always dress up for our little meetings. Somebody researched this garish tartan which I'm told is essential for dress kilts in my clan. Frankly, given the revolting shade of yellow that is all you really see when you look at this thing, I think they stitched me up.'

'I can see it's a bit loud.'

'A bit loud?' he laughed, 'it frightens horses at a hundred yards. Now, come over here and have a drink. I'm sure a vintage malt wouldn't go a miss.'

Tom really didn't feel like drinking, and at the back of his mind he was thinking about the motorbike ride back from the station. But he couldn't really say no.

'That would be very nice, thank you.'

'You and I have a great deal to talk about. Purchasing Anglia Media is just the start over here Tom. It's just a very small stone that I'm throwing into the water. The ripples will grow and grow. I want to build a serious media presence in Britain from which I can launch an all out assault on Europe. I reckon you're the guy that can handle this for me, and as you already know I pay very well. What do you say?'

'I'm very flattered, and of course I'm interested. How will all of this work?'

'You'll report to me Tom, direct line through to the top, no messing. We discuss each prospect, assess how it might fit into the business and if we both think it's a yes, then you go and buy it. I want a serious operation up and running across the whole of the United Kingdom by the end of next year, with footholds in all the key European countries. Doesn't matter if its newspapers, satellite, cable or terrestrial, it's the coverage I want. And I think we should look at broadband, search engines, whatever we can bring in so that we can go to the market and present the whole offering. I loved the way BT bought all those football rights under the nose of you know who. That's the approach I want. He's getting too powerful, and I think we can take him on. We'll fight him on both price and quality. So how does that all sound to you?'

'It sounds pretty good. I assume you want me to pull together a team here in London? We can find a base in one of the emerging areas like King's Cross or parts of Islington.'

'I'll let you lead on all of that. Just choose somewhere that's cutting edge and gives the message that we're innovators. We're the new kids on the block, and we're going to shake things up.'

*****

Wendy and PC Smart had arrived at Farm Lane with Lloyd Evans.

'I'll get the car recovered for you, but we'll need to examine it first. If forensics can do it today we should be able to get it to a garage tomorrow morning. Is there anywhere you'd like it taken?'

'Well I normally go to the dealer in Cambridge,' replied Lloyd.

'Let's hope they're open on Saturday mornings then. Now, please would you retrace your steps for us?'

They opened the bridleway gate, which Wendy noticed had been repaired recently, and Lloyd Evans led them across the field. Wendy was trying to locate the barn, but even when they reached the middle of the field she couldn't see anything.

'I can't see a barn anywhere,' she said.

'It's very well hidden. You have to actually follow the path right into Folly Wood until you find it. It's this way – follow me.'

Lloyd Evans was enjoying his new role as guide to the scene of the crime. He hoped the police would remember how helpful he was being, particularly this troublesome Inspector.

'It's this way,' he said.

They followed him along the bridleway and into the woods. Wendy realised just how perfectly hidden the barn was. It really couldn't be seen until you were almost on top of it. An almost invisible hideaway. Smart pushed the heavy door open and looked around inside. There was the hook, with the rope that had been used to tie up Bounce. He moved across to the side door and entered the workshop. There was a faint smell that he recognised.

'There's something in here. I'm not sure what's been in these jars, but I recognise the smell.'

Wendy recognised it instantly. Having seen the body in the Eagles tent on Tuesday night, she thought it was a smell she would never forget. She walked over to one of the jars and the smell grew stronger.

'Sulphuric acid. Call the SOCOs and get them up here immediately. Don't touch anything. Get some reinforcements up here as well, I want the field, bridleway, barn and wood sealed off and a full search done.'

'Right away,' replied Smart.

'Now Mr Evans, if you'd stay here with Constable Smart until the cavalry arrive, I'm just going to drive down the lane to Folly Farm and see if anybody is in.'

*****

As Wendy walked past Lloyd Evan's car she thought what a sorry state it was in with its bonnet bent and wrenched open. For a moment she imagined it was the result of an accident after drink driving, but she put the silly idea out of her mind. She realised that Chief Superintendent Warren was probably right; she had got it in for Lloyd Evans. He'd just been very helpful and yet she was secretly wishing she could lock him up again. Time to put such thoughts out of her mind as she had much more important business to pursue this morning. Wendy climbed back into the car that Smart had driven to Farm Lane, and drove further down the road to the entrance for Folly Farm.

As the police car entered the drive up to the farm house it was watched by a bleary eyed Lucy Garroway looking out of her bedroom window. She decided she'd better throw on some clothes very quickly. Wendy had rung the bell several times when Lucy eventually opened the front door.

'Is your father in?' asked Wendy.

'No, I think he's going down to London. He set off early this morning.'

'What about your mother?'

'She's gone with my brother to Summer Bible Club. I should have been with them, but I had a bit of a late night. Have mum and dad done something wrong?'

'Nothing for you to worry about,' said Wendy. 'Do you mind if I take a look round? Would that be OK?'

'I suppose so,' said Lucy hesitating slightly. She wished she wasn't dealing with this on her own.

Wendy opened a door off the hallway into what was obviously Tom Garroway's office. It was expensively furnished with a very modern desk, chair and lighting. She decided not to touch the computers. That would be going too far and she needed the experts to go over them. On the desk was a folder with "Anglia Media" handwritten on the front. She opened it and found what appeared to be draft contracts for the purchase of the company by Intermed. She whistled out loud when she saw how much Intermed were paying. No wonder Catherine had been so coy when they'd discussed it.

Apart from the Anglia Media folder, there were various Intermed publications on the desk. The book shelves seemed to be stocked with a combination of business texts and computer manuals. Lying on the bottom shelf Wendy found a glossy marketing brochure for an American church.

"First Church of the Redeemer. Hope, Arkansas: Saving your soul."

Flicking through the brochure, Wendy thought it seemed to be more about savings in this life than the next, as it offered investment and pension advice together with a lot of other services available to members of the church. The picture of the inside of the main church building suggested that it must hold hundreds of people. Bit of a contrast to Quaker meeting on a Sunday morning she thought.

'Thank you,' Wendy said to Lucy. 'I've seen all I need to for now. If either of your parents comes back, please would you tell them that Inspector Pepper needs to talk to them? Thanks.'

On the way out she called Peterson on her mobile and asked him to arrange a search warrant for Folly Farm.

'I'll come back to the station and then we need to go to Bonhunt Academy and see if Jean Garroway is still helping at Summer Bible Club. Get a car down to Castle Lofts Station as well. Make sure they have a picture of Tom Garroway. I want him picked up when he gets back from London.'

*****

Following his meeting with Robert Latimer, Tom was on a bit of a high. He'd turned his mobile off to ensure he wasn't disturbed and he set off on a walk around the West End. The hard work had paid off and this was going to be a fantastic opportunity. He would be working for one of the major players at the most senior level. This was more than just nice converted farm in the countryside territory. It was a smart flat in London, a base in New York and an unlimited expense account.

Jean wouldn't be keen, and he wondered if their marriage would survive. He'd discussed his career with his wife on many occasions. She'd never been happy with all his travelling and the visits to the States. They'd had long talks late into the night, often when he just wanted to go to bed before an early start the next day. She felt he was leaving her with all the difficult tasks, bringing up the kids, looking after the house, maintaining links with all their relatives and friends. Meanwhile he had the 'fun' globetrotting and mixing in the wealthy circles that went with his job while also 'dipping in and dipping out,' as she put it, of doing things with Lucy and Joshua. She clearly felt that he expected to be able to have the enjoyable aspects of parenthood with none of the grind.

Tom wanted to try and sort things with Jean if he could, but every time he tried to make a helpful suggestion it was rejected. Sending the kids to boarding school had been an immediate no. Getting more help in to run the house had been resisted. And Jean didn't want to come to the events in London and the States when he invited her. He really thought she'd have gone for the weekend in New York linked to Intermed's annual ball, a truly extravagant affair, but Jean used the excuse of an eventing weekend that Lucy was riding in not to go, So yet again he'd flown over to the States on his own, being as social as ever and having to explain in every conversation why his wife couldn't be with him.

It was clear to Tom that this new role would be the acid test for his marriage. If things fell apart, well he might just decide to base himself in the States. He was sure that Intermed would pay for him to fly to and from the UK whenever he needed to, and part of him fancied the life that New York had on offer. He was beginning to feel confined by England, and particularly Chipping Bonhunt. Perhaps he needed a bigger country.

How he'd managed to move in his mind from the positive meeting with Robert Latimer to the uncertain state of his marriage, Tom wasn't quite sure. He decided to accentuate the positive. A top quality lunch at one of his favourite restaurants would be followed by a train journey home and a flying lesson with Henry Buske. Better ring Henry and confirm that he would be there around six pm. When he'd completed the call, he ignored all his other messages and switched his mobile off again.

*****

Wendy and PC Smart arrived at Summer Bible Club with a couple of other police constables. A bit over the top Wendy had thought, but they needed to show that they meant business. Sylvia Maitland was on duty in the Reception tent and greeted them with a broad smile.

'This looks official, are you part of the security detail for our Grand Finale this evening?'

'No, we need to find Jean Garroway if she's here.'

Sylvia pointed across the field. 'Over there, in the Eagles tent. I don't think I need to give you lot visitors' badges, everyone will know who you are.'

'Thanks, we'll make our own way over,' said Wendy.

'Before you do, can I just say thank you for the way you've handled everything this week. We feared you might insist we close Summer Bible Club down, but instead you've got on and done what had to be done with a minimum of fuss and helped us keep going as well. We all really appreciate it.'

'Yes, we've tried to work round you, but we haven't caught the killer yet.'

'Are you any closer?'

'We think we're pretty warm.'

The Police set off towards the Eagles tent. When they were half way across the field the children from one of the tents came out onto the field to play games. Wendy had to intervene to stop the two constables joining in playing football with the boys.

'Just remember why we're here, will you,' she said in her official voice of disapproval. The constables shrugged their shoulders and followed her across the field.

They arrived at the Eagles tent just as John Davies was giving out instructions to the children about taking all their chairs up to the big marquee ready for the Grand Finale that evening.

'Now, I want each group to line up behind their table leader outside and follow them up to the big tent.'

He turned and almost bumped into Wendy as she entered.

'Sorry to interrupt, but we need to have a word with Jean.'

'What, me? Oh of course, whatever you want,' Jean said, surprised to be summoned in front of the whole tent by four members of the police force.

'I think it's probably best if we go across to the incident room at the school, we'll have more privacy there.'

'Has something happened, nobody's been hurt?'

'We need to talk through a few things, if that's OK with you.'

'Don't worry Jean,' said John, 'I'll look after the children on your table.'

The children were all talking excitedly about the arrival of the police officers. Jean was sure she heard one of them say 'I bet she's the murderer, she looks the sort.'

Jean walked back across the field accompanied by the police. Soon afterwards, a line of children set off from the tent, all carrying a chair as they headed off towards the big marquee.

*****

Catherine was sitting in the office in the sixth form centre. Originally she had intended to take the day off, but she'd decided she really must catch up on the work she needed to do for the new English exams. This year had been difficult enough. At GCSE the speaking and listening tests no longer counted towards the final mark. Apparently teachers couldn't be trusted to mark those parts of the exam objectively, so it was all back to focussing on the end of year exam. While that might help some of the pupils, it would certainly not help the performance of some of the others who performed better in school assessments. At A level, the loss of the January sitting for exams had already put more pressure on the students that were particularly prone to being stressed. And it was all going to get worse over the next few years.

She looked out of the window and saw Wendy walking across the field towards the school, accompanied by some other police and a woman she thought she knew but couldn't quite recall who she was. Looks as though Wendy might be making some progress, she thought.

*****

Henry Buske arrived at the airfield in order to prepare. He surveyed the tents at Summer Bible Club in the distance and the hive of activity taking place on the school field. It was just after three thirty and most of the children were now being collected by parents. With the exception of the big marquee, all the tables and other pieces of equipment were being assembled outside the tents. A large van was slowly progressing round the field so that everything could be loaded into it.

Henry pulled the main hangar door open. It was quite an incredible building to be located in this beautiful spot. Although the airfield had never had a proper runway, it had been used during the war as a subsidiary site to the other air bases in the area. The legacy was the hangar, and you really couldn't wish for a better building in which to store a collection of small aeroplanes.

Despite the other planes being based inside the hangar, Henry was usually the only person who flew during the week. The others were weekenders, mostly living some distance from Chipping Bonhunt. The exception to this was Lord Bonhunt, who would turn up at random moments to polish his spitfire. However, this was rarely flown and required a huge amount of preparation before it took to the air. It had been out to loop the loop during the concert on Sunday night, making a fine sight as the sun was going down just before the fireworks, but it probably wouldn't be flying again for at least another month.

Henry started preparing the Maule, getting ready to roll the plane out onto the standing area in front of the hangar.

Tom Garroway would probably arrive a little before the lesson he had booked for six that evening, so there was quite a lot of time to get everything ready. But then, there was quite a lot that Henry needed to do.

*****

Peterson had been struggling to get authority for the search warrant. This had taken a lot longer than he had anticipated and it wasn't until around four pm that he was ready to set off for Folly Farm with the search team. They were just about to go when Peterson received the call he had been waiting for. It was a good thing he was still at the police station as they might have had difficulty getting hold of him if he had been on the road. The information he received helped fit some more of the jigsaw together and his American contact at the Sheriff's office had turned up trumps. Now Tom Garroway really was in the frame, and the fact he'd neglected to mention the connection when they had interviewed him surely just reinforced his guilt. A real cool customer, though Peterson. He 'phoned Wendy immediately.

'We've got him. The deal he's involved in with that American media outfit, Inter-what's it?'

'Intermed: he goes to New York for his meetings with the company because that's where they're based.'

'They are and they aren't.'

'You're talking in riddles now Peterson.'

He paused, so that he could saviour the moment of revelation. He could feel his heart racing with the excitement at the news he was about to pass on to his boss.

'Intermed's HQ is in New York, so we all assumed that's where Garroway was going for all of his meetings. He did nothing to suggest otherwise when we interviewed him and certainly seemed happy for us to think that's where he was spending all his time in the States. But a lot of the meetings took place somewhere else, at the home of Intermed's idiosyncratic boss Robert Latimer. And that's in…well boss, I'll let you have a guess.'

'Hope, Arkansas by any chance?'

'Hope, in a huge Dallas type mansion, and that's where he's been going most of the time he visits the States. Tom Garroway is an important figure at Intermed. My source says that only the very top people, the selected few, get invited to the company meetings at the Latimer residence and our good friend Tom Garroway has been brown nosing his way very much into the inner sanctum. Gossip is that Robert Latimer thinks he's one of the best assets his company has, so our friend Tom is destined for very high things.'

'Except that he appears to have been murdering people on the way up. I wonder what threat our two American victims represented. It must have been something serious for him to take the risk of bumping them off here, so near to home.'

'Unless he really is a religious fanatic.'

'I've been giving that a lot of thought, and it still doesn't seem to fit the picture I have of Tom Garroway. But everything is pointing to him so I suggest you go ahead and start the search. I'll bring Jean Garroway back to the house so she can help us. She's in a state of shock at the moment and clearly doesn't know that much about what her husband gets up to, but she may be able to help us if we find anything. I'll tell the Chief Super that we're going to bring Tom Garroway in to help us with our enquiries.'

*****

Tom had arrived at Liverpool Street earlier than he'd anticipated and had just made the three thirty-eight train to Cambridge. Arriving at Castle Lofts Station at four twenty, he'd slipped unnoticed along the path from the down platform to where he had left his bike. The police constables had a good view of the bridge as they drank their coffee in the car, but the train hid Tom's exit from their view, and by the time the train pulled away he was already out of their sight.

Tom put his jacket in the pannier and pulled on his leathers. He loved the anonymity of the biker's gear. Once you had your helmet on, you could be anybody. Hell's angel, city gent, burglar, vicar; he believed biking was a great leveller and, despite his income and status, Tom was a bit of a leveller at heart.

So, some time to kill before getting to the airfield and an opportunity to have some fun on the bike. He drove off towards Chipping Bonhunt.

*****

At the Friends' Meeting House Trevor Sandling and some other members were giving the makeshift foyer and the ground floor circulation area a final lick of paint before putting down the new carpet. 'New' perhaps wasn't an accurate description as, ever mindful of costs and the need to protect the planet's precious resources, Trevor had found something suitable from the excellent second hand furniture shop in Abbey Street.

Trevor had just stopped for a moment to admire his handiwork when he heard a familiar voice.

'Not slacking on the job are you?' said Cllr Hodgkiss as he walked through the door, 'sorry, only joking, I can see you've all been very busy and what a fine job you've done. I wonder if I could have another word with you Trevor.'

'Of course, Mayor. We could go through to the Meeting Room if that's alright with you.'

They went through some double doors and sat at the back of the large room that ran across the rear of the building.

'You know, this would make a fine restaurant in here. It's a lovely setting with the garden at the back.'

'Actually that's the Friends' grave yard and I don't think we'd want to use the Meeting Room as a restaurant, but I believe we might be getting there with the proposal about opening the foyer up and using that with the front room as a café during the week.'

'I'm glad to hear that. It would make such a positive contribution to this part of the High Street, and I'm sure you'd do a good trade. As well as dropping by to see how it's all going, I wanted to tell you that I think we might be able to offer you a small grant from the Town Council's new town centre promotion fund. You could use it towards the cost of buying the equipment you need to run the café. What do you think?'

'How much are you talking about?'

'I like that, direct talking! Probably somewhere between ten and twenty thousand pounds. Depends on what exactly you plan to do. But it might be enough to set up a proper kitchen and servery. What do you think?'

'It'll be up to Meeting to decide, but I would support it. You need to give us some time though; we're not the sort of organisation that rushes at these things. We need everyone to agree before we can move forward.'

'Well don't take too long to consider this. We've just finalised the criteria for the fund and none of it's allocated, but I expect it to be taken up very quickly.'

Outside there was the loud roar of a motor bike and then the sound of breaking glass from the front room. Moments later it was completely engulfed in flames.

'Get out quick,' shouted the Mayor.

The door into the front room had been propped open while the painting had been taking place. Trevor Sandling, two other Quakers and the Mayor dashed out of the front entrance and on to the High Street as the flames spread into the circulation area. It was clear that the fire was taking hold very quickly.

*****

The search team were already well into their work under Peterson's direction when Wendy arrived at Folly Farm. Jean Garroway had recovered her composure from the original state of shock she had experienced when confronted with the evidence about Tom. Joshua was sitting, quiet and sullen, next to her.

'I really don't believe Tom could be involved in this,' said Jean. 'I'm sure I would know if he'd been involved in these killings.'

'But you admitted you didn't know a lot about his job or how he spends his time. Today is a case in point. You know he's gone to London, but you don't know what time he'll be back and you can't raise him on his mobile 'phone.'

They climbed out of the car and went into Folly Farm.

'Mum, what on earth is happening?'

'Don't worry Lucy darling, I'm sure everything will be alright.'

'I don't think it will be, there are police everywhere. They're going through everything. I wish dad was here, but he's having a flying lesson this evening.'

'What was that you said?' asked Wendy.

'Dad's having another flying lesson this evening. There was a message on the 'phone from that Henry guy who works down at the airfield. He asked dad to confirm he was OK for six pm this evening.'

Wendy looked at her watch. It was just before five thirty.

'Peterson,' she called

'Yes boss?'

'You remember when we interviewed him yesterday Tom Garroway said he was at the airfield to book a flying lesson?'

'Yes, that was his reason for going there.'

'Well, I think Tom Garroway is on his way to the airfield now. We haven't heard anything from the constables at the station, but if he's going to turn up for his flying lesson he must be back in Bonhunt by now. I'm going to go to the airfield so I can make sure he doesn't get into a plane. If he knows we're on to him he might well try and do a bunk. I'll call in and get some support on the way. You carry on here, and don't let any of his family try and contact him. Get their mobiles and keep them away from the landlines.'

'You sure you don't want me to come with you?'

'No, I want you to keep things under control here.'

*****

There was a lively atmosphere outside the big marquee at Summer Bible Club as children and parents queued to get in. It looked as though it was going to be a really good turn out, and the chairs were filling up fast. Traffic was taking time to get along Castle Lofts Road because the High Street had been closed again.

'Somebody told me there's another fire,' Sylvia Maitland said to her husband. 'Whatever are things coming to?'

'I don't know, but at least it's not spoiling the atmosphere here.'

'I suppose we should be reassured by the police being on site, but it's not our normal way of doing things.'

'We'll just have to accept it, and it does provide some reassurance for all the parents, given everything that's taken place this week.'

John and Alice Davies were approaching with some of the children who'd been in Eagles during the week. They were accompanied by Sarah and Lewis, who were being pestered for piggy-backs.

'No, Chloe, I'm sorry but I really can't give you a piggy back. Aside from you being far too heavy, we're not really supposed to.'

'Oh, pleeeeeease give me a piggy back.'

'Look, I'll swing you round one last time,' said Lewis, 'but this really is the last time.'

Lewis spun round holding Chloe's outstretched arms. She squealed with delight as Lewis went faster and faster. Eventually he stopped.

'That's me finished now Chloe. I'm completely giddy and can hardly stand up anymore!'

'Thank you Lewis,' Chloe said as she skipped off into the tent, followed by Lewis and Sarah.

'They seem to be getting on very well,' said Sylvia Maitland.

'Yes,' replied John. 'I think Lewis has become a sort of father figure this week, which is no bad thing. I even heard Chloe asking Lewis which church he went to and whether it had a Sunday school. So we might have made some links there.'

'So the young helpers haven't been too much trouble?'

'Apart from the odd problem at the beginning of the week they've been pretty good. You know what Sarah can be like, but she settled down and has been really helpful. They're definitely a plus, not a minus. Eight out of ten, I reckon, what do you think Alice?'

'Oh, I'd go for nine, you're always a bit cynical about the young helpers!'

'John, cynical? Never!' exclaimed Sylvia and they all laughed.

'Well, time for us to get inside and shepherd any loose Eagles down to the front,' said John.

Inside the tent the band had started playing an enthusiastic rendering of *'Sing Hosanna.'* John thought that if the volume rose much more, they'd be able to hear the singing in the centre of the town.

*****

Back at Folly Farm, Peterson was called over to the barn by PC Smart who was helping with the search.

'We've only just started going through the barn. The family use it as their garage. I thought you should come and see what we've found.'

Inside the barn was a maroon Jaguar. It bore the registration E5VNS.

'It looks like Lloyd Evans car,' said Smart, 'but it can't be.'

'Why can't it be Lloyd Evans' car?' asked Peterson.

'Because earlier today that was parked just down the road with its bonnet wrenched open and its wiring ripped apart by somebody who didn't want him going anywhere fast. I know, because I saw it with Inspector Pepper when we brought him back out here to take us through what had happened at Folly Wood.'

'Well, couldn't it have been moved here afterwards?'

'I suppose it could have been, but this Jaguar has a completely different type of damage. Look, the bonnet hasn't been wrenched open, but it's dented on the top. The light at the front had been broken and there's some other damage.'

Peterson examined the front of the Jaguar. He wasn't an expert, but it looked very much as though the car had been involved in an accident: a hit and run perhaps? So there were two maroon Jaguars, for all intents and purposes identical and it wouldn't be a coincidence that this one had copies of Lloyd Evans' personal number plates.

Peterson went back to the farm house and entered the kitchen where Jean Garroway was sitting, holding a mug of tea.

'Mrs Garroway, please help me here. We've just started searching through the barn over there, your garage where the cars are stored. We've found a maroon Jaguar with damage to the front and bearing what we think are false number plates. Whose car is that and what is it doing there?'

*****

Wendy was desperately trying to reach the airfield beside Bonhunt Academy, but it was chaos on the roads because of the fire on the High Street. Things had only been made worse by the tail back of traffic taking parents and children to the Summer Bible Club Grand Finale and a line of cars driven by commuters trying to get back into the town as they drove home from Castle Lofts station. Wendy had decided to try driving the long way round and while this had helped her escape the line of cars entering the school site, it had simply taken her to the back of the queue of commuters. Even with the blue lights flashing and siren on she was making very slow progress. She'd radioed in to ensure she was not alone when she arrived at the airfield.

'Can't give you an ETA at the moment. It's complete chaos in Chipping Bonhunt and we can't take many officers away from the High Street because they're needed to direct the traffic from the road closure and keep sightseers away from the Friends' Meeting House.'

'Friends' Meeting House?'

'Yes, that's where the fire is. I'm told it's bad, whole building alight. Another petrol bomb we think, but more effective than the ones last Sunday.'

Poor Trevor thought Wendy, as she finally managed to reach the drive up to the hangar at the airfield, he'll be heartbroken.

*****

Peterson was just about to call Wendy on his mobile to tell her what he'd learnt from Jean Garroway when he saw the text from Trudy, 'Call soonest re States.'

He called Trudy immediately.

'Ian, I wondered when you would call; I've been trying to get hold of you all afternoon.'

'Sorry, it's been madness here. I need to get hold of the boss, but I've just seen your text about the States. What have you found out?'

'Well, that guy I talked to – the one who was so concerned about the influence of conservative evangelicals – he came up with some stuff about those two Americans whose names you gave me. Apparently there was a real bust up involving the two of them.'

'Jake Kerry and Philip Frost?'

'Yes, Jake and Philip were both student outreach workers at First Church of the Redeemer in Hope, Arkansas. It's one of those mega evangelical churches with over a thousand members. Jake and Philip were the superstars amongst their younger members. But they had a secret which caused a huge scandal when it came out, or perhaps I should say when *they* came out. They were both gay and not just gay but also in the case of Philip promiscuous as well.'

'I can imagine that didn't go down too well in a conservative evangelical church.'

'Too right it didn't. The First Church of the Redeemer isn't just conservative evangelical, it's radical Christian right, what you might call Tea Party with attitude.'

'Tea Party?'

'Yes, surely with your background in history you've read about the right wing grass roots movement in the Republican Party? Takes its name from the Boston Tea Party in 1773.'

'You really are losing me here, the Boston Tea Party?'

'You must have heard of that, Ian! Protestors in Boston boarded ships belonging to the East India Company and threw the chests of tea into the sea, destroying the contents. It was a key event in the American Revolution leading up to independence. Today the "Tea Party" is anti tax, anti big government. The radical Christian right love it. Sarah Palin is one of their heroes.'

'Now I've heard of her.'

'There was another key figure at the church who was involved as well. It was all very big news about six months ago. Somebody slightly older who was one of the elders and who was also a very active member. One day he had a guilt trip about what he'd been up to with Philip Frost and confided what he'd been doing to someone he trusted, a frequent visitor to the church from England. Problem was that the English visitor then talked to one of the church pastors about it, asking that they help the guy. Unfortunately while they may be into the tea party, they're not into tea and sympathy at the First Church of the Redeemer and the elder was publicly condemned the following Sunday and thrown out of the church. He claimed Philip had seduced him during a period when he was feeling weak. Basically this elder then went completely off the rails and vowed that he would wreak God's revenge on everyone involved. Shortly afterwards the pastor who had condemned him had a narrow escape with his family when his house was fire bombed. Then the elder disappeared.'

'How did you're friend get hold of all this information?'

'It was all over the Arkansas papers at the time. The church didn't manage to keep this one quiet and the papers are very big on any church scandal they can get hold of, particularly ones involving right wing Christians and sex. Everybody wants to read about it. The evangelicals love to stand in judgement and everybody else enjoys reading about the hypocrisy of conservative evangelicals, so the press sell the story to both sides!'

'So what happened to the disgraced elder?'

'That's the interesting thing. Last record of him was flying out of a small airport near Hope. He was a pilot and he literally disappeared into thin air, nobody's heard of him since.'

'Did your friend have a name for him?'

'Yes, the guy's name is Hank Bush.'

'Trudy, that's all been really very helpful but I need to go. I need to contact the boss. You and I must try and meet up this weekend. Love you.'

'Love you too.'

Peterson finished the call and immediately tried to 'phone Wendy.

'Damn,' he said. Her mobile was switched off. He decided he'd better get to the airfield quickly.

*****

Wendy climbed out of the car and walked quietly towards the hangar at Castle Lofts airfield. She could hear the excited children attending the Grand Finale at Summer Bible Club. There was clearly a lot of singing and laughing going on. Whoever was leading the event was definitely a big hit. She was sure she could hear the children shouting 'behind you' at the top of their voices.

Beside the hangar Wendy could see two motorbikes parked beside each other. There was no sign of any of the back-up she had requested, so she decided she would have to get closer to the hangar on her own. Once alongside the motorbikes Wendy could feel the heat coming from their engines. Clearly both of them had been used recently.

She walked as quietly as she could along the side of the hangar. There was no sign of anybody, but on the standing area in front of the hangar a plane had been made ready for take-off. Wendy surveyed the scene carefully. The plane was easily in reach, and once she was there it should be possible to use it as a shield to hide her presence from anybody that might be in the hangar. Biting her lip, she walked quickly to the plane.

Never be caught out by the unexpected, she had always told herself whenever she was in a potentially dangerous situation. But Wendy was not prepared for what she saw through the side door of the plane. Inside was the bound and gagged figure of Tom Garroway. He looked as though he was desperately trying to say something to her, his eyes flashing wildly and his head nodding towards her.

'Behind you,' she heard the children in the big Summer Bible Club marquee shouting again at the top of their voices. The words rang through Wendy's ears as momentarily she felt a heavy weight on the back of her head, before she fell to the ground unconscious.

*****

PC Smart was running on adrenalin as he drove Peterson along Castle Lofts Road to the airfield. He loved the opportunity to put on the blues and twos, and with the lights flashing and siren blaring he was forcing his way through the traffic, causing complete chaos as drivers moved out of the way by mounting the pavement, driving onto the verge, and in one case into a ditch. The police car made its way down the middle of the road between the two lines of cars that had become gridlocked in both directions.

Peterson was talking on his mobile to Chief Superintendent Warren.

'I'm really worried about Inspector Pepper and we need back-up here now. She was right about that car in the hit and run. It was a Jaguar just like the one owned by Lloyd Evans and it had a fake set of plates to make it look like his. We've just found it in a barn at Folly Farm.'

'The place you needed the search warrant for?'

'Yes, sir. We were following up our investigation of Tom Garroway.'

'Your chief suspect?'

'Our chief suspect until about half an hour ago.'

'So what's changed?'

'According to his wife, the Jaguar was left there by an American called Henry Buske. He's a pilot working at the airfield. Jean Garroway says he told them that he needed to store the car until he could afford to get some repairs done.' As he spoke the final piece of the jigsaw fell into place. 'Of course, Hank Bush, he was a pilot.'

'A moment ago, you said he was called Henry Buske, now you're talking about Hank Bush. You're losing me Peterson.'

'No sir, it's just come together. Henry Buske and Hank Bush are the same person. It all fits; I'll explain it all later. Tom Garroway and his links to the States are a massive red herring, and they were meant to be. Inspector Pepper always had her doubts about his motives for the killings. It all pointed to him, but that was meant to distract us from the real killer. Hank Bush is a highly disturbed extreme radical Christian. His background, the biblical quotes and the arson, it all fits. Smart will get us to the airfield as quickly as he can, but we need reinforcements. This man is extremely dangerous, and I don't think the boss knows that he's really the killer.'

'We'll get as many people as we can over to you immediately. Don't do anything stupid Peterson.'

'Thank you sir. I'll be as careful as I can.'

They were driving up to the airfield. As they turned towards the hangar, Peterson and Smart were just in time to see Hank Bush taxi off from the standing area, turn the plane onto the grass airstrip and accelerate away from them. Within seconds he was airborne.

Fearful of what they might find, Peterson and Smart went into the hangar. Their quick search of the building found nothing. Beside the hangar were the two motorbikes, with the car that Wendy had used to drive to the airfield from Folly Farm parked a short distance away.

'Well, I don't think she's in the building, unless he's put her in one of the planes and he hasn't had enough time to take her anywhere else.'

'Two motorbikes and a car,' said Smart. 'That suggests at least three people.'

'Inspector Pepper, Tom Garroway and Hank Bush. If the boss and Garroway aren't down here, then they must be up there,' Peterson thought out aloud as he watched the plane climb up into the sky.

*****

The events had made quite an impact in the big marquee. As he had taken off in the Maule, Hank Bush had turned the plane and flown low and very noisily over the Grand Finale taking place below. It was a bright sunny evening, and the combination of the noise and the shadow of the plane over the top of the tent had frightened a lot of the children and many of the adults as well.

'That was a bit close,' said Sylvia Maitland to her husband. 'I'll go and take a look out there and see what's going on.' Outside she found the police were on their radios, all following the plane as it climbed upwards.

'Nothing to worry about,' said one of the constables, 'please keep everyone inside and we'll handle things out here.'

Sylvia Maitland decided to stay just inside the doorway to keep an eye on what was going on. If a policeman said there was nothing to worry about, she thought, then there almost certainly was.

On stage were a couple of familiar figures dressed in school uniforms and caps that were far too small for them. They were doing their best to defuse the tension with a quick bit of improvisation as part of their naughty boys' routine.

'That was a very noisy aeroplane wasn't it?'

'Yes it was, I wonder where it went'

'I think it went over there.'

'No, I think it went over there.'

'Which way do you think it went children?'

'It went over there didn't it?'

'Oh no it didn't.'

'Oh yes it did.'

The children joined in very noisily.

'Oh no it didn't.'

'Oh yes it did.'

'Didn't.'

'Did.'

'Oh look there it is.' One of the naughty boys pointed to the left hand side of the top of the tent. 'Oh, sorry, it's not there it's over here, look.' As the other naughty boy turned, his face met a paper plate covered in spray cream. The children were all laughing and the mood inside the tent relaxed.

'It's time for another song,' said one of the naughty boys.

*****

For a moment, Wendy wondered where on earth she could be. The noise was horrendous and the back of her head was very sore. She felt very cramped and couldn't move her arms because, as she quickly realised, they were tied together behind her back. Cramp was causing extreme pain in one of her legs and Wendy was alarmed to find that they were both tied together as well. As she regained consciousness she had to fight a sudden attack of panic when she became aware that she was in the small aeroplane. Stay calm, she thought, you can cope with this.

There was somebody else beside her. She turned her head and found herself looking into the same wildly flashing eyes that she remembered seeing just before she'd been whacked on the back of the head. It was Tom Garroway, still bound and gagged and looking very uncomfortable. He was also still nodding his head at her and seemed to be directing Wendy to look at the front of the plane.

Afterwards Wendy recalled thinking at the time that he was being very illogical. They were both tied up in the back of the plane and somebody else must be flying it. She followed the direction of his nodding action and recognised the man she had talked to earlier in the week at the Great Eastern, the pilot who worked at the airfield. Well, at least that made sense. They'd have to wait; no matter how uncomfortable it was, until he landed the plane somewhere. Presumably they were hostages or something. Perhaps he thought they were his get out of jail free card, to be used in negotiation. So why was Tom still nodding and flashing his eyes so frantically?

She tried to follow the direction of his nods, and then the shocking truth of their situation became clear to her. Beside Hank Bush was some sort of device, made up of what appeared to be a considerable quantity of explosives wired up to a trigger mechanism. My God, thought Wendy, he's going to blow us all up. But what's the point of that? What is he trying to achieve? She instinctively tried to free her hands but realised that was going to be quite a challenge. As she moved herself along the seat, trying to find something she might use to cut the ties binding her hands together, Hank Bush looked round. He shouted above the noise of the plane

'So you're back with us. Let me introduce myself, Hank Bush is my name. I'm glad you're awake in time to see the Grand Finale. You know, you two are a great couple to have with me. You're one of those Quaker heretics aren't you? You claim to have a faith, but you allow people to question the truth. You consort with sinners, and you're the policewoman who lives with another woman so you have sinned grievously against the Lord.'

Wendy would have liked to try and explain that just because two women shared a house it didn't automatically mean what Hank Bush assumed, and in any case she disagreed with his clearly very judgemental theology. But now wasn't the best time for an argument.

'Tom here is no better,' Hank continued. 'He came to my church, befriended me and in a weak moment I confided something to him that he wasn't supposed to share, but he went and told one of the pastors. I was cast out and made to look a sinner and a fool. He said he believed but he is just another miserable sinner. I've paid a heavy price for my sin, and now you are all going to pay as well.'

Tom clearly wanted to say something, but the gag was not going to allow anything to come out other than some highly agitated mumbling.

'You are neither hot nor cold, so the Lord will spit you out. You're all going to be spat out.' To illustrate the point, Hank drew breath and then sent a mouthful of flem flying in Wendy's direction, landing across her forehead. She could do nothing about it.

'The whole lot of you will be spat out. None of you repent for your sins the way I have repented. You are all sinners and fornicators; you consort with sodomites and accept the devil as a friend.'

Wendy flashed back in her mind to the previous Sunday morning at the Friends' Meeting House. Luke Watson was a friend of Peter Lord's. Hank Bush must have befriended Peter Lord who in turn had shared all this flowery judgemental language with Luke, and he was always easily influenced by other people's strong opinions. So that's where Luke got all the stuff he'd been ranting on about.

'So Peter Lord was a friend of yours?' Wendy shouted.

'He was weak, he was no true friend. I thought he shared the true faith, but he was going to ruin everything. So I spat him out.'

'Killed him you mean.'

'The Lord told me to spit him out. The Lord tells me to spit all the lukewarm Christians out. Lesbian Quakers!' he spat more flem towards Wendy. 'Liberals!' another gob headed in her direction.

'Look, can't we talk about this?' Wendy asked, realising immediately how pathetic this sounded and wishing she could have thought of something better. Somehow all her negotiation training didn't seem to be appropriate to the situation she found herself in. This guy wasn't going to negotiate, he was a complete lunatic.

'There's nothing for us to talk about. There is only one true Kingdom and that's where I'm going. The two of you need to pray hard to God. Repent and pray that he will forgive your sins. Otherwise you're both going where you deserve, the fires of hell.'

They were flying over Chipping Bonhunt and Wendy realised they were slowly turning back in the direction they had come from. As they turned she got a glimpse of the town below. The Friends' Meeting House looked like an inferno, with flames leaping high out of the roof. The painful sight was matched by the acute pain Wendy felt herself as she slowly loosened the tie behind her. She was managing to rub part of the tie against a sharp edge on a broken seat belt socket. She felt it loosening, but it was also cutting the side of her hand horribly, and she could feel the bleeding. However that was the least of her problems at the moment.

'You see, the flames of hell consume the sinners. No more will your heathen folk peddle their heresies. The fire will cleanse and put an end to false witness. But we still have important work to do. I will rid this hell hole of all those that give false witness. This will be a sign that the true will of the Lord shall prevail.'

Suddenly Wendy realised the full horror of what Hank Bush had planned. He had enough explosives to kill a large number of people and they were now circling over the big marquee at the Summer Bible Club site with upwards of 700 adults and children enjoying the Grand Finale inside. In all of her training about suicide bombers, Wendy couldn't recall anyone ever mentioning a fanatical member of the evangelical Christian right in the list of high risk categories. This was probably a first that would have been difficult to foresee, but that didn't provide her with any comfort.

The tie around Wendy's wrists gave way and her hands were free. As discretely as she could, she started to work on the tie binding Tom Garroway's wrists together. She didn't have much time.

'I've packed this little bomb of mine with ball bearings, nails and razor blades. When it goes off the sword of the almighty will slay the heretics in this evil little town.'

Wendy was making some progress on freeing Tom's wrists. Her problem was she couldn't risk Hank Bush seeing what she was up to, so she daren't look at what she was doing. She decided she had to say something.

'Surely you don't want to harm all those children? Didn't Jesus say that the kingdom of God belonged to little children?'

Wendy felt the tie around Tom's wrist fall away. She hoped he heard her as she tried to speak in his ear without Hank Bush hearing: 'We need to untie our feet.' Tom nodded, thinking that she could surely have trusted him to work that out for himself.

'Don't try to be clever with me,' said Hank, 'he visits the sins of the fathers on the children to the third and fourth generations.'

Both Wendy and Tom were struggling to undo the rope tying their feet together. Wendy freed herself and decided she was going to have to go for it. Get rid of the explosives first, she thought.

The plane had flown beyond the Summer Bible School site and was turning back, flying a wide circle over Castle Lofts House. Wendy could feel that the plane was starting to descend and she could see that Hank Bush was lining up towards the big marquee. She lent over from the back seat and grabbed the explosives. Hank tried to grab her with his left hand and pulled them out of her grasp, but he couldn't fly the plane at the same time and it swerved off course to the right. He regained control and lined the plane up again. Meanwhile Tom was desperately looking for a heavy object with which to attack Hank. He saw a metal bar beside the pilot's seat at the front of the plane and lunged forward in an attempt get hold of it. Hank grabbed the other end with his right hand and again the plane swerved alarmingly.

While Hank was fighting for control of the metal bar with Tom, Wendy made another attempt at seizing the explosives. This time she succeeded and ended up with them in her lap. Desperately thinking through her options, she leant forward and started opening the window beside the seat in front of her. She'd just started to make some progress when Hank took a lunge at her and she fell back. But he'd had to let go of his end of the metal bar, and Tom seized his opportunity. He pulled the bar back, lifted it up and brought it crashing down on Hank's head. There was a howl of pain as Hank sank backwards. Wendy pushed hard on the window and managed to open it further. Another push and the opening was wide enough to throw the explosives out. They were over the airfield and the plane was descending rapidly, on the verge of going into a catastrophic dive. She threw the explosives out and they fell towards the hangar that was directly beneath them. Then she grabbed the groaning Hank Bush and pulled him over, so that he lay across the front seats of the plane. Tom managed to climb into the front and, sitting on top of Hank's body, tried to regain control of the plane.

'I hate to mention this, but landing is never my strongest point even in normal circumstances.'

'You didn't have to tell me that.'

Hank Bush was writhing under Tom and trying to push him to one side. Wendy decided there was nothing else for it and having grabbed the iron bar she gave him another swipe across the head.

Behind them there was a massive explosion and the hangar appeared to lift into the air. Corrugated sheets, steel girders, and pieces of aeroplane flew out in all directions. Something hit the back of the plane and Tom cursed.

'Damn, the rudder control has gone. If we don't make it, can I just say I think you're a great policewoman.'

'Apologies for making you our chief suspect!'

'Did you? I hope all your colleagues will realise it wasn't me.'

Tom managed to hold the plane up high enough to fly over the big marquee, but then it plunged to the ground between the smaller tents. For about 50 yards it stayed upright as it sped towards the Eagles tent with Tom desperately trying to slow the plane down. The Maule's wheels caught some heavy guy ropes and the plane somersaulted into the tent, coming to a stop inside and on its roof. There was a slow creaking sound as the huge timber poles swayed and then gave way, bringing the canvas down with them and engulfing the plane.

For a moment there was silence.

*****

The promised police reinforcements had arrived and were followed soon afterwards by Chief Superintendent Warren, but all they had been able to do was join Peterson and Smart as they watched with horror as the events unfolded. Fortunately most of them had moved across to the Summer Bible Club site when they had realised what Hank Bush was trying to do, so only a couple of constables had been standing near the hangar when it was demolished by the explosion. One of them would need hospital treatment but his injuries didn't appear too serious.

Peterson and Warren rushed over to the Eagles tent and fought their way through the torn canvas to the wreckage of the plane. Smart organised some of the other constables to hold all the children and parents back from the crash scene, helped by some of the Summer Bible Club tent leaders. The sound of sirens could be heard as ambulances arrived at the scene together with a fire engine. The fire service were still tackling the blaze on the High Street, but one fire engine was released to attend the crash

It was difficult to get into the plane, as the impact of the crash had buckled the doors and distorted the main structure of the cabin. Peterson and Warren had managed to tear away the canvas tent fabric so that the area around the wreckage was clear. Warren was frantically pulling at one of the doors with little success.

'Give us some room, please,' said Steve Turner as he led two other fire officers carrying some cutting equipment. He set them to work cutting the side of the cabin away while making sure they propped the bottom of the upturned plane to stop the structure collapsing when it was opened up.

'Is Wendy's in there?'

'Yes,' said Peterson anxiously, 'the plane came down too quickly.' He felt stupid that this was all he could think of saying. It was pretty obvious what had happened.

'Well, Wendy's one of our friends, and we don't give up on our friends easily.'

Slowly the fire crew cut away one side of the cabin. Both Wendy and Tom were lying on what had been the top of the cabin and Hank Bush was sprawled across both of them. No sound or movement came from his body, but Wendy was trying to say something.

'My shoulder feels as though my arm's been pulled out and I can't move one of my legs.'

Tom seemed to have suffered less in the crash. 'I think I still need a bit more practice at landing.'

Wendy managed a rather painful laugh, 'Remind me not to come flying with you again.' Then she passed out.

'I think she's going to be OK,' said Steve Turner, 'but we need to get them all to hospital as soon as possible.'

Three of the emergency ambulances had moved up to the crash site. A couple of constables travelled in one of them with Hank Bush, and Peterson joined Wendy in one of the others. Tom had argued with the ambulance staff that he didn't need to go to hospital, but he was showing some signs of concussion and eventually he was persuaded to go in the third. A police escort accompanied all three to Addenbrooke's Hospital on the outskirts of Cambridge.

Saturday

Visiting Addenbrooke's hospital was always a bit of a nightmare. The hospital campus was vast. Catherine had decided to use the Park & Ride service so that she wouldn't get charged the exorbitant hospital car parking fees. She'd been a bit miffed to discover that they'd started charging for the Park & Ride car park as well. Having walked for what seemed like miles from the hospital bus stop trying to find the right ward, she'd eventually located Wendy in a side room on her own.

Her right leg was in plaster and her shoulder appeared to be strapped up. She was just about recognisable despite all her bruises and she was surprisingly cheerful given the experiences of the previous day.

'So how's Chipping Bonhunt's heroine? I gather the Grand Finale at Summer Bible Club was pretty spectacular and you were the star turn!'

Wendy laughed and then winced in pain.

'Please don't make me laugh, it really does hurt.'

'So what's the damage?'

'I've dislocated my shoulder and it's being problematic fixing it. I've got a serious fracture in my right leg and I've broken several ribs, not to mention that I'm black and blue all over.'

'So you won't be back on duty on Monday?'

'I said please don't make me laugh, you're being rotten! I deserve some sympathy here.'

Catherine became serious for a moment. 'Wendy, I'm just glad you're still with us. Steve Turner told me that when he first arrived at the scene his heart missed several beats. He thought nobody would have survived.'

'Well, I hate to admit it, but I think I owe Tom Garroway a drink or two. I really thought we were all goners. How he managed to land that plane is beyond me, although I'd have preferred it if he'd managed to finish the right way up!'

'Now that's just being picky!'

Wendy laughed again and immediately wished she hadn't.

'Oh stop it, it's hurting'

'Well, perhaps this will help.'

Catherine reached into her bag and brought out a bottle of White Zinfandel rosé together with some paper cups.

'Sorry I couldn't run to proper glasses, but I thought you deserved some of this.'

Catherine filled two cups.

'It's only eleven in the morning. You're turning me into an alcoholic.'

'You're definitely off duty and if you remember, this was what we were drinking when it all started at Castle Lofts. I think we both owe Tom Garroway a drink. Thanks to him the sale of Anglia Media is going ahead so I've decided we deserve a celebration. How about I book that trip to Venice that we keep promising ourselves? I reckon we could just fit it in before I have to be back at the school.'

'That sounds a fantastic idea, as long as you don't expect me to steer the gondola!'

A nurse entered the room, and Catherine quickly slipped the bottle back into her bag.

'Are you comfortable? One of the doctors should be round later, but press the call button if you have any problems with your shoulder.' The nurse looked at the two paper cups. 'I hope that's not alcohol that you're drinking there.'

'Grape juice,' said Wendy quickly. 'Extremely good for my vitamin intake I'm told.'

The nurse smiled and left.

'Wendy, you're a police officer. You can't tell lies like that.'

'What lies? It is grape juice. It's just been processed a bit! As a serving police officer I understand how in certain situations the facts have to be presented carefully'

Catherine was laughing when the door opened and Peterson arrived, carrying a bag of grapes.

'Now, which would you prefer?' asked Catherine and they both laughed leaving Peterson looking very confused.

'I can never keep up with you two,' he said.

'Peterson, thank you for your very kind gift,' said Wendy, 'we now have the choice of processed or unprocessed grapes. I assume you'd prefer the processed variety. Would you like to join us in a drink?'

'Oh. I get it. Yes I'd love to.'

'So, what happened after we crashed? I reckon the Summer Bible Club finale was probably a bit livelier than usual!'

'Yes, it took a bit of time to get everyone calmed down after your rather spectacular entry. Apparently they had almost finished, then the hangar next door was blown up and you flew over only just avoiding flying into the big marquee. The kids were terrified.'

'I'm not surprised. I hope the children were all OK.'

'I think so. You know you have to take your hat off to the organisers. They were busy consoling the ones that were upset and making sure that nobody was missing. We decided to let them finish before everybody went home, and that's exactly what they did. Got everybody back together and they all sang *We're marching in the light of God.*'

'I was always a bit cynical about Summer Bible Club, but you know I might even offer to help a bit next year.'

'I reckon they could do with some help on their security.'

Wendy laughed again only to regret it very quickly, wincing in pain.

'So what state is our fanatical suicide bomber in? I heard he was in here somewhere on life support.'

'With an armed police guard, although there's nothing to suggest he was working in conjunction with anybody else after he shot Peter Lord. They think he'll pull through, despite the damage you did to him. I reckon Warren would have been happier if you'd finished him off. He says it's causing a hell of a stink with the Americans. Warren said it doesn't fit with their narrative about terrorists. They'd really like to pretend Hank Bush doesn't exist, but he's one of their citizens so they've got to perform their representative role properly on his behalf. They're also worried about possible copycats. Apparently the FBI is going to review all their files to try and identify other possible violent evangelical Christian terrorists.'

'Something I don't understand. If Tom Garroway knew Hank Bush from his visits to the States, why didn't he suspect him when he turned up at the airfield? Not only did he not raise the alarm, but he signed up for flying lessons with him. Why didn't he question his change of name?'

'Tom Garroway thought he was helping Hank by telling the pastor about his fling with Philip Frost. He had no idea the church would react in the way it did, and he flew back to the UK before it all blew up.'

'Unfortunate choice of words,' said Wendy.

'You know what I mean!' Peterson laughed. 'Tom didn't go back to Hope for a couple of months and when he visited the church next time and asked after Hank, they just told him he'd moved on. Tom missed all the press coverage and didn't think to ask anymore. Then Hank turned up here in Chipping Bonhunt, said he'd decided to give things a try at the airfield having heard Tom speak so glowingly about the town and offered him the flying lessons. It was obviously planned, but Tom had no reason to question what he said.'

'So all of this happened because Tom Garroway tried to help Hank Bush, went to the church pastor thinking they would show some Christian care and concern and instead they stood in judgement on the guy.'

'But what else could Hank Bush expect? He was pretty hard-line himself. It seems to me they gave him a dose of his own medicine.'

'Just shows what damage the church can do when it gets judgemental. What was with the name change?'

'Hank told Tom that he wanted to sound more English and he made a bit of a joke about Hank Bush sounding too like a dissolute son of George W. He said Henry Buske was part of his reinvention as an Englishman.'

'So how's the clearing up going, I expect I made a bit of a mess of the hangar?'

'There wasn't much of it left standing after the explosion. Lord Bonhunt is very uptight about his spitfire and it's going to take quite an effort to find all the pieces. He says you're worse than the Germans.'

'Well, the one thing I shall look forward to whenever we manage to get back into the Meeting House....'

'That's not going to be for sometime I'm afraid,' interrupted Catherine

'…is just how dull and boring our meetings are going to be. No more excitement, and certainly no more flying, for me.'

Made in the USA
Charleston, SC
27 October 2014